LIVING WITH DUPLICITY

A NOVEL BY

JEAN E. ROBINSON

Living With Duplicity

Cover art by Aneitra Coleman of Details R Essential

Edited by Patricia Wentzel

Published in the United States of America

Sunshine Solutions Publishing
3609 Bradshaw Rd H260
Sacramento, CA 95827

ISBN-13: 978-0692747193 (Sunshine Solutions)
ISBN-10: 0692747192

1. Fiction
2. Suspense

"This above all; to thine own self be true,
And it must follow, as the night the day,
Thou canst not then be false to any man. "

- William Shakespeare

Dedication

This book is dedicated to my mother, Mae P., who always wanted to write.

CHAPTER 1

The windshield wipers hardly keep up with the driving snow. The strained rhythm of the wipers matched Mark's fleeting thoughts. What could he say to Candy that would make sense? How could he say it? Would she understand? Could they work something out? What about the children? She's a good person, of course she would understand. She loved him, and he loved her.

The car had finally warmed up; he wriggled out of his coat. The snow was coming down harder and the wind had picked up. The storm was getting worse so he slowed down and gripped the wheel tighter. The memory of his conversation with Candy just before he left the house distracted him ...

"Why did you marry me, Mark?" Candy had asked. "You don't act like you want to be in a relationship at all, let alone a marriage. So why did you marry me? You're gone all the time, and you only interact with the children and me when it's a social occasion. It seems that we're only for show. I need answers, Mark, and I want them now! I deserve to know."

Mark had looked at her. So beautiful, he'd thought. She's right. She does deserve to know the truth, and she deserves a normal life. He had sat down in the chair across from her, put his elbows on his knees, and laced his fingers together, in the manner of confidentiality that he used with his patients. "It was my mother's idea."

"What! What are you telling me?" Candy had gasped as she put her right hand to her cheek, her left arm clutching the baby closer.

Mark had said, "Now don't get hysterical, Candy. You wanted to know the truth, so here it is. Mother chose you because you fit her plan for me. You have the look and the breeding to fit into our family. So I married you to complete the picture. There you have it, and I'm sorry if it's not what you thought it would be. Now I have to go to the hospital and check on a patient. We can talk more, later." He got up and put on his coat, scarf, and gloves, went into the garage, opened the garage door, got into his car, and backed down the drive as if it were an ordinary day. He had left for the hospital rather than face her after that.

He was brought abruptly back to the present when he hit an ice slick and began to slide. He managed to get the car straight on the road again; maybe he should go back home and wait for the storm to let up. He was looking for a place to turn around when he hit another slick spot. It's called black ice because it looks exactly like the road and there's no way to avoid it. Mark was still thinking about Candy when the car began to slide sideways toward the river.

~~~~~~

Candy sat on the sofa, four-month-old Marcus David Procter, Jr. in her lap, her mouth open in disbelief. So typical of Mark to leave like that. They never argued – you couldn't call them arguments, because he never participated. He simply walked away, refusing to engage, leaving her to sort out the details. But this time would be different. She had to have answers.

She got dressed, fed and dressed the children – three year old Bea and the baby Markie – packed them in the van and headed for her mother-in-law's. It was a cold, blustery day. The snow was blowing and the streets were icy.

Candy was an excellent driver. With the children in the car, she was extra cautious. The questions swirling around in her head made it hard to concentrate, but she went slowly, and managed the ten blocks without incident.

Frances Procter was sipping her tea and reading the paper when she heard the doorbell. She called to Robert, her husband, "Bob, can you get that? Who would be here at this time of day and in this weather?" Bob opened the door, and, shocked to see the three, greeted Candy and the baby with a hug. Then he swooped Bea up and twirled her around as was his usual greeting for her. "How's my Bunny Rabbit today, and what are you doing out in this storm?" To Candy he said, "Get out of those coats and things and come on in. Let's get you something hot to drink - warm your bones."

Candy loved her father-in-law and always felt comfortable around him. She said, "Thanks, Bob. Where's Mother Procter? I need to talk with her." She could not bring herself to call her mother-in-law Frances, or Frankie, as others did. Frances was a cold woman –at least that's how Candy perceived her.

As they went into the kitchen, Frances stood, pulled her robe tighter around her waist as if she were gathering herself together, and said, "What brings you out in this weather, dear? I would have appreciated a call first. As you can see, we are not ready to receive company." Then she bent and kissed Bea on the cheek. "Hello, Bea. Would you like some hot chocolate?"

Bea replied, "Oh, yeah, Ganma."

Frances flinched. "It's 'Yes, Grandmother. Thank you.' Now you say it."

"Yeth, Ganma. Tank you."

Frances chuckled. "I guess that will have to do. Bob, would you make the cocoa? Now Candice, have a seat. You look upset. What can we do for you, dear?"

"I had a talk with Mark this morning. He told me something that was very upsetting. He told me our marriage was your idea. What did he mean?"

Bob dropped the kettle in the sink just as the phone rang. Frances startled, and quickly recovered as the phone rang a second time. Time seemed to stop and then the phone rang a third time, breaking the spell. Bob said, "I'll get it," picked up the receiver, and said, "Hello. Yes. Yes. Yes, his wife is right here. What? Say again. Oh, no! I see. I understand. Yes. I'll be there as soon as I can." He looked at the two women sitting at the table. If he had to choose which one to comfort first, it would have been Candy. He said, "There's been an accident. They found Mark's car in the river. It seems he skidded off the road. They are searching for him. I'll go see what's going on."

Candy and Frances said at the same time, "I'm going with you."

Bob said, "No. You wait here. I'll call when I know something." He put on his boots, coat, hat, scarf and gloves and went into the garage.

Bea followed him. "Can I come, Ganpa, can I?"

He knelt down, hugged her, and said, "Not this time, Bunny Rabbit. Not this time."

Frances turned to Candy and said, "I'd better get dressed. Excuse me, dear." She went upstairs leaving Candy in the kitchen with the children.

Candy found the basket Frances kept for Bea's 'busy work', as she called it. She gave it to Bea and rocked the baby as she waited and worried. She told herself, "It's just an accident. Everything will be all right."

Frances came into the kitchen wearing slacks and a sweater. She was a tall woman with a trim figure. She wore her straight black hair pulled back and up into a bun, which gave her a severe look. She had average features, brown eyes, arched eyebrows, and a distinct, cleft chin that jutted out slightly. Mark had that same chin, as did Bea, and baby Markie. She asked Candy, "Would you like some breakfast, dear?"

Candy was incredulous. How could she think of food at a time like this?

She replied, "No. Thank you. I wouldn't be able to swallow. What I need is answers." Frances took out a Danish pastry and poured a fresh cup of tea. She gave Candy a cup and poured tea for her, too. She sat across from her and said, "So, what do you want to know?"

Candice said, "Mark told me our marriage wasn't his idea – it was yours. What did he mean by that?"

"I guess he meant that I approved. If he meant something else, you'll have to ask him. Now let's see if we can get some information about this storm." She got up and turned on the television.

"But he said that I fit your plan. What did he mean?"

Frances turned to her and said, "You hold the baby too much. Put him on the sofa in the living room and drink your tea. I do wish you would eat something. You have to keep up your strength you know."

Candy's eyes watered in frustration. She wanted to scream. The baby squirmed. Her arm was getting tired, so she went into the living room, placed him on the sofa, and tucked pillows around him. Then she looked out the window. The storm was getting worse, the wind blowing the snow into drifts. I should be home instead of here with this woman who always makes me feel inadequate, she thought.

Candy went back into the kitchen. "The storm is getting worse. I think I should go back home. Bob can call when he knows something."

"I think you should wait here until the men come, or until the storm lets up."

Before Candy could answer, the doorbell rang. Frances opened the door, and greeted the state trooper standing there. He introduced himself and told them that he would take them to the hospital where Bob had been taken. They quickly bundled everyone up and followed the trooper to his car. Along the way he told them what had happened.

Bob had arrived at the accident scene as they were pulling the car out of the river. He'd seen what he thought was Mark's coat, and before anyone could stop him, he had tried to reach it, but slipped and fell into the water. He had gone under, but they'd managed to get him out right away, and had rushed him to the hospital. There had been no sign of Mark. The trooper said he might have gotten out of the car before it sank. But Mark hadn't been seen anywhere near the accident.

In this small town, nearly everyone knew each other. So it was no surprise that the nurse took them straight to Bob's side when they got to the hospital. Bob was on a gurney in the Emergency Room being hooked up to tubes and machines.

Frances asked the doctor working on Bob, "How is he?"

He looked at her and shook his head. "With his heart condition, it doesn't look good. Bob, can you hear me? Bob, Frances is here. Open your eyes."

Frances took his hand. "Bob, darling, wake up. It's me, Frankie. Wake up!"

Candy looked around and asked the nurse, "Where's my husband, Dr. Procter?"

The nurse looked at the state trooper who said, "We didn't find him yet. We're still looking." Candy slumped down and the trooper caught her just as the nurse grabbed the baby.

Bea started to cry and wailed, "Whut wong wid Ganpa, Mommy? Mommy, Mommy!" The nurse took a struggling Bea and the baby out into the waiting area, talking softly to Bea, reassuring her that Mommy was ok.

Bob opened his eyes and said, "Frankie, I'm so cold. Where's Mark? I saw him in the water. Where's Mark?"

Frances replied, "I don't know, darling. Let's get you warm and we'll find him."

Bob looked at his wife and said, "You know I love you. I feel funny. I love you Frankie. I'm so cold. I'm so cold. I love you Frankie. Where's Mark?"

Recovering from her faint, Candy heard Bob talking to Frances and tried to move closer. She was unsteady on her feet and the trooper held her up. She heard Bob say, "Where's Mark? Frankie, you have to tell her the truth. She needs to know so she can handle things. I feel funny. Where's Mark? Frankie, I love you."

He closed his eyes, and Frances gripped his hand tighter and cried, "Bob, wake up. Bob? Bob, stay with me. Bob, you can't leave me now. Bob! Bob!" She looked at the doctor and shouted, "Do something! Fix him! I can't lose him! Do something, now!"

The doctor placed his stethoscope to Bob's chest and said, "The strain was too much for his heart. There's nothing more we can do."

Frances screamed, "No! No! I won't hear of it! You fix him! I demand that you fix him! Use that paddle thingy and fix him now!" Sobbing, she grabbed the doctor's arm and pulled him around to the other side of the gurney. "Get busy! He can't die on me! He can't." Tears and mucus were running down her chin, and strands of hair came undone. She grabbed pieces of equipment screaming, "Use this! Fix him! He can't die!" The doctor tried to calm her, but to no avail. He told the nurse to bring a sedative. They restrained her and gave her a shot. Within seconds she was moaning softly as they laid her on a gurney.

Candy was mesmerized. She had never seen Frances show any emotion, and she felt sorry for her, forgetting her own predicament for a few seconds. Then she asked the doctor, "How is Mark? Where is he? I want to see him."

He replied, "We haven't seen him. They didn't bring him in yet."

The state trooper was standing nearby ready to help her if she fainted again, and he said, "Mrs. Procter, we didn't find him yet. They're still looking. He wasn't in the car when we got it out of the river." He paused. "It's become a recovery effort now, not a rescue. Do you understand? The current is strong and with the storm and all, we'll just have to wait."

Candy sat down slowly, "So you're telling me he's gone? Are you telling me my husband is dead? Is that what you're saying?"

The trooper replied, "We don't know, Ma'am. All we know is we didn't find him when we recovered the car. He may have gotten out and found shelter somewhere. We'll have to wait until the storm clears and see what the investigation finds."

"Wait and see," Candy repeated softly. She was optimistic and convinced herself that Mark had gotten out somehow and would be okay. She proceeded to do what was necessary. She made all the necessary phone calls to take care of Bob and asked the trooper to take her and Frances and the children home.

CHAPTER 2

Candy got Cora Mays, Frances' housekeeper, to come and stay with Frances then she went home. The children were hungry and tired. She fed them and put them down for a nap. Waiting was the hardest thing Candice had ever done. She wanted to go to the crash site and look for herself. But with the storm and no one to take care of the children, all she could do was wait. She told herself that Mark had been picked up by some passing motorist who was sheltering him until after the storm. Her unanswered questions about their marriage would have to wait. She convinced herself that Mark would be home later that night, or surely the next day.

Candice got very little sleep that night, startling awake at every little noise, thinking it was Mark. The next morning was very cold, but at least the storm had passed. She called Frances, and Cora answered the phone. She said Frances was still asleep. The doctor had been to see her and had given her another sedative to keep her calm. Candice decided to go to Frances' and see what she could do.

Cora watched the children while Candice went upstairs to see Frances, who was still in bed, but awake. She rose up on her elbow and motioned for Candice to come closer. Candice asked her what she wanted to do about the arrangements for Bob.

Frances said, "We made arrangements for both of us years ago. The mortuary knows exactly what to do. Bob was good about taking care of details."

"That's good to know. It's one less thing for you to have to do. Mother Procter, what did Bob want you to tell me because I needed to know?"

Frances sat up and screamed at Candice, "My husband just died, and my son may be dead, too! Why are you bothering me with your stupid questions? You may be a widow, too, you know! You silly child! I don't know what you think you heard. You have the children to think about now. Leave me alone and go home!"

Candice stammering said, "I'm sorry Mother Procter. You're right. I apologize. Let me know if you need anything..." She looked at her mother-in-law and felt sorry for her. She would just have to wait and hope to get answers later. She didn't know what to think about Mark.

~~~~~~

Robert Procter's funeral was held two days later even though there was no news of Mark. He had been well liked. Friends, relatives and co-workers filled the church. He was a handsome man, graying at the temples, he looked very distinguished in the coffin. Frances was stoic during the service, and only showed a little emotion when Bea climbed into her lap. She hugged Bea, kissed her cheek, and then handed her over to her mother.

Candice cried softly when Bea, clutching the stuffed rabbit that Bob had given her for Christmas, asked, "Why Ganpa not wake up? Where Daddy? Why you cry, Mommy?"

It was hard for Candice to stay in control when people spoke of her loss, and asked if she was going to have a memorial service for Mark. She wanted to tell them that he was just missing, and she was waiting for him to come home. Instead she simply thanked them for their concern, and said she didn't know yet what she would do.

Candice's aunt, Margaret Wilson, came for the services and was a great comfort. She called her 'Aunt Maggie,' but really should have called her Mother, since she was the only mother she knew. Candice's mother and father had died in a car accident when she was two. Margaret had adopted Candice, her brother's child, and raised her as her own. She told Candice that when she was ready to make a move, Candy should consider coming to live with her. – She had the room, and could help with the children. Candice thanked her and said she would think about it. For now, she felt she had to stay put and wait for Mark.

~~~~~~

She felt dead inside as she went about her daily routines and tried for normalcy for the sake of the children. She checked with the police and the fire department for any news, and she asked around her neighborhood. But no one had seen or heard from Mark.

The days became longer, and the weather warmer. The smell of spring was in the air when the hospital called they could no longer keep Mark on the payroll. The bank manager called soon after that to say their funds were getting low and she would need to make a deposit.

Candice knew she had to do something other than wait for Mark to turn up. Two bodies had been found in the river, an old man and a young woman, but no Mark. She had to admit to herself that he might not be coming back. She actually didn't know what to believe. She hoped he was still alive, and if he were, she would have to admit to herself that he had deserted her and the children. If he were dead, she would have to deal with that, too. She hated being in limbo like this, but knew she had to take control. She went to talk to Frances about having a memorial service for Mark.

"Absolutely not," said Frances. "I know he's out there somewhere. Spring is almost here, and they haven't found his body yet so I know he's still alive!"

Candy told Frances about her financial situation. She told Candy not to worry, that she would make a deposit into her account every month. Candice thanked her and said she would pay her back when she found a job. Frances said, "You have the children to look after; concentrate on taking care of them."

Candice was uncomfortable with the situation, but realistically, she knew Frances was right. She hated being obligated to her mother-in-law more than anything. In her mind, she cursed Mark for putting her in this predicament. She felt feverish and tired-- probably from a lack of sleep and worrying about Mark. She thanked Frances again, said she hoped she hadn't upset her, and took the children home. After they ate lunch, Bea threw up and so did the baby. Then Candice threw up while she was cleaning up their messes. Both children had fevers, and she felt faint. She called her friend and neighbor, Phillis, who came to see what was going on. She told Candice to go to bed and she would take care of the children. Phillis had been a nurse when she met and married Joe Roberts. Phillis was about six inches shorter than Joe, with almond colored skin, big brown eyes and dimples. They were a handsome couple.

Phillis called Frances and told her that the family was sick. Frances thanked her and said she would take care of it. A little while later, Cora came to look after them. Frances called Candice and told her she didn't feel well herself so she had sent Cora.

Cora stayed and took care of all of them for three days. Frances never came over or called. On the fourth day, Candice thanked Cora and told her she felt strong enough to take over. She said she would compensate Cora for her time, and Cora said that Mrs. Procter had taken care of it. Candice made a note to herself. She would keep track and pay Frances back for everything - every cent.

CHAPTER 3

A few weeks later Candice and the children went over to Phillis' house for the children to play together. It was a warm sunny day and Candice was feeling stronger. Bea and Phillis' two children, Linda and Jay-Jay, were playing with a litter of pups. Jay-Jay was two years older than Bea while Linda and Bea were only a few months apart. Phillis and Candy had become very close friends; they had moved into the neighborhood about the same time. Jay-Jay had a dark brown complexion and an athletic built like his father, but he had his mother's features. Linda looked more like her father, Joe, with a lighter brown complexion. Markie, as Bea called her baby brother, was kicking and cooing on a quilt. Phillis brought out drinks for everyone. "I saw your mother-in-law at the grocery store last week, all dressed up in a fancy outfit," said Phillis. She said she had just come from a sorority meeting. I mentioned that I thought she was sick, and she laughed at me, said it was just a sniffle."

Candice replied, "I'm learning not to be surprised by anything that woman does. I'm feeling better, and the children are fine. That's all that matters." One of the pups came over to Markie and began licking him. Markie squealed in delight, rolled over and tried to crawl with the puppy. He laughed and the puppy grabbed the seat of his diaper and pulled. All the children were laughing, and Candice couldn't help but laugh, too.

It was as if a dam had broken. Candice laughed until her stomach hurt. It felt so good to just let go and laugh. She felt relaxed for the first time in months, actually since before Mark disappeared.

Phillis said, "I think you should take that one home with you."

"Really? Do you think so?"

"Yeah. And you can take my two kids with you, too. And this next one when he or she comes."

Candice said, "You're expecting again? When are you due? I'm happy for you."

Phillis said, "In about six months. I'll let you have the little rug rat for a quarter."

Candice started laughing again. Then Bea came over to her mother and said, "Mommy, can we hab puppy?"

Candice said, "How about the one that's attached to your brother's behind? If we take him home, you'll have to name him." They all started laughing again.

When they got home, Bea said, "I know. We call him 'Bunny' like what Ganpa called me. Can we take him to see Ganma?"

Candice called Frances and asked if she would like to see the children – they had a surprise to show her. Frances said she would love to see the children.

Frances answered the door, and Bea raced in and hugged her around the knees shouting, "Ganma, Ganma, look what we got! We gots a puppy. We call him 'Bunny' like what Ganpa call me. Look, Ganma! He pulled Markie's diaper off. He so funny!"

Markie, in Candice's arms, was squealing and kicking his little legs. Bunny was jumping up and down, and racing around and everyone but Frances was laughing. She just stood there. "Is this the surprise?" she asked. "I don't want a beast in the house. You'll have to leave him outside."

With that, Bunny stopped running around, looked up at Frances, squatted and peed on the tiled entryway. Candice gave Markie to Frances and went to the kitchen for a towel. After she cleaned up the mess, she said to Frances, "I think we'll be going now."

When she had the children situated in the van, she laughed again. Bea and Markie joined the laughter, and Bunny barked all the way home.

That night, after the children were asleep, Candice took a long leisurely bath and thought about her situation. What was she going to do? She got out of the tub and examined herself in the full-length mirror. If she had to describe herself, she would say she was average. Average height; average weight, though she had lost quite a few pounds since Mark's disappearance; clear peachy complexion; average brown hair that needed a trip to the beauty parlor; average looks, except for her hazel eyes. Everyone thought she had lovely eyes. Bea had the same eyes. They reflected whatever color she wore. She thought about what her aunt had said to her, how she would be welcome to bring the children and come live with her. She put on pajamas, went into the kitchen, made a cup of tea and called her aunt.

Aunt Maggie was delighted to hear from her, and asked when she would be moving back home. Candice laughed and said, "I haven't decided what I'm going to do yet. I just wanted to hear your voice."

"You know I've got this big old house. I need some life in it. You and the children can have the upstairs bedrooms. I can use the one downstairs. We can work out something. I'm not trying to tell you what to do, I'm just putting a bug in your bonnet. You could go back to school and finish your degree, or you could start another career. You're young, pretty, and bright. If that man shows up, he'll know where to find you, if his Momma will let him. Oops, I didn't say that, did I?" and she laughed.

It always made her feel good to talk with Aunt Maggie. She was a public school teacher and loved to talk. Aunt Maggie said her mission in life was to bring joy and lore to people– if they wanted it. Candice told her aunt she loved her. She would think about the bug in her bonnet, and let Maggie know her decision.

She put newspapers down in the kitchen, took Bunny out to the back yard to pee, brought him back in and closed the kitchen off. He started whimpering, then whining, then barking. She knew she wouldn't get to sleep with him carrying on, so she let him out of the kitchen. He immediately trotted to Bea's bed, settled down at her feet, and went to sleep.

Candice looked at the sleeping trio. Bea, hugging her bunny rabbit with Bunny on the bed, and Markie in his crib. I may as well face it. I'm on my own now. They're my responsibility, and my life. I guess I'm pretty lucky to have Aunt Maggie and Phillis. I'll decide what our future will be, and we'll move on together.

She remembered how she and Phillis had developed an immediate bond when they met. They liked each other from the start and shared a lot of interests. She had hoped that Mark and Joe would be close friends, too but she gave up on that idea. When she mentioned to Mark that the four of them could do things together, Mark nixed the idea. When she asked him why, he told her, "If you're white, you're all right. If you're brown, stick around. And if you're black, get back."

She was shocked. "Mark, I'm surprised at you. I didn't know you felt that way. Where did that come from?"

"Oh, I didn't really mean it. It's what the guys in my fraternity used to say. It was a joke."

"Well, I don't think it's funny. It's disgusting and I'm disappointed in you. Phillis and Joe are my friends and I really resent your saying it."

Mark replied, "I'm sorry. I just don't think Joe and I could be like you and Phillis. We don't have anything in common. He's the jock type, and I don't have time for that. We can't talk about sports. I don't even go to games." The memory was a little unnerving for Candy.

She looked at the ledger she had started, got a pad and pencil and did some calculations. When she had looked at everything in black and white, she made up her mind. She would start the ball rolling in the morning. Why wait? She knew she couldn't continue this way, and she didn't want to be obligated to Frances for anything. She hated the position she was in. Since Mark was eight years older, she usually let him do all the decision-making. They would discuss their options and she gave her opinion, but she eventually went along with whatever he decided. Now everything was up to her. She never dreamed she would have to go it alone.

CHAPTER 4

The next day Phillis kept the children while Candice went to see Frances to explain her plans. Frances said, "I don't see why you have to move away, dear. If you feel you must work, we could hire someone to take care of the children. I should think that you would want to keep your own home. But it seems you have given this some thought, and I see you've made up your mind."

"I have given it a lot of thought. I don't know if Mark is alive or dead and I have to make some decisions for myself and the children. I feel that this is something that I have to do. I'll give you an itemized statement of what I owe you before we leave, and I'll give you the money when I can."

Frances said, "Oh, pooh, Candice. Don't even think about it. Now, if you'll excuse me, I have to prepare tea for the ladies this afternoon. I'd ask you to stay, but we have club business to do."

Candice thought, Does she ever let up? She's dismissing me as if I were a child who broke a vase or something like that. Now I know I've made the right decision. "I'll let you know when we'll be leaving and I'll bring the children over for a visit before we go. Goodbye, Mother Procter."

"Goodbye, dear. Call before you come, and please don't bring the dog with you."

~~~~~~~~~~~~~~~~~~~~~~~~~~~~~~~~~~

Aunt Maggie squealed with delight when Candice told her they would be coming to live with her. She could hardly contain herself. "I'm so excited! I'll get the rooms ready for you. You can bring whatever you want, and fix the place up any way you want. You'll have to bring the baby's crib, of course, because he's too young to sleep in a regular bed. Bea should be able to manage. You can have my old room since I've moved to the downstairs bedroom. When the baby gets older, he can have his own room, but for now the spare room can be their playroom. I'll get your old dollhouse down from the attic. And …"

At this point Candice cut her off. "Aunt Maggie, slow down. We'll work everything out. I have to tell you we have a puppy, too. Do you mind having a dog?"

Aunt Maggie replied, "Oh, heavens, no, as long as he can get along with Percy. I'll have Tom build a doghouse for him in the back yard. You remember Tom Andrews, Minnie's oldest boy? Well he's like my handyman. He keeps the yard up, and takes care of any repairs. He's a nice young man. I sometimes wonder if he's all there, but he does what I tell him to do. His work is very neat, and I can depend on him."

Again, Candice had to interrupt. "Who is Percy?"

"Oh, Percy is the cat," Aunt Maggie laughed.

When Candice ended the call, she couldn't help but smile. Dear Aunt Maggie. She always made her feel good, even when she rambled on and on. She had a lot to do. The realtor she had contacted would come that afternoon. She had to plan a moving sale, sort what she would take with her, and what she would sell or give away. She looked around the house, and thought, The only thing I'll miss is being able to see Phillis.

The moving sale went better than expected, and the realtor had a lot of lookieloos come to the house. Then the realtor dropped a bomb. Candice couldn't sell the house without Mark's signature, or a death certificate.

Candice called her lawyer, and he informed her that she would have to wait seven years before she could be issued a presumption of death, or she'd have to petition for a divorce for desertion. This was disappointing, but she refused to let it stop her. She decided to rent the house out and have an agency take care of it for her. This would give her an income – at least enough to pay the mortgage - and maybe some left over. She would work out the details, but she was determined to move.

Phillis had a going-away cook out for Candice and the children. Friends and neighbors came to give their good wishes. Frances arrived late and seemed very uncomfortable. She said her obligatory goodbyes and left after about fifteen minutes. She wasn't missed, not even by Bea. Phillis asked Candice, "What's with her? She didn't even touch the baby, and barely spoke to Bea."

Candice replied, "Now you see why I have to move away from her. I don't think she is good for the children."

They left early the next morning. With frequent stops along the way for snacks and potty breaks, the two hundred mile ride took longer than usual. They arrived at Aunt Maggie's house late in the afternoon. She was in the back yard giving Tom directions on where to put a swing. When she turned around to go into the house, she saw the family standing by the back porch watching her. She threw up her arms, and shouted, "Here you are at last. I was beginning to worry. Come on in. I've got your favorite chicken dinner all ready. Oh, my goodness! Just look at you. I'm so glad to see you. Look how you've grown. Oh, happy day! You're here, you're here!" She was wiping tears away with her apron.

Bea asked Candice, "Why she crying, Mommy?"

Aunt Maggie replied, "Tears of joy, darling. Tears of joy! Come on in."

Bunny bounded up the steps and scratched on the screen door. Aunt Maggie said, "See. He knows he's home. Tom, your next project will be to put in doggie doors."

Beatrice whispered to Candice, "Is she your mommy?"

"No. She's my aunt. She is my daddy's sister. Just like you are Markie's sister, but she's like a mother to me."

"What I call her?"

"What do you want to call her?"

Bea wrinkled her forehead. "Maybe I call her 'Auntie Mom'."

CHAPTER 5

After dinner, when the children were settled in bed, Candice and Aunt Maggie sat at the kitchen table drinking tea and talking. Aunt Maggie chuckled, "That Bea is something else. I like that 'Auntie Mom'. She's a smart little cookie."

"You know, we never talked too much about my mom and dad. How did you happen to get me, and what happened when they had the accident?"

Aunt Maggie said, "The streets were icy, they were going too fast. They lost control and the car wrapped around a power pole. They didn't have a chance.

"I was teaching at the time and still living at home. I had a boyfriend, Don. We were talking about getting married. Our parents were getting on up there in age and there was nowhere else for you to go. It was up to me to take care of you and when I was able, I adopted you. I tried to give you a good life." She wiped her eyes.

Candice reached across the table and took her hand. "You did give me a good life, and I'm grateful. I believe everything happened the way it was supposed to. We'll just make the best of what we have now."

Aunt Maggie looked at Candice through her tears. "You're a sweet girl, Candy," and they laughed at her pun.

"Whatever happened to Don? Did you two stay together? You never married, so what happened there?"

"Don got tired of waiting for me to make room for him in my life and he found another girlfriend. He wanted somebody who would put him first and didn't have the family obligations that I had. He wouldn't take on a readymade family."

"Did you ever have another boyfriend?" Candice asked.

"Oh, I had friends from time to time, but they never seemed to fit into my lifestyle. They had to take a back seat to you and my obligations to my family. That's hard on a man's ego. So I just never hooked-up with anyone. Anyway, I've had a good life. Now I've got you and the children, so I'm content. You know this house will be yours when I'm gone, so let's talk about you for a while."

They talked into the night, and Candice slept soundly for the first time in a long, long time. When she woke the next morning, she could smell bacon and coffee, and she heard sounds of life coming from downstairs. Aunt Maggie was fussing around the kitchen answering Bea's many questions and keeping an eye on Markie playing on a quilt on the floor.

Candice stood in the doorway and watched the group for a while before she made her presence known. "Good morning, my family," she smiled.

Aunt Maggie said, "Come, join us. Sit, sit, and answer some of your daughter's questions. I'm talked out. We'll need to get a playpen for that one, or a cage, or something. He's trying to crawl all over the place."

"The movers are supposed to bring our things today, and we'll get settled in."

"OK. So, how do you want your eggs? We've already eaten, sleepy head. What are your plans for today?"

"I'll start pounding the pavement."

"No need to rush, but you could start at the bank on Elm. John Morris is the branch manager there. He was in your class, wasn't he? And, if I'm not mistaken, didn't he take you to your senior prom? I think he was sweet on you. He's divorced, and has three wild boys. They could use a mother with some sense and a firm hand."

"Are you being a matchmaker? I'm not interested in any romance. I just want a job, but I'll consider the bank. First, I'll look in the paper to see what's available. I'll make a plan, then go from there, you nosy busy-body," she laughed.

There was a loud noise coming from the street, and Bea ran to the front window. "Mommy, Mommy, twuk here!" Candice greeted the movers and showed them where to put everything. Then she changed her clothes and started making the rounds in her job hunt.

Driving around town brought back lots of memories. She teared up a few times when she saw places she and Mark had frequented. She drove around the college campus and watched the students going to classes, sitting around the quad, holding hands and just hanging out. She had an ache in her chest that wouldn't go away. She remembered when she and Mark first met. She was coming out of the library with a load of books. She dropped two of them, and they bumped heads

32

as they both bent to pick them up. He was fun to be with then, and easy to talk to. He didn't get fresh with her like the idiots from high school, and they developed a deep friendship. He was in med school and she was just a freshman. She was thrilled that he even took notice of her. They worked out their schedules so they could have time to spend together. He lived on campus, and she had him over for dinner so often that Aunt Maggie made it a habit to ask, "How many places do I set tonight?"

It was no surprise to anyone when they got engaged. It was his senior year. He took her to his hometown for the winter break, and she spent Christmas with his family. They welcomed her, and she felt comfortable with them, or at least with Bob. Frances was more reserved and distant, but Mark assured her that his mother liked her, that was just her way.

They had a small summer wedding in Aunt Maggie's back yard. Candice looked lovely in an ankle-length dress from Macy's, and Mark was handsome in a navy blue suit. Aunt Maggie made the cake, and friends and relatives brought food. It was a wonderful time. Even Frances seemed to enjoy the festivities. They went to the beach for their weekend honeymoon, then returned to their summer jobs. Candice roused from her reverie and thought, Back to the real world. I don't have time to get sidetracked. I guess I'll start at the bank.

That evening they celebrated Candy's new job with cake and ice cream. She began her training as a teller the following Monday.

CHAPTER 6

Things settled into a routine, and Candice's life became predictable. Her days were filled with work and the children's needs. There was tension at the bank, however, as John began making inappropriate remarks, standing too close to her when he was explaining things and watching her all the time.

John was a little taller than Candice with receding sandy hair and the beginnings of a beer belly. Candice was not attracted to him at all, and tried to be tactful in avoiding him. It became harder and harder in the small branch. One day John pressed himself against Candice from behind, on the pretext of showing her a new procedure, and whispered in her ear, "There's more where that comes from."

Candice was outraged! She whirled around and shouted for everyone to hear, "Get away from me, you sleaze-ball. I quit!"

The other tellers were not surprised. They had seen what was happening. When Candy went into the breakroom to get her belongings, some of the other tellers shared their stories with her. Candy realized that she was not the only one he had harassed. As Candice was leaving she told John, "You can send my paycheck to my home. No wonder your wife left you."

When Candice told Aunt Maggie, she said, "Good for you, girl. You don't have to put up with that. Now sit down, have a cup of tea, and let's talk about what you really want to do. You don't have to work unless you just want to."

"I have to, Aunt Maggie. I can't stay here and sponge off of you. That was why we didn't stay in Newburn. I want to be independent. It's enough that you are taking care of the children for me. I have to work."

"I understand. But don't take any job just to be working. Let the job be something you really want to do. Find your passion. What did you want to do before you got hooked up with Mark and his dreams?"

Candice thought for a minute then she said, "You know you're right. I haven't thought about myself and what I want to do in a long time. I've been practical and put other people's needs before mine for so long that I don't even know myself anymore. I've got some thinking to do. I'm going for a walk."

Millerton was a typical college town with tree-lined streets and cottage-type houses. Candice walked toward the college and was reminded of her childhood growing up in this comfortable environment. Except for the recent trauma, her life had been uneventful. I've been lucky, she thought. It could have been worse. The children are healthy and happy. What do I want for them? No, what do I want for myself? What do I want to do with the rest of my life?

Before she and Mark married, she had thought about going into the teaching program. Instead she got a job at an insurance company while Mark did his residency. She smiled as she remembered their first small apartment. When Mark could get away from the hospital, they had fun playing house. She worked. He studied. They laughed a lot. The meals they concocted were enough to make you gag, now that she thought about it. They really enjoyed each other's company, like they were brother and sister. When Mark was not studying, they played board games. They were each other's best friend.

Then she got pregnant with Bea but was able to work for a few more months. Mark was attentive but his time was limited. The demands of his residency, meant there was little togetherness time. Mark became more distant, but she told herself that it was because of his increasing responsibilities.

Candice realized that she was beginning to frown, and she became aware of the people walking past her. She had walked onto the campus so she headed toward the quad. She sat on one of the benches looking at her surroundings, when she heard someone say, "Candy? Is that you?" She looked up to see a high school classmate.

"Dotty! You haven't changed a bit. I'd recognize you anywhere."

Dotty had been chubby in high school, and she was stout now. She wore her hair in the same short bob now graced with a little gray streak starting at the middle of her forehead. She was wearing glasses now, but her dimpled grin gave her face an open quality that invited people to trust her.

Dotty laughed, "Liar. But it's good to hear. What are you doing here? Have you moved back home? Let's go have a cup of coffee and get caught up."

By the time they had shared their stories, the sun was beginning to set. Candice said, "This has been good for me.

I have to get home to the kids. I'm so glad we got together like this. We have to do it again."

Dotty said, "I remember John from high school. I didn't think much of him then, and I think less of him now. Come by the admin office tomorrow. I'm sure there is something you can do there. You have experience we need. And the good thing about working at the college is you can schedule your work around your classes. I think a divine hand had something to do with you coming on the campus today. I usually go the other way when I leave work, but I had to deliver some papers to the library, and there you were. The Lord works in mysterious ways."

Candice was delighted. She couldn't wait to get home and tell Aunt Maggie her good fortune. "Just think," she told her. "This time last year, I was big as a tick waiting for Markie to be born. And now, a year later, I'm starting a new life."

~~~~~~~~~~~~~~~~~~~~~~~~~~~~~~~~~~~~~

Markie was walking and getting into everything, with Bunny always by his side. Bea was a big help watching him and playing with him. They had a quiet birthday celebration for him in early October. Candice took pictures of him eating his birthday cupcake. He had never had one before, and he took the whole thing and tried to put it in his mouth at once. He looked up with icing all over his face. Bunny proceeded to lick the icing off, and everyone laughed. There was lots of laughter in the house, and Candice thought, I wish Mark could be here to share it. This is good for the children and me. I've made the right decisions.

Bea was excited about Halloween, and decided that she wanted a bunny rabbit costume. She wanted Markie to have one, too. Aunt Maggie made the costumes, and Candice took them 'trick-or-treating.' It was early evening, and the streets were full of little ones dressed up as ghosts, goblins, Princesses, and various get-ups. Bea's eyes were big with excitement, and Markie was bouncing around in his stroller, trying to see everything. Returning home with their bags of loot, a group of teenagers wearing masks came running by. One of them grabbed Bea's bag. Bea screamed, and Candice shouted, "Come back here!" Just then a tall figure came running from behind them and caught up with the group of teens. In a minute he was back with the bag of goodies, and gave them to Bea.

"Here you go, Bea. Don't cry." It was Tom. He had been following them to make sure they were safe. Candice thanked him, and Bea gave him a hug, and told him to take all the candy he wanted.

~~~~~~

Candice wrote to Frances often and sent pictures of the children. She always enclosed a check with an itemized statement. Frances called and thanked her then commented how the children were growing and they looked happy. When she received the pictures of Markie's birthday, she said, "You know it's not sanitary to let an animal lick a child in the face, don't you?" Candice ignored the remark, and thought, Do you ever lighten-up?

They invited Frances to visit for Thanksgiving or Christmas, but of course she refused, saying she had other plans. Aunt Maggie said, "That's a relief. I want to enjoy the holidays. One turkey is enough for me," and they laughed 'til they cried.

The hustle and bustle of the Christmas holiday kept everyone busy. Bea was excited and Aunt Maggie helped her write a letter to Santa. They decorated the house, and Tom hung lights on the eaves. Aunt Maggie said she hadn't had lights strung since Candice was in college. She thanked Candy for making the house come alive again. Bea had a hard time getting to sleep on Christmas Eve. Candice read two books to her, and reminded her that Santa would not come until she was asleep.

When she turned out the light in the children's room, she adjusted the shades and looked out the window. It had started to snow and she saw a tall figure standing by the tree in the front yard. The person seemed to be looking at the house. She stood at the window and watched for a while. At first she thought it was Tom admiring his work. But as she watched, she could see that the figure was larger than Tom. She felt uneasy and wondered if she should confront the person. She went downstairs and told Aunt Maggie what she had seen. Aunt Maggie assured her that it was probably one of the neighbors admiring the house's decorations. Candice went into the living room and looked out the window. The figure was gone, but she still had an uneasy feeling. Aunt Maggie told her to forget it, then they had a glass of wine and proceeded to play Santa Claus, spreading the children's gifts under the tree, filling the stockings and snacking on the cookies and milk left for Santa.

When Candice went to bed, she allowed herself the luxury of a good cry. She missed Mark, but at the same time, she was angry with him. She thought to herself, if you were here, Mark, I would like to punch you out Mark Procter. Last Christmas they had played Santa together. She had made a romantic advance toward Mark, and he had given the excuse that it was too soon after the baby's birth. She realized they had not made love since Markie was conceived.

That night, she had fallen asleep on the sofa while reading a book. Mark had come home late from the hospital, and she was awakened when he put his hand in her robe. He cupped her breast as he kissed her neck. She reached up and kissed him on the cheek. Then he kissed her ear, her nose, her forehead, and finally, her lips. When their lips met, she tasted a hint of Scotch. They slipped to the floor and her robe fell open. Mark's hand pushed up her gown. He entered her, and they thrust in rhythm until they were both spent. Remembering that night filled her with longing.

The memory made her cry harder, and she curled up in a fetal position and moaned, "Mark, Mark, what happened to us? Why did you change? Why did you have to leave us?"

The day of the accident they had awakened early and she had made his breakfast. She looked at him as he sipped his coffee and she wanted him. She took his cup out of his hand, straddled his lap and began kissing him all over his face. He pushed her away and said, "What's wrong with you, Candy? You're acting like a slut. That's vulgar. I have to get ready for work." And he left the kitchen to get dressed. While he was dressing, the baby woke. Candice took care of him, gave him a bottle, and when Mark came into the living room, she confronted him with the question, "Why did you marry me, Mark?"

She drifted off to sleep remembering the events of the past year. A lot had happened since the accident.

CHAPTER 7

Vic was literally bouncing down the street. He was walking so fast it was almost a trot. Every now and then he would hop and kind of skip. He was whistling and humming to himself. He was happy. He was free. He felt good. He was going home to Pat.

He stopped at the top of a hill and admired the view. It was one of those perfect days in San Francisco when there was no fog, and you could see all the way to the bay. He loved it here. He loved his job. He loved Pat. He loved life. He felt like a new man. He chuckled to himself. New man. That was the name he gave himself. Victor Newman. It sounded legitimate. Everyone called him Vic. They thought it was short for Victor. Only he knew it was short for Victory. Victory over his old life. Victory over his mother. Victory over a career he didn't enjoy, and never wanted. Victory over pleasing everyone else, never himself. His only regret was leaving the children. He loved them even though he never wanted them. But that was not their fault. It wasn't Candy's fault either. She had been a good wife and mother. She was a good person. He had been the liar in the relationship.

He remembered how they had had fun in the beginning. They were best friends. They enjoyed each other. Their relationship was easy and the sex was good. What happened was not Candy's fault. He just didn't want the traditional lifestyle that his mother had carved out for him. He wanted something different. He wasn't sure just what, but he knew he didn't want what his mother had planned for him. He tried to talk with his father about it, but that went nowhere.

Bob did whatever Frances suggested. He tried too hard to please her. The more he gave, the more she took. This had been a turbulent year. For the first time in his life, Vic had made snap decisions without weighing the consequences. It started the morning of the accident. He had left the house with a determination to talk things over with Candy that evening. He needed her to understand what kind of pressure he was under. He hit a spot of black ice in the road and the car went spinning and sliding towards the riverbank. He could see that there was no way to stop the slide, so he opened the door and jumped out. He rolled away from the car onto the frozen ground. With just a few scratches and bruises, he watched as the car slid slow motion into the river.

He went across the road and started back towards his house. He was hunched over against the storm wishing he had grabbed his coat, when a truck stopped beside him and the driver rolled down his window. "You want a ride, Buddy?"

Mark reacted quickly "Yeah. Thanks," and hopped into the truck. A car had stopped near where his car was slowly sinking, and other cars were slowing down. He could see a fire truck coming in the distance with the sirens blasting.

The driver of the truck said, "Looks like an accident. Where're you headed in this weather?"

Mark thought quickly. "I'm not sure. The Old lady and I had an argument this morning, and I just stormed out without my coat. Dumb, huh?"

"I understand, good buddy. Been there myself. Sometimes it's best to just walk away and give yourself some time. You want me to drop you off somewhere?"

"Hmm. I'm not sure. Where are you headed? Maybe I'll just ride with you for a while."

"Fine with me. I could use the company. I'm Vance. What can I call you?"

"Buddy, is fine. Just call me Buddy," and Mark reached out and shook his hand.

CHAPTER 8

The anniversary of the accident, Candy called Frances. She just wanted to talk with someone who had shared the experience with her. Frances was her usual cold self, but besides being distant, she seemed depressed. Her speech was slow and her answers to Candy's questions were vague. She sounded listless. Candy tried to cheer her up with stories about the children. She talked about Bea's birthday gathering. Bea had drawn a picture of herself with the doll Frances had sent. It was Bea's way of saying thank you. Candy asked her if she had received it, and Frances replied in a monotone "Oh, yes. Thank her for me." Candy asked her if she would like to see the children, and her reply was, "Ok, if you want to bring them here."

Conversations with Frances always left Candy feeling uneasy, as if there were things unsaid. She talked with Aunt Maggie and asked her if she would like to drive with her and the children to visit Frances during the spring break. Aunt Maggie said, "That would be a nice trip. But don't ask me to stay at that woman's house. She might poison me or something. We'll get a motel. There's nothing like a motel room to bring people closer together," and she chuckled.

Phillis was delighted to hear that they were coming to visit and insisted that they stay with her; the children would have fun getting reacquainted. They had room for all of them, and she would love to spend time with Candy and her aunt.

The day after their arrival, lunch with Frances was tense and not very tasty. Cora gave them a warm greeting, and when she hugged Candice she whispered, "We need to talk." Bea was her usual outgoing self and tried to interact with Frances, but with little response from her. When Bea showed her the pictures she had drawn, Frances just smiled and stared off into space. Aunt Maggie worked hard to keep a conversation going, but even she was at a loss for words. Frances spent most of the time staring into space and seemed unaware of their presence.

Walking through the rooms to take Bea to the bathroom, Candy noticed that all the family pictures were missing from the walls and tables. She thought, this is very strange. She asked Frances, "What happened to the pictures?"

"They are no longer necessary. I remember Bob and Mark."

Cora was chatting with Aunt Maggie and the children, trying to make things pleasant. When they were ready to leave, she walked to the van with them. Candice asked her, "What's going on? She really seems to be out of it. How long has she been this way?"

Cora said, "Ever since Mr. Proctor died, she's been slipping away. She walks through the house muttering. She talks about when Mark comes back. She has his room fixed up like when he was a boy, and she goes in there and sits for hours. Sometimes when I arrive in the morning, her bed has not been slept in and I find her in Mark's bed. She needs help, but she won't talk to me. I don't know what to do."

Candice said, "I'll see what I can do."

The next day Candice called Dr. Richards, whom she knew as a family friend, and told him what Cora had told her. He was unaware of Frances' condition. She had not been to see him since the accident. He told Candice he would make a social call and try to talk with her. Candice thanked him and asked him to keep her informed. She was Frances' only relative; she had not met or ever heard Frances mention any family on her side – only Bob's relatives. Dr. Richards went with Candy to the bank to sign the papers so Candy could handle Frances' finances until she was better.

She called Bob's sister, Paula, who was glad to hear from her. Paula inquired about the children and seemed genuinely interested in what was happening in Candy's life. They chatted for a long time. Then Candy told her what was happening with Frances. Paula lived in another town and she told Candy she would try to visit Frances when she could. "We were not that close. Frances never wanted anyone around except Bob. We didn't share holidays or things like that. So I didn't really get to know her. I tried to talk with her several times after the accident, but she's not the easiest person to converse with. It was always a strain, and I would have to make the conversation work. It was a relief to hang up the phone. She didn't even send a Christmas card this past holiday. She must be depressed. I'll try harder to communicate, and you do the same. It's not good for someone to isolate themselves. You keep in touch and send pictures of the kids. Maybe that will help. We'll have to keep in touch, too. I would love to see you and the children sometime."

Candy assured her that they would continue their relationship. The children needed to know their father's relatives. She wanted them to know Frances, too, but she didn't want them hurt by her coldness either. There was no reason for Candy to feel responsible for Frances, but she did. After all, Frances was the children's grandmother, and Mark would have expected me to look after her, she thought. Besides, I feel sorry for her. Frances has no one, and I am surrounded by love and people who care about me.

~~~~~~~~~~~~~~~~~~~~~~~~~~~~~~~~~~~~~

They stayed another day and enjoyed visiting with Phillis and her family. Candy thought she would feel nostalgic when she saw her house, but she felt nothing. The renters were taking care of the yard and the house looked the same. She would be glad when six more years had passed and she could sell it. This was no longer her home, and she was anxious to get back to her real home. By the time they arrived home it was late evening and the kennel where they had boarded Bunny was closed. They would have to wait 'til the next day to get him. Markie tottered from room to room calling, "Bun, Bun." He couldn't understand why Bunny was not there. Candy tried to make him understand, but he only got more upset. Bea assured him that he would see Bunny in the morning. He slept with Bea that night, and cried himself to sleep.

The next morning they went to get Bunny before they had breakfast. Markie was so excited when he saw Bunny that he started laughing and crying at the same time. Bunny seemed to be grinning as he wagged all over. After breakfast, Bunny lay down to take a nap, and Markie lay beside him.

He patted him until he too was asleep. Candy took a picture as she and Aunt Maggie smiled and wiped away tears.

Cora and the doctor kept Candy informed of Frances' condition. The doctor had prescribed medication for Frances' depression, but Frances refused to take it. She went further and further into herself. She no longer conversed with Cora, and barely ate. She lost weight and no longer took care of her personal needs. She wore the same pajamas day and night for weeks.

In June, Cora called Candice, "Mrs. Proctor ate her breakfast this morning, took a shower and got dressed. She said she was going to get Mark. I asked her where was she going, and she said where they're keeping him. I asked her where that was, and she said, 'You'll see.' So when she left, I got in my car and followed her. She was headed toward the river. So I stopped at a pay phone and called Doctor Richards. I told him what she was doing, then I drove to the river. There she was just sitting in her car and staring into space. I went over to the car and asked her what she was doing. She looked through me, not at me, and said, 'He's in there. I know he is and I'm going to get him.'

"I told her she couldn't go in the river, and she said, 'You can't stop me.' I tried to keep the door shut, but she pushed me aside. I continued to try to talk to her and to hold her back, but she was as strong as a mule. By that time the doctor had arrived. He tried to calm her down, but she fought him, too. He had to wrestle her to the ground and give her a shot. She stopped struggling and he was able to get her into his car. He took her to the hospital, and now she's in the psych ward. I don't know what to do."

Candice thanked her for helping Frances and asked her to continue looking after the house until she could get there. Then they would decide what to do.

When Candice told Aunt Maggie about Cora's call, Aunt Maggie said, "I feel so sorry for her, poor thing. She has no one but then she pushed everyone away. Maybe she had mental problems all along. No one can be that removed from people without something being wrong. You go see what you can do for her. I'll take care of things here."

Candice went directly to the hospital to see Frances and found her in a trancelike state. She could not communicate with her at all. Dr. Richards said it would be awhile before she would show any response to her treatment. They would place her in a facility where she could get the care she needed with Candy's consent.

Candice stayed at Frances' house and while she was there she looked through the rooms for the pictures. She found them in Mark's room in the closet, stacked on top of a box. She looked at each picture closely hoping to find a clue as to what was going on with Frances. She didn't know what she was looking for, but something told her to continue looking. When she reached the box and opened it, inside were snapshots of different activities – Mark and Bob fishing, Frances and Bob on a picnic, Mark in his baseball uniform, etc. Then near the bottom of the box were silhouettes of a little girl at different ages. Each picture had been trimmed so that whatever, or whoever was in the picture with the child was gone. On the backs of each one were fragments of dates or names remaining from the original picture. It was never enough information to tell when or where the picture had been taken. As Candice looked at the pictures she could see a progression of the child's growth from a tot to an older child. Clearly they were pictures of Frances.   Obviously Frances wanted to be disassociated from the other people in the pictures – probably her family? This might explain a lot if Candy knew more about Frances family. Why would Frances literally cut away her family? Candice wondered if this had anything to do with Bob's plea to Frances the morning of his death and Mark's disappearance. Could it be the key to what Bob wanted Frances to tell her?

She looked at the backs of the silhouettes again and tried to piece together the fragments of names and dates to try to get a clue. Nothing seemed to come together. She got a piece of paper and wrote down all the parts of words and the numbers. It was like assembling a puzzle. Perhaps if she worked at it she could make some sense of the pieces. If she could get a name, maybe she could figure out where Frances was from and – then what? What would she do with the information? She wasn't sure what she was looking for. If she found something, how would it affect her life? Did she really want to pursue this or should she even care?

She put everything back like she found it and decided she would leave the next day after a visit with Phillis and Dr. Richards. She had to get back to her children and her job. Frances' enigma would have to wait.

CHAPTER 9

With treatment, Frances' condition improved and she returned to her home after a year. Candice continued to converse with Dr. Richards and Cora and she talked with Frances often. She sent her pictures of the children, and Candice could tell she was getting better because Frances started criticizing what they were wearing or the activity they were doing. Aunt Maggie said that Frances would never change. "She's a negative person. Nothing you can do about that. Just keep on doing what you're doing."

Candice got her degree and completed the credential program, She took a job teaching in an elementary school. She loved her work, and the house was constantly filled with activity. She developed lots of crafty projects for her students and had Bea and Markie try them out first. The other teachers at her school were quite impressed with her work and frequently borrowed her ideas. The principal told her she was a treasured addition to their school.

She and Dotty had become close friends since the day they had met at the quad. She had a busy social life but Aunt Maggie fussed that she needed to find male companionship. One day while they were sipping tea and talking at the kitchen table, she told her, "Let's face it, girl. You're not getting any younger. Mark is gone. You're still young and pretty. You need to move on with your life."

"I'm not ready. And besides where do you find someone who is available in my age group? If he's not attached, there's something wrong with him. I have enough to deal with. I don't need a man getting in my way, causing problems. The children and my work keep me plenty busy. I'm happy with the way things are. Bea is doing very well in school, and Markie loves preschool. As long as they are okay, then I'm okay. Why don't you get a boyfriend?"

Aunt Maggie laughed. "Girl, if I could find one standing up straight, without his teeth falling out when he talks, and not wearing diapers, I'll grab him." They laughed until their tea got cold.

That night, before Candice went to sleep, she thought about what Aunt Maggie had said. It would be nice to have some companionship. Someone to go to a movie and share popcorn with, and maybe a dinner. I haven't had a date in so long, I wouldn't know how to act, she sighed. Oh, well, if it's meant to be, it will be. And with that thought, she drifted off to sleep.

The school principal had talked with the district superintendent who approached Candice with the idea of going to other schools in the district and giving workshops to show them her artsy-craftsy projects. Candice was flattered and said she would think about it. She knew it would require a lot of preparation and organization and she didn't know if she wanted to spend a lot of time out of the classroom. She talked it over with Aunt Maggie.

Aunt Maggie's advice was to tell the superintendent that if she chose to do this, it would have to be on a full time basis. She would not be able to teach and do what he wanted at the same time. She would need an office and an aide to help prepare material and take care of scheduling and other details.

Candice wrote down her conditions and took them to the superintendent. He agreed. They decided to start the next school year. Candice was excited and began planning during the summer. She shared her plans with Frances, who said, "If you're so good, why don't you write a book?"

Candice refused to let Frances get to her. Then she thought, for once the old biddy might be right. It's the first time I've ever received any constructive advice from her, and she didn't even mean it that way. She was being sarcastic. .

As Candice began organizing her lessons, she kept copious notes. She set up a file and took lots of pictures of project steps from different angles. She looked at How To books and studied their layout and organization. She contacted publishers with her ideas, but received little response and no offers. She convinced herself not to get discouraged, and continued to hone her ideas.

~~~~~~~~~~~~~~~~~~~~~~~~~~~~~~~~~~~~~

When school started in the fall, she hired Dotty's daughter, Megan, as her assistant. They coordinated Megan's schedule with her college classes. Everything was falling into place.

The first workshop went smoothly enough, however Candice realized that teaching teachers was the same as teaching children. She had to constantly ask them to keep the noise level down, and to pay attention. Some of the older teachers responded negatively towards her, or refused to use her ideas. Some whined about not being able to do them, so how could children do them. They said some projects were too hard or too easy. The complaints went on and on.

54

When Candice shared her experience with Aunt Maggie, she told her, "I could have told you that, girl. When teachers get together, all they do is talk. They don't want to listen. They act just like children. You'll have those who want to learn, and those who just put in their time. They'll go back to their classrooms, but use the same old ideas they've had for years. Just do the best you can. About half of them will take your ideas and use them. Don't get discouraged. Don't blame yourself. Keep doing what you're doing. It will all fall in place. Don't stress over it. Things have a way of happening in their own time. In the meantime, take care of yourself. Now, sit down and share a glass of wine with your old aunt."

CHAPTER 10

Creativity feeds on itself. Candice got more and more ideas. Some worked and some didn't, but she was not discouraged. She created booklets for her workshops which became very popular – especially with the younger teachers. The district began publishing her booklets and they reached a wider distribution.

One evening a man called and asked to speak to Candice. He said he had seen her booklets and wanted to talk with her about being her agent. He thought there was a chance he could get her ideas published. He invited her to lunch to discuss the details. It was hard for Candice to control her enthusiasm and she tried to sound nonchalant. She agreed to meet with him the next day.

When she hung up the phone, she punched the air with her fist and shouted, "Yes!"

The children and Aunt Maggie asked, "What? What?" When she told them the news, they were all jumping up and down and dancing around.

Aunt Maggie said, "This is cause for a celebration. Get out the ice cream!"

~~~~~~~~~~~~~~~~~~~~~~~~~~~~~~~~~~~~~~

Lionel Brownell was a tall man with regular features, horn-rimmed glasses, a little on the heavy side. He had a friendly, likable manner, and Candice was comfortable with him from the first firm hand shake. They talked about their families, and what was expected from each of them. He offered her a contract. Candice said she would think about his offer, have a lawyer look over the contract and get back to him. He said, "I'm impressed. I've had people get so caught up in the excitement of getting published, that they sign the contract without even reading it. I think we'll work well together."

Candice's confidence was so heartened, she felt like she was walking on air when she left the restaurant. She smiled all the way home. Aunt Maggie called the children in from the back yard, and said, "Sit, sit, sit. Start from the beginning. Tell us everything. What did he look like? What did you eat? What did he say? Don't leave out anything. I want all the details. How do you feel about him? What did you talk about?"

Candice had to interrupt her, as usual. "Calm down. I'll tell you everything if you'll let me get my breath." She could hardly contain her excitement as she described the afternoon. She showed them the contract and exaggerated how cool she was when she told him she would have a lawyer look at the contract and get back to him. The three of them said, "Ooh! Cool!"

The lawyer said the contract was a good one and Candice should have no problem with the agent or the publishing company. Candice signed, and began a long and profitable relationship with Lionel. She went to educational conventions and had book signings. She enjoyed the travel, but missed her family. She was never gone long, usually just a weekend, but it always seemed long to her. The children were growing up so fast and she felt she was missing out.

They were both active in sports and their games were almost always on weekends.

Candy occasionally travelled to teaching conferences. One of her trips was to San Francisco. During a break, she and a group of ladies went to the De Young Museum to look at some of the exhibits. She glanced around the room, and she thought she saw a familiar figure leaving through the outside doors. She had to take a second look. Her heart was pounding fast as she went as quickly as she could to the doors. By the time she got through the crowd, though, he was gone. She went out to the front of the building and looked to the left and then to the right, but she didn't see him. She thought to herself, I could have sworn that I saw Mark. Maybe my mind is playing tricks on me. It was probably someone who looks like him. They say everyone has a double.

She went back to her group, and someone asked her what made her run off like that. She said that she thought she saw someone she knew, but it wasn't them. She paid little attention to the exhibitions, and vaguely joined the conversations. For the rest of the weekend she struggled with the nagging feeling that she had seen Mark.

When she returned home, she told Aunt Maggie about the incident. "If you think it was Mark, hire a detective to investigate and put your mind at ease. I know you won't rest until you have some answers. At least you'll know if it was him, and if he is still alive."

~~~~~~~~~~~~~~~~~~~~~~~~~~~~~~~~~~

The detective Candice hired reported his findings. The last bit of information he could find on Dr. Marcus Procter,

MD was from the hospital where he had been employed. He had been reported missing since the date of the accident, a possible drowning victim. He could find no activity since that date. There was no record of a Dr. Marcus Procter in or around San Francisco. He was presumed dead.

Candice paid him and thanked him, but she wasn't satisfied. She still had this awful feeling that the person she had seen in San Francisco was Mark. However, she couldn't think of anything else to do so she kept busy with her everyday activities and tried not to think about it.

~~~~~~~~~~~~~~~~~~~~~~~~~~~~~~~~~~~~~

Every now and then she tried to make sense of the fragments of numbers and words that she had copied off the pictures of Frances as a child. Maybe if she could find the name of a person or a place, she would have something to go on. She usually ended up frustrated and put the paper aside to look at later. The Procter mysteries would have to wait.

She toyed with the idea of talking with Frances about the pictures, but decided that that would not be a good idea, given Frances' fragile mental state. Besides she would have to admit that she had been snooping. It would be best to leave well enough alone.

One day, when she was sorting some of her files, Bea came to help her and she spotted the paper with the fragment of words on it. She asked, "What's this – some new game?" Candice replied, "Oh just some idea I had, but it's not working, so I put it aside."

Bea loved puzzles and challenges. She was analytical and excelled in math. She said, "Hmmm. Let me give it a try." The phone rang and Bea took the piece of paper to her room before Candice could think of an excuse to stop her.

It was the hospital. Markie had been hit on the head by a ball at baseball practice. Candice said, "I'll be right there." She and Bea went as fast as they could to the hospital. When they got to the Emergency Room, Markie was sitting in a chair holding an ice pack on the side of his head.

He looked up at them and grinned, "Hey, what's up?"

Bea said, "We heard that you mistook your head for a bat and tried to make a home run."

Candice laughed through her tears. She hugged Markie and said, "We were so worried about you. Are you all right? Does it hurt? What happened?"

A voice behind her said, "The doctor said he'll be ok. It wasn't as bad as we thought. We brought him here just as a precaution."

It was Wesley Knox, the coach for the Little League team. He touched Candice's shoulder and said, "He'll be Ok. Don't worry." His hand was comforting, and his voice was reassuring. She could feel the warmth of his hand even after he took it away. Candice thanked him and went to take care of the paper work.

On their way home, Bea said, "The coach seems like a nice guy. Why don't you invite him to dinner some time?"

Candice sputtered, "Why Bea! Are you trying to be a matchmaker? The man looked after Markie, that's all. He probably has a wife and fifteen children, for Pete's sake."

Markie said, "He has a wife and a son. But he is a nice guy. I like him."

Candice said, "So there, Miss smarty pants. You're out of business. Now leave it alone."

Bea replied, "You do need to have a date now and then. I'm going to start looking for someone for you. You're too young and pretty to be an Old Maid. I'll take care of it."

Markie said, "Yeah, Mom. I'll start looking, too."

Candice giggled and pretended to be outraged. "Will you two stop? I can find my own man if I want one! Okay? I think that knock on your head rattled your brain, Markie."

When they went into the house, Aunt Maggie said, "This is the first time I ever saw people come from the Emergency Room laughing. What happened?" Bea gave her the details, and Aunt Maggie said, "I think that's a good idea. I'll start looking, too. We'll fix her up with somebody."

Candice said, "I hope you three are enjoying yourselves. If I want a man, I can get one just like that!" She tried to snap her fingers, but couldn't, and they all laughed harder.

That night, before Candice fell asleep, she thought, It would be nice to have some companionship. But I have enough to keep me busy. If it's meant to be, it will be. She drifted off to sleep with the memory of Wes's hand on her shoulder.

Whenever she went to Markie's games, she tried hard not to look at Wes and avoided talking to him. She chastised herself for over-reacting and felt foolish when she found she could not avoid looking at him. He's a married man – with no interest in me at all, she told herself. Nothing can come of this, so why are you even thinking about him? She tried to come up with reasons to miss Markie's games, but she quickly abandoned that idea. After all, she wanted to be there for her son.

At one game, Markie slid into home base just before the ball and made the winning score. Candice was jumping up and down with the rest of the parents when the woman next to her asked, "Is Markie your son?"

Candice replied, "Why yes he is. Is your son out there?"

She answered, "Yes. He's the one who was at bat. Markie has improved a lot. He's very athletic, and so polite. He's a nice boy."

"Thank you. Now if I could get him to clean his room, I might keep him."

They both laughed, introduced themselves, and started sharing stories about their children. Candice really liked her and felt that they could be friends. They were still sitting and chatting when almost everyone had left the field. Markie and another boy came over to the bleachers and everyone exchanged names. Then Wes came over to the group and said, "I see you've met my wife, and this is my son, Fred."

When they got up to leave, Wes helped his wife, Nicole, with her braces and they went slowly to the parking lot. They waved goodbye and Candice watched as Wes situated Nicole in the car. As she drove out of the parking lot, Markie said, "Fred's mom has what they call MS, whatever that is. She has a hard time walking sometimes, so she uses those brace things. She's a good cook. She's always bringing treats for the team."

Candice said, "That's a good idea. I can bring treats sometimes, too. I'll talk with her about it so we won't bring them at the same time. I am really proud of you – not just for making that winning slide, but for being the good son that you are," and she reached over and mussed his hair.

Markie grinned, "Ah, Mom. Cut it out." But she could tell that he liked hearing it, even if it did embarrass him.

CHAPTER 11

Halloween was always a special time for Vic and Pat. They enjoyed it as much as Eric, Pat's son. They would spend days getting Eric's costume ready, no matter how outlandish his ideas were. This year he wanted to be a robot, and they tried to make it as authentic as they could. It was fun shopping for the right material, and going to unique shops for different parts.

As they worked, Vic was reminded of the Halloween when he almost went back to his family. He had been bumming around, living off his wits, and decided it was time for him to go home. But he enjoyed his freedom – no responsibilities for anyone but himself – his only worry was where he would sleep and where his next meal would come from. He met interesting people, and made friends with truck drivers, always eager for a companion on the road. It was fun being a vagabond. He was unrecognizable with his long hair, mustache, and full beard. He knew where his family was by eavesdropping on conversations he heard in a coffee shop in Newburn. So he went to Aunt Maggie's house with the idea that he would say he had had amnesia. He had only just remembered his family and wanted to come back to them.

When he walked near the house, no one noticed the man dressed like a bum with scraggly hair and dirty clothes. They probably thought he was just another trick-or-treater. Just as he was about to cross the street, he saw Candy come out of the house with the baby in a stroller and Bea by her side. They looked so cute in their bunny costumes. He followed close enough to watch, but not be seen by them.

When the teen-agers ran by and grabbed Bea's bag, he grew angry and started to run after them, but then he saw a young man grab the teen, and take the bag back to Bea. He saw that they obviously knew the man. So he decided to disappear again.

In his imagination, after he returned, they would move back to their home in Newburn. He would resume his work at the hospital. Life would be good. But the more he thought about it, the less he wanted to do it. He didn't want that life anymore. It would be unfair to the children and Candy, as resentful as he was. None of them would be happy. He loved Candy, but he was not in love with her. Things could never be the same as before. He was sure she would never trust him again – why should she? Her distrust and his duplicity would wreck their lives.

He moved about the town unrecognized for the next few weeks, struggling with his decision. As the days passed and the nights grew colder it became harder and harder to find a warm place to sleep at night. He had no trouble finding warm clothes at thrift stores and church giveaways, but finding a place to sleep was not easy. So on Christmas Eve, he took one last look at Aunt Maggie's house before he hitched a ride with a trucker going west. The house was lovely with lights strung around the eaves and on the bushes. It was a Currier and Ives picture – tranquil and inviting. He saw the light go out in one of the upstairs windows, and he knew they were safe. The children would be fine in Candy's care. He hunched against the cold, buttoned his coat and headed for the truck stop.

His reverie was interrupted by Eric. "What's this supposed to be?" He was holding a spear and laughing. "Is this part of the robot costume? A robot wouldn't carry a spear."

Vic laughed, "You're right. I thought we could use it for something else. Maybe next year, or maybe I'll dress up this year as Sir Laugh-a-lot. What do you think, Patricia?" He knew Pat hated to be called Patricia.

Pat came out of the kitchen. "I think that deserves fifty lashes with a wet noodle."

Just then, the chandelier began to sway, and the floor moved sideways. Pat said, "Earth quake! Get under the table!" They scrambled to the heavy dining room table, and crowded together, holding each other. After what seemed like an eternity, but was only about sixty seconds, the shaking stopped. They cautiously emerged stepping gingerly around books, broken glass, and other debris, and went outside.

Some of their neighbors were slowly coming out, also. Their house didn't seem to have much damage, but some of the houses on the other side of the street were slumped on one side, or had broken windows and cracks in the walls. Vic asked, "Is anybody hurt? We need to take care of the injured."

Those who could went door to door looking for people who might need help. Vic administered to the injured as best he could with limited supplies until they could get them some emergency medical care. His training came back to him as if he had never stopped.

When things were more settled, Pat said to him, "I watched how you handled yourself today. You looked very professional. Me thinks you were a doctor in your other life, eh? Do you want to confess, or are you going to leave me guessing?"

Vic answered, "Could be, but right now, we have work to do. We'll talk about it later." They went back into their house, assessed the damage, and decided it was structurally sound enough for them to stay there. They cleared away as much as they could to get to their beds and fell into them, exhausted. Eric was asleep as soon as his head hit the pillow. Vic and Pat found a bottle of wine and two mugs that were not cracked and toasted their good luck. They, too, were soon asleep. Talk would have to wait 'til another time.

CHAPTER 12

The Martin's cat was sitting on the fence flicking its tail and Bunny was barking as loud as he could. Aunt Maggie called to Markie, "Come and take your dog for a walk so he'll stop that infernal barking."

Markie came into the kitchen and said, "If I take him, what do I get?"

Aunt Maggie shook her wooden spoon at him and said, "One cookie. Now get out of here."

Markie reached into the cookie jar, grabbed two cookies and ran back out the door. "Come on boy. Let's go for a walk."

He hooked Bunny's leash onto his collar, picked up his skateboard and went around the side of the house through the gate. He stuffed both cookies in his mouth, and they started leisurely down the sidewalk with Bunny pulling Markie on his skateboard.

The Martin's cat sauntered by and meowed at Bunny. Bunny gave chase as the cat ran towards a tree. He pulled the leash out of Markie's hand before Markie could get a firm grip on it. He could not control the skateboard and he was hurled into the path of an oncoming car. Markie was catapulted onto the hood then into the street. The driver stopped and jumped out of his car. He looked at Markie and ran to the house on the corner. He banged on the door, and Mrs. Martin answered quickly. The driver told her what had happened, and she called an ambulance.

Wes was driving in the opposite direction when he saw the accident. He rushed over and saw that it was Markie. He knelt by Markie, checked his pulse but didn't try to move him. He could tell that his leg was broken just by looking at it. He heard the ambulance's siren and knew that they would know what to do for Markie. He told the driver of the car to stay with him and he would tell the victim's family.

When Aunt Maggie heard the persistent banging on the door, she wiped her hands on her apron. "All right. I'm coming. I'm coming." She saw that it was Wes and heard the siren, "What is it? What's going on?"

Wes told her that Markie had been in an accident and was on his way to the hospital. Candy was on her way down the stairs when she heard Wes talking to Aunt Maggie. She slumped down, grabbed the banister and said, "I'll get my keys."

Wes said, "You'll do no such thing. You're in no shape to drive. Come on. I'll take you." Candy called to Bea and the three of them got into Wes's car.

When they reached the emergency entrance, Wes let them out, and Candy thanked him. They went inside and didn't see Markie anywhere. They inquired at the nurses' station and she told them to have a seat and wait for the doctor to come out.

They sat down, and Candy looked up to see Wes coming through the door. "You don't have to stay," she said. "It might be a long wait."

Wes replied, "Don't worry about it. I'll wait with you."

After about an hour, a doctor came out and told them that Markie was in very serious condition. He had internal injuries, a broken collar bone, a broken left arm, broken left leg in two places and a possible concussion. They needed Candy's permission to operate, and it would be a long wait. They could go home and someone would call when he was out of surgery.

Candice said that Aunt Maggie and Bea could go home, but she would wait, no matter how long. Wes said he would take them home, and they left.

Candice took care of the paper work, and the nurse directed her to the surgical waiting room. It was more comfortable, with magazines and roomy chairs and sofas. Candy couldn't get interested in a magazine as she flipped through the pages. There were other people there, but she didn't want to talk with anyone. She only wanted her baby to be well. She said a silent prayer.

She startled awake when she felt a hand on her shoulder. Someone was calling her name. She looked up into Wes' worried eyes. She could see that it was dark outside. "Oh, I didn't know I had drifted off to sleep. I'm sorry."

"Don't apologize. Here, Nichole sent you a sandwich and some coffee. You need to keep your strength up. I bet you haven't eaten anything."

"You're right. I didn't even realize that I was hungry. That's so like Nichole, - always thinking of other people.

She's such a good friend. Thanks Wes," Candy said as she began eating. "I've taken up enough of your time today. You don't have to stay. I appreciate everything you've done."

"I know I don't have to stay. I want to."

"I'm glad Markie has you for a coach. He really likes you. You're like a father to him."

"He's a good kid. I like him, too. If you don't mind my asking, what happened to his father?"

Candy told him the story of the accident and what had happened afterwards. He told her about Nichole's illness and its impact on their family. They talked through the night.

"Mrs. Procter. Your son is out of surgery," the doctor touched her on the arm. She had nodded off, her head resting on Wes' shoulder. His arm was around her shoulder. He opened his eyes and stretched. They had both drifted off to sleep. It was getting light outside.

"Mrs. Procter, you and your husband can see your son in about an hour. He'll be in ICU. We'll let you know when he regains consciousness. Then you can come one at a time."

Candy replied, "Thank you, Doctor." To Wes she said, "He assumed that you're my husband," she giggled.

"Well, it's no wonder. You bold woman, you had your head on my shoulder," he laughed. "I'll tell your aunt and Bea that he's out of surgery, and I'll see you later."

He walked to the door, turned around and their eyes locked. Candy could not look away, and she was not sure

71

what she saw in Wes' eyes. "We talked a lot last night," said Wes. "We need to talk some more. We both know it." Candy could only nod. He turned and went out the door, closing it behind him.

Candy ran to the door and she could see his back as he turned the corner down the hall. She put her hand to her throat. "What am I doing? The man is married. His wife is my friend. What kind of hussy am I? Why do I feel guilty? I haven't done anything to feel guilty about. And I won't do anything. I won't." As she turned away from the door, she admitted "but I haven't felt this way in a long, long time."

She went to the vending machine and got a cup of the swill they called coffee and tried to get interested in a magazine. After about an hour, Aunt Maggie and Bea came into the waiting room with bags of food, and together they waited to see Markie.

A nurse came to tell them that Markie was awake and his mother could see him. Candy began crying when she saw him. He had a cast on his left leg which was in traction. His left arm was also in a cast, propped up on the cast encasing his upper torso. He had a soft cast around his head, too.

He opened his eyes and whispered, "I'm so sorry, Mom."

Candy took his right hand in hers. "Hush. Hush. You have nothing to be sorry about. It was an accident. It wasn't your fault. We're just glad that you're going to be ok. It's going to take a while, but you'll be fine. Are you in pain? That's a stupid question, isn't it? You're my baby. I don't care how big you get. I'm just glad you're going to be all right."

When they moved Markie out of the intensive care unit the next day, Bea and Aunt Maggie were allowed to see him.

Bea said, through her tears, "You dork. You'll do anything for attention. I have more to worry about than a duffus on a skateboard. You scared us, you knuckle head."

Markie whispered, "I love you, too, Sis. Thanks for the endearing remarks."

Aunt Maggie said, "Just so you know, Bunny has been moping around the house and whining. Percy chased the Martin's cat off the fence yesterday afternoon. We heard a lot of yowling and we haven't seen that cat since. Percy sits on the back porch watching the fence, thumping his tail. I think he taught that cat a lesson he won't soon forget. So everything is under control at home. You just concentrate on getting well so you can come home."

Markie whispered, "Hey Coach."

They turned around and there was Wes with a bunch of yellow flowers. "These are from the team. They send their best, and they'll be coming to see you as soon as they're allowed. It may be a while before you're back in the game, but you'll always be on the team."

Markie got tears in his eyes. "Thanks, Coach."

"Ladies, I've got to get to work. I'll check on our patient later." Wes touched Candy on the arm and walked out of the room.

Bea sighed and looked at Candy, "Too bad he's married."

Aunt Maggie said, "Yeah, too bad." They both looked at Candy.

"What? What are you two looking at?"

Then Markie croaked, "Yep, too bad."

They started laughing, and Markie cried, "Stop! Stop!! It hurts to laugh."

"That's what you get for trying to be funny. We're going to leave now so you can get some rest. We'll be back later today. I need to shower and get out of these clothes. I've been in them since day before yesterday." They each kissed him on the cheek and he was drifting off to sleep as they were leaving the room.

CHAPTER 13

Markie's recovery was slow. He had lots of visitors and he made friends with the hospital staff. He was fascinated with the details of his treatment, besieging the medical staff with questions. He was allowed to go home when he no longer needed to be in tractions, but was still in casts.

Candy rented a hospital bed and they set it up in the living room where he could watch television. A "WELCOME HOME, MARKIE" banner was strung over his bed. His little league team and some of his classmates were there, along with his teacher. They had ice cream and cake. Markie was delighted. Bunny's whole body wiggled with his tail and he wouldn't stop licking Markie. He stayed next to Markie the entire time. Percy waited until everyone had left. Then he got on Markie's bed, sniffed at all the casts, and rubbed Markie's cheek. He began purring and kneading his right shoulder. Bea said, "Percy's giving you a massage." They laughed as Percy curled up next to Markie's side then went to sleep. Bunny jumped up next to his right leg and settled down watching everyone with his head resting on his paws. Candy got the camera and took pictures.

As usual, she sent pictures to Frances. When Frances received them she called. "I'm disappointed in you Candice. I thought you would know better than to let those animals contaminate the boy. They have all kinds of germs you know, especially the cat. Cats go into all kinds of unseemly places, and it might suck the breath out of the boy while he's asleep. Let me speak to him."

Candy rolled her eyes. "Mother Procter, I wouldn't let Percy and Bunny hurt my son. Cats sucking someone's breath while they are sleeping is an old wives tale. I'm surprised you believe something like that. Markie can't come to the phone, and the phone can't reach him. I'm sure he would love to hear from you though. You could send a card. I'll tell him you called. What would you like for me to tell him?"

"Just tell him that I hope he heals soon, and to be careful from now on. He is the only grandson that I have, and I do love him. I love Bea, too. I want them to come see me as soon as he can get around."

Candy sighed, "It's going to be a long time before he'll be well enough to travel, Mother Procter. But you could come here if you want to see the children. You are able to travel, aren't you?"

"Yes, I suppose I could. I'll have to think about it. I'll let you know. I have to go now, dear. Take care, bye."

Candice put the receiver on the wall phone and shuddered, "That woman always makes my blood boil. How could anyone be so insensitive?"

Aunt Maggie replied, "When you only think of yourself, it's easy. I don't think she knows any better. Here, have some chamomile tea and settle down. Don't let her get to you. You should know by now not to expect a typical response from her."

Two weeks later, Bea and Markie were watching American Band Stand on television, and Bea was trying to imitate the dancers on the screen. Markie said, "Hey, you're pretty good, Sis. Where'd you learn those steps?"

Bea replied, "Mostly from watching Band Stand. We'll have to practice when you're up and about. You can do it, too."

Just then, Candy came into the room, "What's going on?"

"I'm trying to do this new dance, Mom, but it's not as easy as it seems. Bet you can't do it," and she winked at Markie.

"You want to bet?" Candy responded. Then she joined Bea, and they were laughing and dancing when Aunt Maggie came out of the kitchen and joined in. She started dancing, too.

Bea began laughing so hard she missed a step. "You're supposed to twist your hips, Auntie Mom, not wag your behind."

Aunt Maggie said, "You dance your way, and I'll dance mine," and they continued to dance. Bea heard the knocking on the screen door, and she motioned for Wes to come on in. When he saw what Candy and Aunt Maggie were doing, he joined in. Candy had not noticed him, and was engrossed in dancing away when she turned around and saw Wes. She stopped dancing, and put her hand over her mouth in embarrassment. Wes just laughed. "That's pretty good. Keep it up." Candy shrugged and returned to dancing.

Bea said, "There's nothing like watching old folks dance, if you want a good laugh."

Aunt Maggie said, "Watch your manners, girl. You're just scared we'll out shine you."

Bea joined them, and Markie said, "Stop, stop, stop. It hurts to laugh like this!"

Aunt Maggie said, "Laughter is good for the soul, boy. So is dancing – good for the soul, but not the back. Whee, I've got to give it a rest."

Just then, the music stopped. They all were breathing hard when they heard, "Ahem," from the doorway. They turned to see Frances and Cora standing in the doorway. Frances was dressed in a suit, hat and gloves, clutching her purse, looking more severe than ever.

"Is this how you're helping you son get well, Candice? You were gyrating like some common person. What are you teaching your daughter? And who is this man? "

"Mother Procter, Cora, you should have let us know you were coming. Bea was showing us a new dance. This is Mr. Knox, Markie's baseball coach. Wes, Frances Procter, Cora Mays, Mother Procter, Cora, Wes Knox. Wes came over to check on Markie, and he saw us dancing, so he joined in. Won't you join us? I don't mean to dance, but won't you come in and sit down?" Candice sputtered.

"How do you do, Mrs. Procter, Mrs. Mays? Nice to finally meet you." To Candy, Wes said, "I really came over to see if we could have the team over here to watch the game tomorrow? Nicole and I will bring the treats. We thought it would be fun for Markie to have the team here. You might enjoy watching the game, too, Mrs. Procter. What do you think, Candy? If it's an inconvenience, we can do it some other time."

"I think that will be fine. What do you think, Aunt Maggie? We could make brownies. Is it ok with you, Markie?"

Markie said he would love it, and Aunt Maggie said she'd be delighted.

Candice went to the door with Wes. "Thanks for coming over. I'll call Nicole and we can work out the details. You're a good friend. Don't let Mother Procter get to you."

Wes said, "I'll see you tomorrow. Good luck. You're going to need it with that one."

Candy's mind was racing as she went back into the living room. "Well, I wish you would have let me know you were coming, Mother Procter. Are you hungry? Make yourselves comfortable. Cora, you can sleep in Markie's room. Mother Procter, you can have my room. I'll sleep out here on the couch. I do that quite often anyway. Let me get you something cool to drink. How about some lemonade?"

Frances interrupted her. "Don't fuss about so, Candice. We've taken a room at the hotel downtown. A glass of lemonade would be nice, though. What do you think, Cora?"

For the first time, Cora spoke. "I'm so glad to see you, Candy. Maggie, it's good to see you, too. My, how the children have grown. Bea, you're such a pretty little lady. I knew you would be. Markie, you should be proud of yourself. It took your accident to get your grandmother to leave her house. I would love some lemonade," and she laughed.

Aunt Maggie said, "I'll get the lemonade. You stay here with your 'company', Candy."

Cora said, "If you don't mind, I'll come with you."

Aunt Maggie replied, "I don't mind one bit. Come along."

When they reached the kitchen, Aunt Maggie asked Cora how Frances was getting along. "She seems better. At least she can focus now-- not as depressed, -- but still a little off. Between you and me, I don't think she's never been quite on – if you know what I mean. She's always been a little strange, even before the accident. I've worked for her for so long, I just accept that she's different, and let it go."

The next day, Wes, Nicole, and Fred came over right after church. They brought hamburger patties, wieners, rolls, chips, condiments, and sodas. People began dribbling in around 1:00. Most of the gang was there by 2:00 when the game started. It was noisy and crowded with kids sitting anywhere there was an open space. Everyone seemed to be having a good time, when Bea answered a knock on the screen door. It was Frances and Cora. "Hey, Grandma. Come on in." She tried to hug Frances.

Frances turned away slightly. "You've got mustard on your face. Don't get that hot dog on me."

"Sorry, Grandma. Hi, Miss Cora. Come on in." and she hugged Cora. Cora hugged her back, and they went into the living room. Frances just stood in the doorway looking as if she didn't know what to do. "I think you'd be more comfortable in the kitchen, Grandma."

The three went around into the kitchen and Maggie greeted them. She said, "Sit here at the table, ladies, and I'll fix you a plate. Do you want hot dogs, or hamburgers, or both?"

Frances said, "A hamburger, please."

Cora blurted out, "Both." They all laughed, including Frances.

Aunt Maggie asked what they would like to drink. Frances chose iced tea, and Cora picked beer.

They sat at the table chatting and eating. They could hear the cheers and laughter coming from the living room, and Frances unbuttoned the two top buttons on her blouse. She said, "It's getting warm in here, isn't it?"

Aunt Maggie said, "It sure is. Let me get you some more iced tea."

Frances said, "That would be nice, thank you. It sure is good tea -- just a little sweet, but not too much, and such a nice flavor. What kind is it?"

"Just plain black tea, but I brew it a special way, with a secret ingredient," and she winked at Cora.

"I need to use the lady's room. Which way is it?" asked Frances.

Aunt Maggie showed her the way, and when she came back, she called Cora to the sink and showed her the secret ingredient. Cora giggled and asked for another beer.

When Frances returned, she said, "This really is a lovely home, Maggie. It's so comfortable. Warm and cozy, not pretentious, but welcoming. Yes, that's the word – welcoming."

Aunt Maggie said, "I'm glad you like it. Here have some more iced tea."

They retired to the back yard when they finished eating, and sat in the shade of the big tree sipping their cool drinks. They could hear the noises from the house, but it was not unpleasant – just young people having a good time.

Frances sighed and said, "This is really very nice. No wonder Candice and the children love it here."

Aunt Maggie looked at Cora and they winked at each other, and made pretend toasts with their drinks.

In the house, Candy noticed that Nicole was very quiet. She looked pale, and Candy whispered to her, "Do you need to lie down for a while? You can stretch out on my aunt's bed and rest until the game is over."

Nicole looked up at Candy. "I think that would be a good idea." She managed to get up with her braces. Wes saw her struggling and stepped over a couple of kids to get to her side. By the time he was near her, Nicole was up, and she and Candy were making their way to Aunt Maggie's room. Nicole told Wes, "I'm all right. I'm just going to lie down for a while. Go back to your game."

When they got to Aunt Maggie's room, Candy helped Nicole situate herself on the bed and placed a light weight throw over her. Then she pulled down the shades to darken the room and started to leave. Nicole called to her, "Candy, wait. I need to talk with you."

Candy said, "What is it, Nicole?"

Nicole said, "I consider you a dear friend. We've become very close since Markie's accident. I can feel that I'm getting worse, and I don't think I'll be around much longer. No, don't say anything, just listen. I want you to take care of my boys for me when I'm gone."

"Nicole, what are you talking about? You'll be around for a long time. You'll see Fred become a grown man, and you'll play with your grandchildren. And what do you mean by 'your boys'? You only have one son, don't you?"

"I know my body, and it's giving out. I'm so tired of this struggle. And by 'my boys', I mean both my boys – Fred and Wes. I'm not saying that you and Wes are having an affair. I'm saying that I see a connection between you two. I know you wouldn't act on those feelings. You're not that kind of person, but you can't deny that they're there. I just want you to know that I want Wes to be happy when I'm

83

gone, and I want to know that Fred will be looked after and loved. I think you could do that. You're a good person."

"Oh, Nicole, I don't know what to say. It's like you're giving me permission to take your family. I think Wes should have something to say about this. It might not be what he wants. He loves you so much. I feel like we're plotting against him. I can't do this. You're my best friend, and I love you like the sister I never had."

"Hush, Candy. You can do this. And besides, I'll be around for a while longer. You have plenty of time to think about it. Don't say anything to Wes about what we've discussed. He has enough to deal with as it is. As you said, he might have other ideas after I'm gone. He might want to remain single, or hook-up with some floozy," and she laughed a little.

"Okay. We'll leave it at that. You get some rest. I'll check on you later. Can I get you anything?"

Nicole replied, "No, thanks, Candy. Go watch the game. Don't worry about me. I'll be fine."

Candy joined the group, and signaled to Wes that Nicole was okay, but she couldn't concentrate on the game. She considered the conversation she had had with Nicole as she watched Wes and Fred. She sighed. I don't know what the future will hold, but it's going to be interesting.

When everyone was gone, Aunt Maggie, Bea, and she cleaned up, then relaxed. Candy asked Aunt Maggie how things went with Frances and Cora. Aunt Maggie laughed and said everything went swimmingly. She told them about the iced tea and how mellow Frances had become. "She even made compliments. Can you believe that?"

Candy asked, "What is your secret ingredient, Aunt Maggie? Or do I want to know? I'll bet it's not the chamomile tea."

Aunt Maggie went to the sink and showed her a pitcher of 'water'. Candy said, "That's just water. Is it some special kind?"

Aunt Maggie said, "It's been distilled. Here, smell," and she let Candy take a whiff.

Candy gasped, "It's vodka! You sneaky little devil, you. You should be arrested!"

They laughed. Bea said, "It worked. She was feeling pretty good when they left. She was actually pleasant. Markie was shocked when she kissed him on the cheek, patted Bunny's head, and didn't scold him for having the dog on the bed. She even hugged me. It's a good thing Cora was driving. Well, good night, ladies. I'm tired. I've got school in the morning."

"Good night, sweetie. See you in the morning." Candy said. Then she turned to Aunt Maggie. "I think I'll turn in too, after I check on Markie. Good night. I didn't know you could be so sneaky," and she laughed.

In bed, Candy reviewed the events of the day. She thought about what Nicole had said about her connection to Wes. Then she fantasized about what life would be like with Wes. She reminded herself that it probably never would be.

She tried to put the thought out of her head. She had not realized that she was so tired, and she soon drifted off to sleep. She dreamed about Wes that night. She dreamed that she was pregnant and giving birth. When the doctor showed her the baby, it was Fred in his Little League uniform, and Wes said to her, "I'm so proud of you."

CHAPTER 14

Pat was dead. That was a fact, but Vic was having a hard time coming to grips with it. Pat's spiritual presence was everywhere in the house. He didn't know what he was going to do, or where he was going to go, but he realized that he couldn't stay in the house that was Pat's. There were too many memories. Eric had been taken by Pat's parents, and they would not let him see Vic. He had grown very fond of the boy, and he missed him. It was like having his own son with him. Eric was only one year younger than his son Mark. Sometimes he wondered what kind of relationship he would have had with Mark if he had stuck around.

As he walked through the rooms, he noticed that things were out of place and in general disarray. Drawers left open, books knocked off the shelves, closet doors left open, and cushions askew on the sofa and chairs. In the kitchen, pots, pans and dishes littered the counters, and cabinet drawers and doors gaped open. When he went into Eric's room, he got teary-eyed. All reminders of Eric were gone -- his clothes, toys, books, posters. The room had been stripped bare except for the furniture.

He went into the bedroom he and Pat had shared and found his belongings strewn about. Pat's things had been removed by his parents.

He sat on the side of the bed, put his head in his hands and wept. Vic had never felt such profound emptiness, and he sobbed aloud, calling Pat's name over and over, falling over on the bed and pounding the mattress. He was hurt and angry. How did things get so out of control? Were there signs he had missed? Who was Pat, anyway? He had thought he knew the person he loved so deeply. How could this happen to them? He rationalized that everyone has a side that they hide he told himself. He could attest to that. Who was he to judge? Vic sobbed, "Oh, Pat. It hurts so much. I'm so sorry."

He heard pounding on the front door, and the bell ringing persistently. He got up, went into the bathroom and threw cold water on his face, then went to see who was at the door. He asked, "Who is it?" He didn't need the press in his face anymore, and was not about to open the door to them.

"It's Mrs. Malone from next door. Are you all right?"

Vic opened the door and said, "Hello, Mrs. Malone. Come in. I wasn't going to answer, but since it's you, come on in. I want to thank you again for your testimony. If it were not for you, I don't know where I would be now."

Mrs. Malone answered, "Think nothing of it, ducky. I just told what I saw, and what I knew to be the truth. You, Pat and Eric have been good neighbors. You're good people. It's such a tragedy, what happened. Sort of a freak accident, you might say. Just one of those things that happen to people, but it was made worse when the newspapers got through with it. Those people make me sick. They're like vultures looking for some carrion to pick over." She walked into the living room. "Oh, my goodness! Look what they did! I guess it was the cops. They messed up your place. What were they looking for? I don't suppose they even thought about putting things back like they found them. Listen, come home with me and have some supper. You can spend the night and sleep on the sofa. You could sleep with me, but I don't think my hubby would like that. Hey? At least I got a smile out of ya. We'll see what we can do over here tomorrow."

Vic started to protest. The last thing he wanted was to try to be sociable. He wanted to be left alone, but, had it not been for Mrs. Malone, he would be in prison now. So he agreed. He owed her, and besides he liked the old couple, and was hungry, and she was an excellent cook.

Dinner was mostly small talk – the weather, politics, what was a good dinner wine,– anything except what was on all their minds. After dinner, Vic helped Mrs. Malone wash the dishes, then she made up a bed on the sofa. She and Mr. Malone went to their room. Vic could hear muted talk, then the sound from the television. He lay down on the sofa, surprised at how comfortable it was. Anything would be comfortable after that jail bunk. He lay there going over the events of the last three weeks.

He remembered it as if he were watching a movie. They went to the neighborhood bar for a drink after dinner and to socialize with some of the regulars. They sat at the bar and exchanged quips with the bar tender, as they usually did. A guy came in and immediately came on to Pat. Pat responded as if they were old friends. Vic asked Pat if they were friends, and to introduce them. Pat responded that Vic didn't need to know who he was – just a friend. Pat was surly and in a bad mood. Vic didn't want an argument – especially in the bar, so he introduced himself to the man. Pat slurred, "Get away from him. He's my friend, not yours."

Vic realized that Pat was getting drunk, so he suggested they go home. Pat said, "You go home. The night is just beginning for me. Bye, bye."

Vic knew he couldn't leave Pat, so he told the man, "Excuse us. We're leaving." Pat said, "No, we're not. I'm staying with my friend – my good friend. . You're not my good friend," with the emphasis on the word 'good.'

Vic looked at Pat and realized that he had never seen this side of him before. It was like looking at a stranger. He excused himself. "I'm going home. You do what you want. You're in some kind of bad mood, and I'm not dealing with it. I'll see you back at the house. I suggest you sober up before Eric sees you, if he's still awake. He has school tomorrow and needs his rest. You're getting loud and making a fool of yourself."

Pat's words were slurring, "He's my son, and I'll deal with him. Don't you worry about my son. You ran away from your son, so don't you worry 'bout my son."

Vic said, "You're drunk, or crazy, or both. What's wrong with you? I'm leaving, Patricia, and you can do whatever you want."

Vic walked out the door and started up the hill toward their house. Pat came staggering after him, talking loudly and screaming obscenities. When they reached the steps leading up to the house, Vic turned to Pat. "Stop all your confounded noise. You're going to wake the neighbors. You don't want Eric to see you like this, do you?"

Pat said, "Yesh. I want evabody know. You called me Pu tricia. You know I don like be called Pu tricia. You just bein' nasty. You nasty to me, damned punk. Don turn away fum me. Look at me when I talk to you. Hear me?"

Vic turned away from Pat and started up the steps. Pat grabbed his arm and slurred a stream of obscenities. Vic jerked away, and Pat's foot slipped on a step. Pat tried to grab the wrought iron rail, missed, fell sideways, hit his head on the newel and landed on the cement.

Vic jumped down the steps crying, "Are you hurt? Get up, Pat!"

Pat didn't move. Vic felt for a pulse, and finding none, he yelled, "Help, somebody! Call an ambulance! Pat's hurt! Help!" He tried to start CPR, when he pushed Pat's head back, he felt something sticky on his hand. He realized that Pat was bleeding. Blood was streaming from the left temple.

Mrs. Malone came running and shouted, "We called the ambulance! I saw Pat fall. Is he all right?"

Vic looked up at her with tears in his eyes. "I think he's gone! Oh, God! I think he's dead. It was just a stupid argument. He fell and hit his head on the newel. Oh, God! What did I do?"

"You didn't do a thing, ducky. I saw you coming up the street. I hadn't seen Pat like this in a long time. He could get obnoxious when he drank too much. You never saw that side of him before, did you?" Mrs. Malone was trying to console Vic. "From my window, I could see that it was an accident."

91

The ambulance came down the street with the siren blasting. The Emergency crew came over and examined Pat. One turned to Vic and Mrs. Malone. "This man is dead. We can't do anything for him. We'll call the police."

Neighbors were coming out of their houses to see what was going on. A blanket was placed over Pat, and a police car was there in a short while. They examined the scene, talked to Vic, Mrs. Malone, and the neighbors. Photographers snapped pictures and Vic was taken to the police station for questioning.

As Vic lay on Mrs. Malone's sofa, the events of the weeks following the accident were a blur. He had been in a state of shock, inundated with questions, statements, finger prints, photographers, lawyers, a judge, police, accusations, more questions, and insinuations. Pat's parents accused him of murder, and insisted the district attorney prosecute to the fullest extent of the law.

At the hearing, Vic was surprised by all the support that he had. Friends from the bar testified that Pat was so drunk he could hardly stand up. Mrs. Malone gave a detailed account of the accident. Mr. Malone corroborated her story. Other neighbors testified to what they had seen, and they knew Pat's reputation. They also testified about how helpful Vic had been during the earthquake.

All the physical evidence showed that Pat had hit his head on the newel of the wrought iron rail. There was blood on the newel that matched Pat's blood. Even with all the evidence and the testimonies in Vic's favor, Pat's parents still insisted that Vic had killed their son. They were relentless, and went so far as to give interviews to the tabloids.

As Vic was leaving the court room after the hearing, there was a woman standing outside the door. She came up to Vic and introduced herself as Pat's ex-wife, Wanda. She told Vic that she was glad the judge had ruled Pat's death an accident, and that she needed to share something with him.

She invited him to have coffee with her so they could talk. She told him that when she discovered that Pat was homosexual, she wanted a divorce. He told her the only way he would give her a divorce was if he got custody of Eric. He let his parents believe that she had deserted her child to be with another man. They never knew about his homosexuality. Pat's parents were rich and powerful, but she was going to try to get custody of Eric anyway. She loved her son, and knew he had a good relationship with Vic. She said she would try to make arrangements so Eric and Vic could see each other sometimes.

Vic was overwhelmed, and he thanked her. When she left, Vic sat at the table a long time, trying to digest the events that had twisted his life around. He felt lost. He didn't know where to go or what he wanted to do. He went back to the house he and Pat had shared, and found the chaos there. And now here he was, sleeping on Mrs. Malone's sofa, not knowing what his next step would be.

CHAPTER 15

TWO-HEADED BABY BORN IN CHILI, the headlines on the tabloid jumped out at the reader. Candy picked up a copy and chuckled to herself, "Aunt Maggie will love this." She put it in her grocery cart and proceeded to the checkout lane.

When she got home, Bea helped her unload the bags and take them into the kitchen. Aunt Maggie laughed when she saw the tabloid. "Ho, boy! This will be some high, intellectual reading tonight. Thanks, Candy. I can see you went by the library on your way home."

Bea looked at it and laughed. "I don't know how an ex-teacher can read this garbage. Let me see it when you finish." All three laughed.

Markie, on crutches, came into the kitchen and wanted to know what all the fuss was about. Candy showed him the headlines, and he started to laugh, too. "I want to read that article when you're done. That is too funny."

Markie's recovery had been slow, but he was making steady progress. The last part to heal was his leg. He had had two more surgeries and the doctors decided it would do more harm than good to attempt another. When his leg healed, and they took the cast off, he would walk with a limp for the rest of his life. The stairs were still a challenge for him, so he continued to sleep in the living room. Candy marveled at how good-natured he was even when she knew he was in a lot of pain. Markie never complained when he had to go through his exercises, and was fascinated with the orthopedic procedures. He questioned the doctors who took time to talk with him. He had made up his mind to become an orthopedic surgeon and read medical books and journals instead of comic books like his other friends. So Candy was happy to see that he wanted to read something a little more entertaining.

A week later, when Candy was tidying the living room, she saw the tabloid and asked if everybody had finished with it so she could throw it out. They all said they were. She looked at the front page and saw at the bottom, in smaller print, was written, "ACCIDENT OR MURDER? What Does Murdock Family Say? See page 16." She was curious about the two-headed baby, and decided to read about it. That night, in her room, propped up on the pillows in her bed, she started to read the tabloid.

She chuckled about the two-headed baby. I knew it was a hoax all along but I fell for it. I guess that's how they make their money. Then she thumbed through the rest of the paper. When she got to page 16, she did a double-take at the picture she saw there. It showed a man being led by two policemen. His face was in the shadows, but she could see the profile. The man looked like Mark. I wish it were clearer, she thought. She read the article; she could hear her heart pounding. Could it be? Could Mark be alive and living in San Francisco, accused of murder? Oh, my God! I don't want to believe it. I'll have to find out. He must have changed his name.

Sleep did not come easily for Candy that night. It was fretful and filled with weird dreams. The next day she went to the library and looked at the San Francisco papers for the past month. She read every article about the Murdock case -

- the hearing, the eye-witness testimony, and anything pertaining to the accident. But mainly, she wanted to look at pictures of the accused. Most of the pictures showed him shielding his face from the cameras. Finally one picture showed him coming out of the courthouse. It was taken from quite a distance, and his face was in three-quarter profile and hard to distinguish. Candy made a copy of the picture so she could take it home and look at it with a magnifying glass.

When she was alone in her room, she looked closely at the picture. She was almost sure it was Mark – older and with a mustache. She decided not to say anything to her family. How could she explain something like this to her children? Their father was a homosexual accused of murdering his lover. They would never understand how their father could desert them. She didn't even know if they knew what a homosexual was. They had grown up thinking their father was dead. She would let them continue to believe that. And, if this person was Mark, then he was dead to them and to her. He was calling himself Victor Newman, so Victor Newman he would be. Her gut feeling was that it was Mark, but she would say nothing to anyone about it – not even Aunt Maggie – no one. It was his secret and his lie.

CHAPTER 16

How do you forget something as life-changing as the information Candy thought she had discovered? She needed to talk with someone about it. She thought of the possible ramifications. She went for a walk and thought about what she would say to the children if she ever had to talk with them about it. Would it be better to bring it up now, or just leave it alone? After all, she didn't really know whether it was Mark or not. She had no proof – just her gut feeling. She was getting a headache. She looked around and realized that she had wandered on to the playground. She saw the swings, went over and sat down. She swayed back and forth, still thinking what to do; she stopped and put her head in her hands. "Oh my God, what a dilemma," she said out loud.

"What's the dilemma?" Candy looked up and saw Wes. She was glad to see him, but felt embarrassed at the same time.

"Do you make it a habit to come to the playground and listen in on private conversations?" she laughed.

"No, but I saw you walking aimlessly, and you seemed to be worried about something. I thought I might be able to help."

Candy's attempt to lighten the moment didn't work. "Oh, Wes, you always seem to show up when I need a shoulder to lean on. How do you do it?"

"I think I'm tuned in to you, little lady. So what's bothering you? Talk to me."

Talking to someone about her suspicions was the last thing she wanted to do, but Wes was someone who could be objective and listen to her without judging, and maybe give some advice. "You know I told you how my husband had an accident and was presumed dead. Well I never believed he was dead. Somehow, I thought he had survived, and maybe had amnesia or something; there never was a body. So, even though I went on with my life, that has always been at the back of my mind. Now I've come across something that makes me think Mark is alive and I don't quite know what to do about it." Wes sat in the swing next to her. She told him about the pictures, her suspicions and her doubts. Wes listened without giving any comments. Then he said, "It seems like you have some decisions to make. You can leave it as it is, or you can try to prove that he's still alive. If you prove it, then what? If you leave it as a mystery, your life will go on as before. The information you have is supposition. It could be someone who looks like him. If it is him, do you confront him? Do you try to track him down? Do you tell the children? Think carefully, Candy. Whatever you decide doesn't just affect you. It will have an impact on the children, too. I can't tell you what to do. I can only point out your options. Have you mentioned it to your aunt?"

Candy replied, "No, because I have no proof. What do I say? And then there's Mark's mother. I think news like this would send her over the edge. She's already very fragile mentally. I don't have any proof. Besides, if it is him it's obvious that he doesn't want anything to do with his family. Oh, Wes this is driving me crazy! I have more questions than answers. What to do, what to do? I suppose I could hire a detective like I did before, but what do I do then? Teenagers

98

have enough to deal with without this kind of burden. I can't put this on them, I just can't."

"Then don't. Leave it alone – at least for now. You don't have to decide today. It will become clear to you when the time is right. You can trust me to keep your secret, or rather his secret. It will be our secret. Buck up, little lady. You're strong. You've weathered bigger storms than this. Put your mind at ease." As he said this, he pulled her up out of the swing and put his arms around her shoulders. She leaned into him.

Having someone to talk to was such a relief that she slumped onto his chest and started to cry. "Oh, Wes, I'm so sorry to burden you with this. I wish, I wish …" and she began sobbing.

Wes hugged her closely, and whispered, "I know, Candy. I know. I wish, too."

"All right, you kids. Break it up and go home." It was Tom. He made it a habit to police the playground several times a day for vandalism and kids making out. "Oh, it's you, Coach, and you, Mrs. Procter. I'm sorry. I thought it was some kids just..." and his words trailed off. He was embarrassed, and so were they.

"It's Ok, Tom," said Wes. "Mrs. Proctor was sharing a problem with me and I was trying to comfort her. Everything is fine now. She just needed a shoulder to cry on. Sometimes it helps to talk with someone, you know."

Tom knew how that felt. He wished he had someone to talk to about his feelings for Candy. "Yeah, I get that. You Ok, Can... er, Mrs. Procter?"

"Yes, Tom. Much better. I think I know what to do now." She patted Wes on the chest as she walked away, "Thanks for the shoulder, Coach."

By the time she reached the house, she had decided not to tell anyone. She thought, Leave it alone, and go on with your life. She went into the kitchen to make a pot of tea. Aunt Maggie was starting dinner, and she said, "I guess that walk did some good. When you left you looked worried. Now you look like you don't have a care in the world."

"I don't. It's amazing what fresh air can do. Would you like some tea, too?

Auntie Mom said, "I think I would like that. Well, looky here. Don't you look fancy?"

Candy turned around to see Bea standing in the doorway in the new gown she had bought for the prom. "It's too big in the waist. What can I do?" she whined.

"Now, now, dry your tears," said Auntie Mom. "Take it off, turn it in-side out, put it back on, and I'll pin it, sew up the sides, and you'll be set to go trip the light fantastic."

Bea did as she was told, and before she could take the dress off again, Markie came into the kitchen and started laughing. "Now that's a fashion statement if I ever saw one. You look great, sis! Who you going with?"

Bea grinned, and said, "Jerry."

100

"Jerry, who? Football Jerry?"

"Yeah. Football Jerry."

"Oh, wow. I hope you have a good time. We call him Jerry the Jerk." And he ran out of the kitchen with Bea in hot pursuit.

"Don't tear your gown, Bea," Candy shouted.

Auntie Mom said, "Now that's what I meant about some life in this house. It was too quiet before."

"And I bet you wish for some of that peace and quiet now, don't you?"

"No way. I love it," and they both laughed.

Bea was the smartest girl in her graduating class. She was valedictorian. She was pretty in a not flashy way, and she was quiet, but not nerdy. She had a small circle of friends, but she was not the most popular girl in school. So she was surprised when Jerry, the star quarter back and captain of the football team asked her to the prom. Since she was not a part of the 'in crowd', she had no idea why he was called 'Jerry the Jerk.'

The next evening Candy helped her get ready for the prom. Bea was nervous and changed her hair several times. "I just can't get it right, Mom."

Candy said, "Calm down, sweetheart. Here, let me help you." Within two minutes, Candy had her hair swept-up with a cascade of curls hanging down. "Oh, my," she said, "You're so beautiful."

Markie peeped through the door, gave a long, slow whistle, and said, "Wow, Sis, you're really going to knock 'em out. I do believe you washed your face." He ran out of the room just as Bea threw a book at him. "You missed, Cinderella!"

Markie made it his business to answer the door when Jerry came for Bea. He invited him in and called to Bea, "Your date is here." Then he got close to Jerry and whispered, "I've heard about how you've treated some girls. I better not hear about you treating my sister that way."

Before Jerry could say anything, Candy and Auntie Mom came into the living room. Markie introduced them, and Candy said, "Pleased to meet you, Jerry. Bea should be down shortly. The flower is beautiful. Let me have it, and I'll pin it on her for you."

Bea came down the stairs, and Jerry looked up with his mouth open. It was still open when Candy told him what time to have Bea back home.

Auntie Mom said, "He looks Ok, but he didn't have enough sense to close his mouth," and they all laughed.

Markie stayed up until he heard Jerry's car in the driveway. Candy, in her room, had fallen asleep reading a book. Markie went down the steps as quietly as he could trying not to wake his Mom. He heard the car doors close and waited until he heard their footsteps on the porch. He could hear them talking.

"Thanks for taking me to the prom, Jerry. I had a good time. Goodnight," said Bea. But to herself she thought she didn't have fun with Jerry, and she had already made up her mind that she really didn't like him, she didn't care how popular he was. She put her hand out to shake his, and he grabbed her hand and pulled her close to him.

"The night ain't over yet, Bea," and he tried to kiss her, holding her tight with one arm while unfastening her bra with one quick move.

"What are you doing?" Bea said in a loud whisper. "Let me go!"

Jerry whispered, "Shhh! You don't want to wake everybody, do you?"

Whispering a little louder, Bea said, with her teeth clenched, "I said let me go! And I mean it!" As she tried to push him away, he tried to lift her gown.

As she was struggling with him, Markie came out on the porch and said, "I think my sister told you to leave her alone. Now back off!"

Jerry laughed in a sinister way and said, "You gonna make me, Gimp?"

Markie replied, "I sure am." He pulled out a baseball bat from behind him and said, "The Gimp Club is private, but I can make you a member real quick. Do you want me to start from the top, bash your hard head in, and work my way down, or do you want me to start at the bottom, crack your shins, and work my way up? There is a third alternative. You can leave quietly after you apologize to my sister."

Jerry let Bea go and backed down the steps saying, "I'm sorry Bea. I didn't know your brother was crazy."

Markie lunged at him with the bat in the air saying, "I'll show you crazy!"

"I'm sorry, Bea. I won't bother you again." He looked back as he ran to his car.

"Are you Ok, Sis?" He hugged her.

"I am now. Thanks, Markie. Every girl should have a brother like you. I'm lucky."

They went into the house. Markie locked the door, and as they went up the stairs, Markie said, "And don't you forget it. Nobody messes with my sister except me," and they hugged each other all the way up the stairs. When they got to Bea's room, he kissed her on the forehead. Even though he was over two years younger, he was taller than Bea.

Candy said in a sleepy voice, "Is that you, Bea?"

"Yeah, Ma. Go back to sleep."

"Did you have a good time?"

"Yeah. I even got a good night kiss." They both giggled.

"Is that you, Markie? Go to bed."

"Yes, Mother. Good night." They put their hands over their mouths and laughed some more.

Markie whispered, "Good night, Sis." He went to his room and looked in his mirror. He flexed his muscles and thought, Not bad. I'm glad my voice didn't crack when I threatened Jerry the Jerk.

He remembered the first time someone called him a gimp. His feelings were hurt, and he went home downcast. Auntie Mom, always in tune with the kids, asked him what was wrong. When he told her that someone had called him a gimp, and he wanted to punch him out, Auntie Mom told him to sit down. "Listen, Markie, what happened to you was not your fault and you can't change it. So you must deal with it. People always look for a weakness in someone else, so they can deal with their own weaknesses. If you let them know that it bothers you to be called a gimp, they will continue to use it against you, and others will join in because you've become an easy target. Now you can continue to let it get to you, try to punch everybody out, get in trouble for fighting, and become their victim, or you can laugh with them, make fun of yourself, and turn it around. When they realize they can't get to you, it won't be fun anymore, and they'll leave you alone. The ones who were your friends all along, will still be your friends tomorrow. Now it's up to you how you want to handle it."

Auntie Mom was right, and Markie had come to terms with his condition. People like Jerry were the only ones to call him names. And he decided that they didn't count.

The next day after church services, Markie talked with Wes about what had happened. "I don't want him spreading rumors about my sister like I've heard him do about other girls."

105

"Hmm. I hadn't heard about that, but I'm not surprised. He's a good enough football player, but not as good as he thinks he is. It's obviously gone to his head. You see, Markie, sooner or later a person's true character comes out. Don't worry about it. I'll talk with him tomorrow at practice."

When Wes thought it was the right time to approach Jerry, he went over to him, and put his arm around his shoulder. "Come with me for a minute, Jerry. I want to talk with you about your athletic scholarship."

Jerry grinned and let out a sigh of relief. "Ok, Coach. See you later, guys." He wasn't sure what the coach had heard when he came over to the group, and he thought the coach would reprimand him for talking about Bea.

As they walked away from the group, Wes said, "I hear you got a scholarship and I want to congratulate you. Now you know that the scholarship depends on my recommendation, don't you? You get my meaning?" While he was talking and they were walking, Wes's hand moved up from his shoulder to the nape of his neck. His hand got tighter and tighter while he said, "You seem to be an upstanding young man, and I don't think you would spread false rumors about a nice young lady who rebuffed your advances, now would you?"

Jerry choked, "No, uh uh, no sir. I would never do that."

"I'm sure that if you accidently let a few words slip, that you, being the gentleman that you are, you would set it straight with your friends, now wouldn't you?"

"Oh, yes, sir. I sure would. That is if I did something like that --- but of course I wouldn't." Jerry was sweating, licking his lips, and trying to look calm.

"I think your conversation would go something like this: 'Guys, Bea is not only smart, but she's too smart to let a jerk like me even get to first base, let alone make a home run. And if I led you to believe otherwise, it was a mistake.' Now don't you think that would be a nice conversation?" and his hand got tighter around Jerry's neck.

Jerry stammered, "Yeah, Coach. I believe that would be a nice conversation."

Wes released his neck, "Now let's go have a good practice. Have you decided whether you want to go out for football or baseball?"

"Not yet, Coach. But I'm thinking about it."

Jerry was so relieved that he almost wet his pants. As he was about to run away, Wes called after him. "You know Markie is the record keeper, and he's getting pretty good at it, too." Jerry knew what he meant.

CHAPTER 17

"I know what you're trying to do, Dotty, and I appreciate your efforts, but I'm just not interested in anybody right now," Candy said as she took a sip of coffee.

Dotty laughed and said, "Am I that obvious? I thought I was being subtle. I just think two nice people like you and my cousin should get together. You're both unattached and well established. Neither one of you is getting any younger. You're pretty and he's handsome, if I do say so myself, and not just because he's my cousin, and he's the District Attorney. So what's the problem?"

"The problem is I have two teenagers to worry about. Markie is a senior, and Bea is in college. I don't have time to invest in a relationship right now."

"All the more reason you should be dating. Pretty soon you'll be an empty nester. You need a life of your own, Candy and my cousin is a good catch. Stop being so standoffish and cast your net in that direction," Dotty said as she gestured with her spoon.

Candy laughed. "You do have a way with words. But he hasn't asked me out or even acted like he's interested. And, as good looking as he is, he probably has a girlfriend."

"Well, come to think of it. He does have a lady friend that he takes places, but she's not good enough for him," Dotty laughed.

"Leave it alone, Dotty" Candy glanced up when the door opened. "Speak of the devil. Did you arrange this?"

Dotty turned around and looked towards the door as Brandon walked in. "Why, no, but that just goes to show you, it's meant to be."

Brandon was tall with brown hair and piercing dark brown eyes. He had a good physique and was always neatly dressed. A people watcher, he usually sized-up someone in a few minutes. He put them into categories as he watched them – a sort of mental check list. Most of the time, he was right about their character.

Brandon walked over to their table. "Hello, ladies. Enjoying yourselves? What's new, Dotty?" he said as he kissed her on the cheek. "It's good to see you, Candice," and he shook her hand.

"Call me Candy. It's good to see you, too."

"How are the wedding plans going?" he asked Dotty.

"Everything is moving along smoothly. You'll be getting your invite soon. Start thinking about which of your ladies you'll bring as your guest."

"Oh, Dotty, you're a sly one. You'll just have to wait and see. I'll let you ladies finish your lunch in peace. I'm meeting a client, so I'll go find a table. Good to see you again, Candy. Would you mind if I call you sometime?"

"No, I wouldn't mind at all," Candy stammered.

Brandon nodded his head and sauntered off.

Dotty giggled, "See what I mean? 'Call me Candy.' I saw how you said that, trying to be sexy."

"Oh, Dotty, stop it. I wouldn't know how to be seductive if I tried. It's been so long since I dated, I don't know what I'll do even if he does ask me out."

"You'll do fine. Just be your own sweet self, Candy. He'll eat it up."

Candy threw a piece of lettuce at her and they laughed so hard they cried.

~~~~~~

During the spring break, Phillis and her youngest daughter, Judy, came to look at the college campus and stayed with Candy. Bea, Markie, and Judy had fun together, and Candy and Phillis got a chance to catch up; they had remained close friends through the years.

"Can you believe how fast the time has gone by?" Phillis asked. "It seems like only yesterday that they were all running around getting into everything."

Auntie Mom said, "Yeah, and the older you get, the faster it goes." They were sitting in the kitchen sipping tea when the phone rang. "I'll get it, though I don't know why. It's never for me anyway, especially when the kids are home."

She picked up the phone, "Hello. Oh, how are you? That's good to hear. Yes they're all here. Phillis is here with her youngest, Judy. Yeah, that's the one. OK. I'll let you talk with Candy. She can tell you all about it. You take care, you hear. Nice talking with you, too. Well, keep enjoying your tea. I'm sure Cora will try to make it taste like mine.

Here's Candy. Bye," and she made a face as she handed the phone over to Candy.

"Hello, Mother Procter. Yes, everyone is fine. Yes, I'm enjoying their company. What was that? Could you repeat what you just said? I don't think I heard you clearly. I don't believe you just said that. Well I hope it does. I always knew you were different in your thinking, but I never dreamed you were so prejudiced. I don't know what to say. And I don't appreciate this conversation. The guests in my home are none of your business. So keep your biases to yourself. Goodbye!" and she hung up the phone.

Auntie Mom said, "Now, Candy, that's not what you really wanted to say, was it?"

Candy replied, "No! It wasn't!" She picked up the phone and shouted into the dead receiver, "You bigoted old bitch!!"

Auntie Mom said, "Now don't you feel better?"

Candy put the phone back on the hook and said, "I've wanted to do that for a long time." She heard clapping behind her, and turned around to see the teenagers standing in the doorway. She took a bow, and everybody laughed and clapped.

"That old woman really pisses me off!"

The teenagers looked at each other and Bea said, "Oooh. I've never heard that language before. It's hurting my ears," and they all laughed harder.

Markie said, "What did she say that set you off?"

111

Candy replied, "She said something stupid like 'their blackness might rub off.' And 'be careful who I let my children associate with.' I think she's lost her mind."

Phillis said, "You'd be surprised how many people think that way, Candy. I guess that's why we've remained friends all these years. Color never seemed to be a problem for us. In fact I don't think it bothered either of us. I suspect it was the reason your mother-in-law was so uncomfortable and didn't stay long when she came to the good-bye get-together that we had when you moved.

"She's a cold woman." Phillis continued. "I've never been able to relax around her. I suspect there's more to her story than we realize. But, hey, she's your mother-in-law. Every family has its weirdoes. Well, Judy, dearest daughter, what do you think about what you saw? Would you like to come here for school? You'll have another year to think about it. You should check out other colleges before you decide."

"I'll take a look at Bea's school and maybe one more, but I think my mind is made up."

Candy hugged her around the shoulders. "Well, if you decide to come here, you know you'll have family nearby. You can walk from the campus any time and have dinner with us. Auntie Mom and I will be here for you."

The phone rang, and Candy said, "If that's Frances, I'm not here."

Auntie Mom said, "Hello. Yes, just a minute." She handed the phone to Candy and said, "It's for you – a man."

Candy took the phone and said, "Hello. Yes. I'm fine. And you? Well that sounds like fun. I'd love to. I'll be ready. Good-bye."

Markie said, "Who was that, Mrs. Procter? You're blushing."

Candy put her hands to her cheeks and said, "I am not. That was Mr. Brandon Moore, a lawyer friend of mine. Why do you ask?"

Bea replied, "Just nosy. So, when are you going out with him?"

Markie said, "Where are you going? When will you be back?"

Auntie Mom said, "Who's his mama? Who's his daddy?"

Phillis said, "Where was he born? What's his blood type?"

Markie said, "Does he have any hobbies? Does he drink?"

Candy said through her laughter, "Stop, stop! You people are impossible. I'm not telling you anything."

CHAPTER 18

Vic was eagerly waiting for Wanda to show up. He was pacing back and forth in front of The Japanese Tea Garden when he saw them coming up the street. Eric had grown a lot since the last time he saw him. He was as tall as his mother. They greeted each other awkwardly and went through the gate. Vic wanted to hug Eric, but felt that the boy wasn't receptive. Each time Wanda was able to get Eric away to see Vic the gap grew wider, and Vic felt more estranged. Eric was not only growing up, but he was growing away from him.

The first time they met after things had settled down from the trial, Eric cried when he saw Vic. He hugged him and told him how awful it was living with his grandparents. He wished he could live with his mother and be able to see Vic all the time. As time went on it became harder and harder to connect, and now Eric was distant and vague. They had little to talk about. Vic surmised that the grandparents had done a good job of brain washing Eric to believe that his father's death was not an accident. Wanda was not allowed to see him often enough to make a difference. Eventually, Eric would be old enough to decide things for himself. He wanted to live with his mother, but that was a battle they were still fighting. Wanda had managed to get more visiting privileges, and could have him every other weekend. When she could arrange it, she brought Eric see Vic, but with his work schedule, Eric's activities, and her schedule, it was hard to co-ordinate. So they always planned some special outing for his visits. This time it was the tea garden. Vic had a feeling of foreboding as they wandered through looking at the various plants. He could sense coolness from Eric and the conversation was strained. Every question that Vic could think of was met with a monosyllabic response.

By the time they finished lunch, Vic wanted the visit to be over. Eric was very uncomfortable, Wanda was on edge, and Vic couldn't even swallow his food. When they said their goodbyes, Vic knew it might be the last time he would see Eric.

As he walked back to his apartment, Vic choked back tears. He felt so alone and desolate. He had a few casual friends, and the people he worked with, but no one special. Pat's friends had rallied around him for a while, but they were not the kind of people he wanted to hang out with. Funny he hadn't noticed how shallow and vapid they were when Pat was alive. At least he had his work – which he loved. He was so glad that Pat had insisted that he go to culinary school. He had enjoyed messing around in the kitchen when he was a youngster, that is whenever Frankie let him in the kitchen. Funny, he had not thought about his mother in years. He chuckled to himself, - and thought I don't even feel guilty.

He had an idea for a new dish he wanted to try. He stopped at the market then rushed to his apartment. He would present the dish to the restaurant's owner before the dinner crowd arrived and see if it could be added to the menu.

Phillipe's was a high-end restaurant where the "in" crowd dined. Philip Ross, the owner, was always open to new ideas when it came to food. He loved to eat and it showed; to say he was rotund would be putting it mildly. He and Vic worked well together. He would come into the kitchen, rubbing his hands together, and, with a gleam in his eyes, say, "Anything new for me to try, Vic?"

And Vic would present his latest creation with a flourish – "Ta da!!"

Philip would go to his favorite table and wait to be served with the right wine and all the accompaniments. Vic would stand by and wait for the critique. Philip always savored the moment and kept Vic waiting. Finally, he would smack his lips and look as if he were making the biggest decision in his life, mention what might be added – a dash of this, or a smidgeon of that, then he would give his blessing. Once in a while he would nix the dish, but most of the time he would give it the go-ahead. Today, the scenario was the same. The new dish would be on the next week's menu. Vic was pleased.

The following Tuesday, the editor of Gourmet Magazine asked to meet the chef who had created the new dish. Vic was reluctant, he liked to keep a low profile and usually stayed in the kitchen; he didn't want any attention that might stir up the past. But Philip insisted. He said it would be good for the restaurant. Vic went over to the table where Franko Forbes, the editor, was seated with his entourage. They shook hands and Mr. Forbes introduced Vic to the group. There were praises all around, and Mr. Forbes said he would like to interview Vic for his magazine. Vic agreed to the interview with the stipulation that they could take pictures of the food, but not of him. Mr. Forbes was reluctant at first, but eventually agreed.

A week later, when Vic came to work, there was a van parked in back of the kitchen with people milling around as if they were waiting for a movie star. When he walked through the door, he was greeted as if he were the movie star in question. The other cooks were dressed in their best aprons and hats, grinning from ear to ear. They obviously liked the attention. Vic asked who was in charge, and when he was introduced to Charles Bundy, the lead photographer, he felt his heart skip a beat. They shook hands and Vic explained the agreement to him. Charles said, "But you're so photogenic. Why not? We could put you on the cover. Won't you reconsider?" Vic was adamant, and the rest of the shooting event went smoothly. Charles was pleased with what he saw. He assured Vic that he would have the final say-so for the layout and the pictures before it went to press. He would call him and let him know when the layout would be ready for review. They shook hands. Each seemed reluctant to be the first to let go. A look passed between them, and Vic felt alive again. He hoped he was not blushing. When everyone had cleared out, Charles turned and waved to Vic, and with a wink of his eye, was gone.

CHAPTER 19

Candy met Brandon at the restaurant where they would have dinner. Being the independent person that she was, she preferred to meet him, so if the evening didn't go well, she could leave any time she wanted.

When she went into the restaurant, the hostess greeted her and asked her name. Candy told her, and the hostess produced a single red rose in an arrangement then showed her to a table and gave her a glass of wine. Candy was speechless. She thanked her and sat there feeling awkward. She took one sip of wine and looked around. It was dim and almost all the tables were occupied with people talking softly to each other. There was elevator-type music playing softly in the background. She looked toward the door and saw Brandon coming in. He said something to the hostess and headed toward the table, greeting several people on the way. He gestured for Candy to stay seated and greeted her with a kiss on the cheek. He sat down and said, "I hope you don't mind, but I ordered ahead so we wouldn't have to wait; that way we won't be late for the concert. I think you'll like my selections."

Again, Candy was speechless. She had never been treated like this before. She didn't know whether she should be flattered or angry. How dare he presume he could tell her what to eat? But his reasoning made sense. She decided to let it go, it wasn't that important.

She enjoyed the delicious meal. "You made a good choice, Brandon. That was very thoughtful, but next time, I would prefer to decide for myself, if you don't mind."

Brandon chuckled, "I thought you might be that kind of independent woman, but as you can see, time is of the essence. I'm pretty good at planning, in my business, I have to be."

Candy thought of a come-back, but decided to stay quiet. She didn't want to argue on the first date. She had a mental giggle, and thought, This is a date. I told Dotty I wouldn't know how to act.

Brandon said, "You look lovely tonight. That's a good color for you."

"Thank you, Brandon. You look very nice, also."

How long is this politeness going to go on? Candy wondered. I'm uncomfortable with him. I'd rather be home working a jigsaw puzzle. "Do you go to the symphony a lot?"

"Yes, I have season tickets. Tonight should be delightful. It's mostly Chopin. I've heard the pianist often. He was a client of mine for some time, an interesting fellow; a little off the mark, if you ask me, but a lot of artistic people are," Brandon said, and he proceeded to monopolize the conversation until they finished the meal.

They arrived at the theatre on time. Brandon spoke to several people as they were escorted to their seats – three rows back, center. When they were settled, Brandon whispered to Candy, "Nothing but the best for me. That's why I asked you out."

It was almost too much for Candy, and just as she was about to tell him off, the conductor came on the stage, and the

119

program began. She took a deep breath and focused her attention on the concert. In spite of herself, she enjoyed it. She felt transported to another place, and let the music sweep over her. It was beautiful and very relaxing. She forgot that Brandon was sitting next to her. The rest of her surroundings faded away. She closed her eyes and was startled when she felt Brandon take her hand.

He whispered, "Candy, it's intermission. Would you like some refreshments? Let's go to the lobby."

"Oh, Brandon. Yes, I need to get up and stretch. The music was so wonderful, I just got lost in it."

"I could see that. I'm so glad you're enjoying it."

While they were in the lobby, Brandon did a lot of schmoozing and introduced Candy to everyone they met. He had something to say about everyone, and Candy thought he sounded gossipy and petty. The second part of the program was just as enjoyable as the first, and again, Candy got lost in the music.

After the concert, Brandon asked Candy if she wanted to go somewhere for a night cap, and she declined saying she was tired and would rather go home. Brandon took her to her car, kissed her on the cheek, and told her he had enjoyed her company. They said their good nights and Candy drove home.

"Well, how was it, Missy?" Aunt Maggie asked.

"The concert was wonderful. I really enjoyed the music."

"You know what I mean. How was the date?"

"I'm not sure if I enjoyed that part or not. There's something about that man that is unsettling."

"Well, it's been a while since you've dated, give it a chance. You never know."

"You may be right. We'll see. Maybe he won't call again."

"Here, sit down and have a cup of chamomile and tell me about it. Maybe I can help you sort it out," Auntie Mom bustled around the kitchen.

Candy told her about the evening and Auntie Mom told her, "Go with your gut feeling. But I'll bet you a fat man that he'll call you again. He likes you and he's making plans that include you. I don't know what they are yet, but that will come to light soon enough."

"How can you say that after just one date?" "Because he wouldn't have made you a part of his schmoozing if he didn't want to include you in whatever he's working on. I suspect he's got big plans for his future and he wants to make you a part of it. You just wait and see. Mark my words."

"You may be right, but for now, I'm going to bed. See you in the morning, Miss Know-it-all."

Auntie Mom was right. Brandon called the next day and asked her out again. Candy decided that she would give it a chance and not be so critical.

After that she was a little more relaxed with Brandon and she tried not to analyze everything he said. They had fun most of the time, going to movies, dinner with his friends, horse-back riding, picnics and hiking. She found that they liked some of the same things, but more often than not, their dates involved activities that he preferred.

When he asked her to be his guest for Megan's wedding, Candy told him she had promised Dotty that she would be on hand to help her with the details. Bea was one of the bridesmaids, and Candy felt she should help out as much as possible.

Brandon pouted and said, "Well, I'll just have to ask someone else then since you don't want to go with me."

Candy couldn't understand why he was angry and told him so. It was their first disagreement and she didn't like the way he was acting. She told him he could do whatever he wanted and she would see him at the wedding or not.

When Candy told Aunt Maggie about the incident, she said, "Make note. He's acting like a jealous twelve-year-old. That was nothing to get upset about. He'll apologize and be contrite until the next time."

The wedding was lovely, and Megan made a beautiful bride. Bea was very pretty in the "foo-foo" bridesmaid's dress (as Auntie Mom called it) that Megan had chosen. Bea laughed and said, "It's the price you pay to be a bridesmaid. I'll never wear it again."

At the reception, Brandon sat off by himself and watched everyone. Candy sat with Nicole and helped by getting her food. Wes danced with Nicole and he realized that he had to practically hold her up – she was barely able to stand. They danced around and laughed at her awkwardness. Candy was glad to see her having a good time.

Markie came over and asked Candy for a dance.

"Why, of course, my prince. I thought you would never ask," she laughed.

"You know we'll have to go around in circles, don't you," Markie laughed, and they danced onto the floor.

When they came back to the table, Wes asked Candy to dance and Fred asked Bea. Markie asked Nicole to dance, but she declined saying she was too tired. She asked Markie to get her something to drink.

Wes said, "Where's your date? I thought you were seeing your lawyer friend, Brandon Moore."

Candy was surprised and replied, "I don't have a date. Brandon is just a friend, and I haven't seen him here."

"Oh, he's here all right. He's been watching you the entire time. He's keeping his eye on you, and I think he's a little jealous."

"I haven't seen him. Are you sure? Is he with someone?"

"I'm sure, and he's not with anyone. Did you two have a falling-out?"

Candy stuttered, "I... I guess you could call it that," and she told him about the disagreement.

Then Wes surprised her again by asking, "How much do you like this guy? Are you two an item or what?"

Candy replied, "I'm not sure what to call it, Wes. I have my doubts. Sometimes I can't stand his pompous ways. Then there are times when he's fun to be with. I just don't know. I shouldn't bother you with this, but I've always thought of you as someone I could talk to – sort of like a big brother."

Wes pulled her closer to him and spun her around saying, "I don't want to be your brother, Candy. You know that, but there's nothing I can do about it now."

"I think the music has stopped, Wes."

As they were walking back to the table, Brandon came over to them. "Hello, Candy. You look lovely, as usual. Won't you introduce me to your friend?"

Candy made the introductions and Brandon asked her to dance. When they were on the dance floor, Brandon said, "I'm sorry I acted like such a jerk, Candy. I can see how you were needed. It was selfish of me to try to monopolize your time. I'll try to do better if you'll give me another chance."

Candy smiled. "It's ok, Brandon. Let's just dance."

While they danced, Brandon tried to make small talk, but Candy's mind was on what Wes had said. Dancing with Brandon was nice, but dancing with Wes felt so natural. It was easy being with Wes. Even when he was acting jealous, and she smiled to herself.

Brandon said, "You're smiling. I see you are enjoying yourself."

"Yes, I am. It's was a beautiful wedding, and a lovely reception. I hope they'll be very happy."

On the way home, no one said much, except Auntie Mom. She chatted on and on about the dresses, the food, the music, the flowers, and she shared all the gossip she had heard at all the tables where she had stopped. Then she turned to Candy and said, "So, Missy. I see Mr. Moore finally acted like a man and made his move. He tried to keep you all to himself after he saw you dancing with the coach. What's his story?"

Candy laughed. "He apologized and said he had been a jerk."

"Good for him. I always said, 'know thyself.' Nothing like an honest man, but we'll see what he has up his sleeve."

Markie, sitting in the back seat said, "Yeah. I'll keep my eye on him." And everybody laughed.

CHAPTER 20

"Oh, for heaven's sake, Percy. Stop all that noise. Go out the doggie door the way you usually do," said Auntie Mom. Percy was meowing at the back door and pacing back and forth. "Okay, okay. I'll let you out. You're acting funny this morning. I haven't even had my cup of coffee yet." She got up from the table and opened the door, but Percy didn't go out. He stretched up and tapped her on the knee and went towards the door again. "Alright, I guess you want to eat. I'll get your food, but it's a little early, even for you." She went to the cabinet and took out a can of food and opened it. She placed the dish on the floor. Percy smelled it and walked away back to the door and began meowing again. "Oh, it's going to be like that this morning. Okay, mister. I'll just ignore you. See how you like that." Percy tapped her on the knee again.

Upstairs, Markie turned over and stretched. He realized that he could stretch without encountering the weight and warmness of Bunny in the crook of his legs. He got up, put on his robe and went down stairs.

"Good morning, Auntie Mom. What's with Percy and all his noise?"

"You tell me. He's been acting funny this morning. He acts like he wants to go out, but when I open the door, he doesn't. I fed him and he won't eat. He keeps making noise as if he wants to tell me something. But I don't speak cat. Maybe you can figure him out."

Markie bent down and said, "What's the matter fella?" Percy rubbed against him and meowed then went to the door. Markie asked, "Have you seen Bunny this morning? He wasn't on the bed when I woke up. I guess he went out early."

Auntie Mom said, "Come to think of it, I haven't seen him." With apprehension she said, "Maybe Percy is trying to tell us something. Go see if Bunny is in his house and if he's ok."

Markie bounded out the door with Percy running in front and Auntie Mom close behind. Markie called, "Bunny, Bunny. Come on boy! Bun, where are you?"

They went to the dog house and Markie said, "Oh, here you are. What are you doing out here this early? Come on boy, let's get some breakfast." Bunny did not move. Markie bent down and shook him. "Come on Bun, wake up!" There was no response from Bunny. Markie shook harder and realized that his body was not warm, and it was slightly stiff. He pulled him out of the dog house and hugged him close and knew that he was dead.

"Oh, no! Auntie Mom, it can't be! Oh, no, Bunny! Bun, Bun, no! We have to get him to the vet. I'll go get dressed.

Auntie Mom tried to hug him and said, "I'm afraid it's too late, Markie. He's gone. You know he's old for a dog. He's had a good life."

Candy and Bea had been roused by the noise and they came running out the back door. "What's going on?" Candy asked. When she saw Markie holding Bunny's body, she knew. Bea was on her knees touching Bunny, too. "Oh, Markie, I'm so sorry. He was such a good dog."

Markie could not be consoled. He was rocking back and forth and crying. Candy thought her heart would break. She wanted so much to ease his pain, but knew there was nothing she could say or do to help him. She laid her hand on his shoulder. "Honey, come inside. We'll decide what to do with his body." Markie continued to moan and rock back and forth.

Auntie Mom said, "Let's leave him alone. He'll have to work it out for himself. He needs to grieve in his own way. He'll come in when he's ready."

Markie pulled Bunny's old blanket out of the doghouse and wrapped his body in it. He was crying the whole time. He continued to rock him and crooned to him as if he were a baby. "You won't be cold now, boy. This will keep you warm. Oh, Bunny, why did you have to go and die on me? What will I do without you?"

The women were watching from the back porch and they, too, were crying. They clung to each other. Auntie Mom said, "We knew it would happen one of these days, but you're never prepared for it. Poor Markie. He loved that dog so."

Bea said, "How long can we leave him like this? Can't we do something for him?"

Candy said, "Leave him alone. He'll work it out. Let's go inside and wait until he's ready to come in. I could use a cup of tea."

Over an hour later, they were sitting at the kitchen table sipping tea when Markie came in with dirt on his robe and pajamas. "We can bury him under the tree now." His jaw was set and his eyes were red, but his demeanor was that of a man in charge.

The three women said almost in unison, "Okay, Markie." They all went to the back yard followed by Percy. Markie placed the blanket with Bunny's body inside in the grave he had dug. They all watched as Markie covered it with dirt. Nobody said a word or tried to help. They knew Markie had to do this by himself. Percy paced around the hole and kept an eye on the Martin's cat who was sitting on the fence watching everything.

When the hole was filled, Percy got on top of the pile of dirt as if he were patting it down. The four of them joined hands. Auntie Mom said a prayer and they took turns saying good-bye to Bunny. They could not hold back the tears, and they stood there for a while and just cried. Then Auntie Mom said, "Let's go inside and get some breakfast."

As they turned to go, Markie fell to his knees and started sobbing again. Candy got down beside him and Bea and Auntie Mom went inside. Candy took him in her arms and rocked him as she tried to console him.

"Oh, Mom. It hurts so much. Why did he have to die?" Markie sobbed.

Candy crooned, "I know, baby. I'm so sorry. We'll all miss him. He's been with you since you were a baby. He's been your constant companion. I know it hurts now, but it will get better. You'll see. Seventeen is really old for a dog.

We were lucky to have him this long. He'll always be with you in your heart."

"Mom, how do you do it? You're always so strong. . Tell me about my dad. You never talk about him. What was he like? I've only seen pictures. How would he have handled this? What kind of man was he?"

Candy was not expecting this kind of response from Markie. It took her a moment to gather her thoughts. "Well, darling. I don't think he would have handled this situation any better. You were the man in charge today." She hugged him close. Then he put his head in her lap and she rubbed his temple as she talked about Mark.

As she talked, she remembered the Mark she had known. She told Markie every good thing she could think of. She talked about his favorite color, food, hobbies. She remembered the good times they had had – how they met, the fun they had in school and the struggles they had when he was in med school and when they first got started when he became a doctor. She realized that Markie had missed the father he never knew, and she missed him, too. It was good for both of them.

"I'm glad we had this talk," she said to Markie. "I want you to know you can talk to me anytime you want to, and ask me anything."

Markie replied, "I know, Mom. Thanks. Let's go try to eat some breakfast. I can smell the bacon. And you know how Auntie Mom hates to be kept waiting."

Candy chuckled and said, "Somehow, I don't think she would mind today. Let's go eat. I need you to do a favor for me, though. I want you to go with me tomorrow to take Bea back to school. I need you to help me drive."

Markie replied, "Sure, Mom. I'd like that."

~~~~~~

"Emergency warning!" said the voice on the car radio. "Severe storms in the area for the next twenty-four hours. You are advised to stay inside. Go out only if necessary. This is an emergency warning!"

Candy said, "We'd better find a motel and spend the night. Pull into the next one you see." They were on their way back home after dropping Bea off at her dorm.

"I think I see lights up ahead. I'll pull in there," said Markie.

He and Candy talked quite a bit on the trip, and Candy was seeing him in a different light. He had developed into a fine young man. He was tall, handsome, thoughtful, and polite. His voice was deep, resonant and pleasant to hear. Candy thought to herself, I'm very lucky with both of my children. Bea had her choice of scholarships, and Markie will qualify for one, also. I've been blessed.

She asked Markie if he had given any thought to where he wanted to go to school after graduation. They talked into the night about his options. To her surprise, he had given it a lot of thought, and by the time they were ready to leave the motel the next morning, it was decided that he would stay in Millerton and go to the college in town. He was making announcements on the school intercom, and calling the plays at the games, and he had been offered a job at the local radio station. He thought it would be perfect for him. He could work at the station and co-ordinate his schedules.

They asked the clerk at the motel to direct them to a good place to eat. He told them to go to Pearl's across the street. "They have the best food around here or anywhere, and they open early for breakfast."

Pearl's was clean, fresh-looking with quaint decorations. Family photographs lined the walls. While they were waiting for their orders, Candy glanced at the photos. She gasped, "Oh my!" Markie said, "Mom, what's wrong? You look as if you've seen a ghost."

Candy quickly recovered. "Oh, it's nothing. I just thought I recognized someone in the photo. But as I look closer, it's just a look-alike."

When the waitress returned with their orders, Candy asked her, "What can you tell me about the photos on the wall. Are they all the same family?"

"Oh, yes, ma'am. This restaurant's been in the Thompson family since forever. All the Thompsons worked here at one time or another. I'm a fifth generation Thompson myself, on my mother's side."

"Thank you. That's nice to know." Candy made a quick decision to return some other time and find out more about the Thompson family. She didn't mention anything to Markie. They ate quickly and got back on the road.

"Mom, wake up. We're almost home," Markie said. Candy opened her eyes and realized that the rhythmic swish, swish of the windshield wipers had lulled her into a much-needed sleep. She had dreamed that she was in a carnival fun house, and everywhere she turned there were pictures of people grinning at her, but one face was somber, and it was the same face in every picture.

Markie said, "You must have been really tired. You zonked out completely."

"It's only because you're such a good driver. Thanks, Honey."

CHAPTER 21

Vic was nervous as he entered Charles' studio. There was no reason for him to feel that way except that he was anxious about seeing Charles again. He had not felt this way since Pat. Charles had been on his mind every day since their encounter at the photo session. When he thought about him, he felt giddy and he would admonish himself thinking, You're acting like a school girl. Man up and get over it.

Charles was busy spreading pictures out on different surfaces and making adjustments – switching photos around at different angles. Vic stood and watched for a few minutes before he made his presence known. Charles looked up and his face seemed to light up. "Come on in. Take a look. I still think you should let me put you on the cover. You are so photogenic."

Vic was taken aback. He said, "I asked you not to take pictures of me. Why did you do that?"

Charles replied, "I know, but I couldn't resist. You are just so handsome. I thought that once you saw yourself, you would see what I see, and you would let me print them."

Vic grabbed one of the pictures and ripped it in half. "Absolutely not! I told you to take shots of the food, but not of me! No way can you use these!"

Charles was surprised at his reaction, and he stammered, "OK!! Don't get your nose out of joint. I won't use them. I'm sorry, man. I didn't think you were serious. Most people like to see themselves in print."

Vic replied, "It's all right. I'm not like most people. I have my reasons. Now let's get down to business. I have other things to do."

Charles cleared his throat and said, "Ahem. Umm – Yes. Let's look at these and see what you think of this layout. Maybe use this one with your hand holding the plate on the cover. What do you think?"

Vic said, "I think that's a good idea. I'd like this dish featured first, though. And maybe this one just under it like that." They continued working together for about an hour until they finally agreed on how the pictures would be displayed. The text would be added later after the editor approved the display.

Charles said, "That was fun. How about a glass of wine and we'll make a toast."

Vic agreed and they spent the rest of the afternoon sipping wine and getting to know each other. Vic looked out the window and said, "It's getting late. I had no idea we'd talked so long. I'd better be going. Thanks for everything."

Charles walked with him to the door and said, "It is late, but I don't want you to go. Are you hungry? There's a little Italian restaurant around the corner. We could get a bite to eat."

Vic replied, "Maybe some other time. I have to go to work." He didn't want Charles to think he was too eager, and he was reluctant to get involved with him. He didn't want to be hurt again. The way he was drawn to Charles, he felt he could be.

A week later Charles called Vic at the restaurant, "There's been some changes that I think you need to look at before it goes to press. I need your approval. When can you come by the studio?"

Vic was reluctant to go, afraid of what he was feeling. "How about tomorrow afternoon, around two o'clock?" He felt the afternoon would be safer.

Charles said, "I look forward to it. See you around two."

Vic tried to deny his feelings, but he could hardly wait to see Charles again. He arrived at his studio before two and hung around outside the building until a few minutes after two. He didn't want Charles to think he was too anxious. Before he could knock on the door, Charles opened it. With a big grin on his face, he said, "Come on in. I've been waiting for you. I hope you haven't had lunch. I've prepared a feast that I would like you to critique."

Vic couldn't help but laugh. Charles had a round table set with a cloth, napkins, wine glasses, lit candles, and dishes covered with silver domes. He said, "You shouldn't have. I mean it. You shouldn't have. This is more like a dinner than a lunch."

Charles laughed and said, "I know. I just wanted to impress you. So have a seat and let's eat before it gets cold."

They ate and talked very little. Charles said, "Hmm? What do you think? Do I pass muster?"

Vic said, "I think you pass. It was delicious. Now where are the changes you wanted me to look at?"

Charles said, "Right over here." They went over to a table where Charles presented a magazine to Vic and said, "There are no changes to be made. Here's the finished copy. I wanted you to be the first to see it before it is issued. And I wanted to see you again. Was I wrong in thinking there is something between us?"

Vic replied, "No, you are not wrong. I feel it, too. I haven't felt this way since Pa.....," and his words were cut short with Charles' kiss. Vic pulled away saying, "No, Charles. I'm not ready yet."

Charles said, "But you are. I feel it. Come with me." He took him by the hand and led him into another part of the studio that was partitioned off to make a space for a bedroom. It was decorated to look like something out of a magazine and very neat, unlike the rest of the studio.

Vic said, "No. I'm not ready for this. Not yet. I can't. I killed my last lover." He told Charles about Pat. Charles said that he had known about it and knew it was an accident. He surprised Vic when he said he had known Pat and knew how Pat could get when he drank.

Vic was relieved to hear that Charles understood, and he sat on the edge of the bed and put his head in his hands and cried. "I'm sorry. I haven't cried like this in a long time. I'm sorry."

Charles sat beside him and soothingly rubbed his back saying, "It's all right. It's all right. Let it out. I understand."

He took him in his arms and held him until Vic's sobs subsided. Then he turned his face up and kissed him again. Vic did not struggle this time and kissed him back.

Charles very deftly undressed Vic and himself, pulled the covers back on the bed and motioned for Vic to get in. Vic surrendered to Charles. It was good to be touched again. Charles was an expert lover and Vic had never felt that way with Pat or anyone else. He was ecstatic.

At six o'clock, Vic called into the restaurant that he wouldn't be in because he was under the weather. Charles laughed and said, "Come to your storm."

CHAPTER 22

"Yoo-hoo! We're home," Candy said as they entered the living room.

Auntie Mom replied, "We're in the kitchen."

Candy and Markie looked at each other and mouthed, "We?"

When they reached the kitchen they could see two people sitting at the table. Janet Rice, a friend of Markie's, was seated across from Aunt Maggie who said, "We're having a nice visit. Janet came over to see Markie not knowing that you were gone. Come join us."

Candy said, "Hello, Janet. I have something to take care of. We'll visit some other time. Markie can stay and chat. Nice to see you."

Markie stammered, "Hi, Janet. You wanted to see me? About what?"

Janet said, "Oh, nothing in particular. I just wanted to visit and chat awhile."

Auntie Mom said, "I'll just let you two talk, and I'll see if I can help Candy with her project. See you later, Janet."

Aunt Maggie found Candy upstairs looking through her files. "In my day, a young lady let the boy do the courting. I don't know about this new generation. She is just as bold as a brass monkey – sitting there pretending she wanted to talk with me. Have you had the talk with Markie? You'd better tell him about rubbers because that girl wants to get her

139

hooks in him, and she'll do anything to get him. I know her type, and I know she'll do whatever it takes – and I do mean anything. She'd get pregnant on purpose, if she got the chance."

"Aunt Maggie, you say the most outrageous things! But I think you're right. I have talked with Markie a little. I think Wes talks to the boys about things like that, but I'd better do a refresher. I'm not looking forward to it. I have to remind myself that he's not a child anymore. I expect he knows a lot more than we think he knows. We had a nice long talk on the trip." And she proceeded to tell Auntie Mom what they had decided about college.

"I think that's a wonderful idea. We could use a man around the house. It will save money. It's an excellent college. I just hope he can juggle the radio job and his studies. He's a smart young man. You lucked out with both your children, Candy."

Candy replied, "Luck had nothing to do with it. It was your guidance, and the two of us working together. It's not over yet, but I feel good about the future."

Auntie Mom said, "What are you doing in your files? You should be resting."

Candy said, "I thought of something while we were on the trip, and I just wanted to check my notes. I don't remember where I filed it though, so I'll just keep looking for a while. I'll come down when your guest leaves." And she laughed at the look on Aunt Maggie's face.

Candy looked in every folder for the list of words and numbers. Then she remembered that Bea had taken it to her room years before and hadn't returned it. She went into Bea's room and looked in her desk. She found the paper under what appeared to be a diary. Do I dare read her diary? What if there is something I shouldn't see? Then she convinced herself that she would not say anything to anybody if there was something not meant for her eyes.

She opened it and began to read. Just a little girl's thoughts – very well written, with the correct spelling and punctuation and everything – even indentations. She smiled to herself and thought, Typical Bea. Always doing the right thing.

She was about to put it back in the drawer when she turned another page and noticed some words that made her look twice. "I wish I had a daddy. I wish my daddy had not killed himself. I wish my grandma was not so mean. I wonder if she made him kill himself."

Candy was shocked. What had made Bea think Mark had killed himself? She couldn't ask her because Bea would know that she had read her diary. Bea had never mentioned it to her. She wondered if Frances had put that idea in her head. She thought, I wouldn't put it past her. She is a vicious old woman with funny ideas, and she can be cruel.

She looked at the letters and numbers on the paper and they still didn't make any sense. She put the paper in a special folder so she could find it easily, and went downstairs.

Markie and Janet had gone outside and were sitting on the steps talking. Markie had told her about Bunny and he had started to cry. Janet was sympathetic, trying to console him.

Auntie Mom said, "See, I told you she'd be all over him like a leech the first chance she could get. I bet she would love to "comfort him", the little hussy."

Candy laughed, "Aunt Maggie, you are so funny. But I believe you're right. We'll have our talk tonight. I want Markie to have every opportunity to have all that he wants without some floozy side-tracking him."

Auntie Mom laughed, too, and said, "Ah-ha. So you see what I see. Floozy, hussy, Jezebel. Leave him alone!"

Markie said, "Did you say something, Auntie Mom?"

"I was talking to Percy. I told him to leave it alone." She and Candy laughed.

~~~~~~

Janet was a pretty girl with blonde curls and almond shaped blue eyes. Unlike most cheerleaders, she didn't go for the football players. She had her eyes on Markie. She told all her girlfriends that she was going to marry him. She never missed an opportunity to be around him. They were both seniors, and whenever anyone asked her about college, she would give some vague answer about not having made up her mind yet. After Markie told her about his plans to stay in Millerton and go to college, she said that was her plan, too. She got a job in the college admin office sorting mail so she could be near Markie.

After dinner that night, Candy went into Markie's room and asked if she could talk with him. To her surprise, Markie said he already knew what Janet was up to and he was not about to get caught in her trap. She had asked him to take her to the prom and to keep from embarrassing her, he said he would. Candy told him that she was relieved to know that he was not fooled by her, but he would have to be very careful. "She's sneaky, and she would do anything to try to trap you. Don't trust her at all."

"Don't worry, Mom. I think I can handle her. She's pretty, but she's not as smart as she thinks she is."

When Candy told Auntie Mom about their conversation, she said, "I hope he can handle the situation. You know when they stop thinking, that second head takes over, and they're lost."

Candy laughed, and said, "You may be right. Let's just hope for the best." She decided she would ask Wes to talk with Markie in more specific terms. It dawned on her that she never thought to talk to Brandon about any of her problems. It never occurred to her that he would be a resource. She just didn't feel that relaxed around him and she certainly couldn't talk with him about this. She'd be too embarrassed to mention intimacy to him in any form. He had made advances toward her and she had avoided entanglement so far. The most he had gotten was a very light kiss – not a lover's kiss. Because she was not attracted to him in that way at all.

Candy talked with Nicole when they were watching a game, and Nicole said that she had noticed how Janet was

143

always up under Markie. She said that she would ask Wes about talking to both the boys. The boys were very close and people who didn't know them thought they were brothers.

~~~~~~

"Wow! Look at you, you handsome devil. Don't you look snazzy in your tux? Some girl is gonna grab you tonight, and I bet you know who it's gonna be. Don't forget to take your rubbers in case it rains," Auntie Mom snickered.

"Aunt Maggie, you're awful! Leave him alone. You are mighty handsome, though," said Candy.

Markie said, "Don't worry, ladies. There are no clouds in the sky. I don't think it will rain." They all laughed.

Markie let out a long low whistle when he saw Janet in her blue dress. He gave her the corsage and helped her pin it on her dress. She did look lovely. The blue complimented her blue eyes, and anyone could see that she thought she looked pretty. Her father told Markie what time to have her home, and they left for the prom.

The gym had been transformed into a magical kingdom complete with live band, snacks and punch. Everyone was dressed up and looking their best. There was an air of excitement and the dancing began. Janet whispered in Markie's ear, "I made reservations at the new motel on the edge of town. Tonight's our special night, Markie. I want you to make love to me."

Markie drew back and looked at her and said, "I thought the guy was supposed to make the first move, Janet. You're too bold."

She looked at him with tears in her eyes. "It's just that I love you so much, Markie. I want you to be the first. I have condoms in my bag. Don't worry, I won't get pregnant. Please, Markie?"

Markie looked at her again. In the shadowy light, she was more beautiful than ever, and with the tears glistening in her eyes making them look shiny, he found it hard to resist. He said, "Okay. When can we leave without making people suspicious?"

She said, "Leave it to me." And with that she put the back of her hand up to her forehead and asked Markie to walk her over to one of the chaperons. She told her that she felt faint and she wanted Markie to take her home. The chaperon said, "You do look flushed and glassy-eyed. I hope you feel better."

When they got in the car, she started to laugh and said, "See how easy it is to fool people."

Markie said, "Yeah, I see what you mean."

They checked into the motel and found their room. As soon as Markie closed the door, Janet locked it and began unzipping her gown. She turned to Markie and said, "I think I need help. I can't reach that far." She took off his bowtie and started removing his coat. Then she turned around so he could unzip her gown. She stepped out of it, laid it on a chair and began unbuttoning his shirt. As they undressed Markie did what any healthy young man would do. He became hard and he wanted to consummate the act. Janet said, "Uh-uh. Not so fast. Here's a condom." Markie took the condom and went in the bathroom to put it on. Janet got in the bed and held the covers back for him. He got in beside her, kissed her on the mouth, then the neck and each breast. His hand went between her legs and he touched the moistness of her. Then he tried to enter her, and she made a whimpering sound. He said, "Am I hurting you? Do you want me to stop?" She pulled him closer and said, "Don't stop. Go slow, but don't stop. I want this. I want you so much. Oh, Markie, don't stop."

They lay in each other's arms. Markie was spent and Janet had a wily smile on her face that Markie could not see. He felt good and wanted to go to sleep. He rose up on his elbow and said, "We'd better be going. Are you ok?"

"I'll be all right. I love you Markie. I hope I proved how much. We belong to each other."

Markie said, "I hope you know that this isn't something to brag about to your girlfriends. This should be our secret."

"Oh, I won't tell, if you won't tell," and she giggled.

They dressed and Markie took her home. They arrived just five minutes after the time to be back and he kissed her good-night at the door. Janet's father opened the door and said, "I guess your watch was slow. Anyway, five minutes isn't so bad. Did you have a good time?"

Janet replied, "The best. Good night, Markie."

When Markie got home, he went into the bathroom and examined the condom that Janet had given him by holding it up to the light. He could see tiny pin holes. He laughed to himself and thought, well Miss Janet, you think you're so clever. Let's see what you try to pull next. I'm glad I listened to the coach. 'Always carry your own. Don't leave anything to chance.' It's a good lesson.

CHAPTER 23

For Bea, college was one hundred eighty degrees from high school. She was very popular with girls and boys. Girls liked her because she seemed confident and not haughty. She was very diplomatic, thoughtful, and sincere. Being a math major put her in classes with a lot of boys who liked her because she was smart and could talk on their level without being flirtatious or silly. They could relax around her and sometimes they came to her for advice about their girlfriends.

All the sororities were giving her the "rush" but she was not interested in joining any of them. To her, they seemed so petty and insipid – sometimes even silly. They gossiped and talked badly about each other and seemed to have no purpose except to be exclusive with their own. She watched with detachment the young women who pledged, and wondered why they put up with such debasing. It wasn't worth it.

One girl in particular seemed drawn to her and tried to be near her all the time. Mona Graham was rich, but she was very shy and quiet. She did not make friends easily and was very insecure about most things except singing. Bea encouraged her to join the choir. Bea joined with her and discovered her own rich voice. They were both altos, and they became breathing partners. When they had to sustain a long note, they would take turns breathing so that there was no break in the tone. The director placed them side by side and loved the way it worked out. The overall sound was beautiful when blended with the rest of the choir.

People thought they were related and began calling them cousins. Their facial features were similar – both had the jutted chin with a cleft in the middle, except Mona's chin was more prominent.

One of the young men in the choir began to court Bea, and she soon had to extricate herself from Mona to spend time with Bruce. Sometimes they were a threesome. This didn't bother Bea because she was not serious about Bruce, but it seemed to bother Mona. Bea could not tell if Mona wanted Bruce for herself or if she was jealous of Bea and Bruce's relationship.

Mona went out of her way to sit or walk between them. So Bea decided to let Mona get closer to Bruce whenever she could. That way she could have some time for herself. Bruce was trying to get too serious, and she didn't want that. She joined the thespians and got involved with the theatre in her spare time.

One evening Bea was going to the dorm when she saw Bruce and Mona in the shadows of the bushes kissing passionately. She thought to herself, That's good. He's made his choice. Now we can just be friends, and Mona can give me some space.

When Mona saw Bea in the hallway later that evening, she looked embarrassed and tried to make light chatter. Bea told her what she had seen and that it didn't bother her at all. She hoped that they could all be friends and that she and Bruce would be happy together. Mona was so relieved, she almost cried. Bea told her, "We were friends long before Bruce came into the picture. We won't let a guy come between us. Okay?" Bea felt sorry for Mona because she seemed to need to be with somebody all the time. Bea enjoyed her solitude whenever she could and didn't need to have company.

As the year progressed, Bruce and Mona became an item. Where you would see one, you would see the other. Their only time apart was when they were in classes. Bruce was a junior and was carrying a heavy load of classes. Whenever he had spare time from his studies, there was Mona. He tried to be diplomatic and asked Mona to give him some space. She became upset and he gave in.

Mona talked to Bea about their future. She had it all planned out. They would spend the summer together. Bruce could work for her father during the summer, and the next year, after Bruce graduated, they would get married. Bea asked, "Has Bruce agreed to this plan?" "Oh, he doesn't know it yet. But he will. He loves me, and wants to be with me," Mona replied.

Bea warned her that people like to make up their own minds about their future, and that she should talk with Bruce and consider what he wanted too. She suggested that the summer would be a good time for them to assess their situation. They might benefit from time apart to see what they, each one, wanted to do with their lives.

Mona reacted angrily. "You're just jealous because I took your boyfriend. You don't want me to be happy!"

Bea couldn't understand this outburst. She assured Mona that it was not true. She wanted her to be happy. And she and Bruce could do whatever they wanted to do. After that scene, Bea tried to avoid Mona as much as possible except at choir rehearsal. She always found some business to take care of, or someone to see during breaks so she wouldn't have to be around her and Bruce.

One evening, when Bea was going to the dorm after play rehearsal, Bruce got in step beside her and said, "Hi, Bea. Can we talk for a minute?" Bea replied, "Of course. Where's Mona?"

"That's what I want to talk with you about. She wants to be with me all the time. I can't breathe. Can you get her to let up?" He seemed desperate.

Bea said, "I have tried to talk with her, but she seems to think that I want you to be my boyfriend. I think it would be best if you handle it. If you don't want this relationship, don't encourage it." She paused "Do you know what your plans are for the summer? That would be a good time to put some distance between you. Make up your mind, tell her what you want to do, and do it."

"Thanks a lot, Bea. I'll try to do just that. Can I walk you to the dorm?"

Bea hesitantly said, "I guess so. I don't want to stir up anything between you and Mona."

"Oh, it will be alright. I already walked Mona to the dorm. She's inside."

When they reached the dorm, Bruce pulled Bea into the same shadows of the bushes where she had first seen him kissing Mona. As she protested, he tried to kiss and fondle her. She pushed him away and slapped his face. "How dare you! Get away from me, you creep. You have Mona pining for you, and then you try to seduce me! I feel sorry for Mona. She loves you."

"I'm so sorry, Bea. It was you I wanted, but Mona always seemed to be there. Please don't tell her. Please, Bea?"

They heard a voice saying, "She won't have to. I can see for myself. I thought you were my friend, Bea. I should have known all along. You wanted my boyfriend. Now you've stolen him away. I hope you're happy!" It was Mona. "Oh, Brucey. I'm so sorry she did that to you. I know you never would have bothered her if she hadn't come on to you like that."

Bea looked at the two of them and said, "You two deserve each other." As she walked away, she thought to herself, now I know what crazy looks like. She was glad to be going home the next week, and she went to her room and began packing. She had enough to do with finals and the play. She was too busy to be bothered with those two.

She phoned Candy to let her know when she would be ready to leave the dorm so she could pick her up. She was so happy to hear Candy's reassuring voice, and glad to have the year over. She would get a summer job and enjoy the quiet.

CHAPTER 24

"You're mighty silent, Bea. Do you feel like talking about it?"

"Not now, Mom. I'll tell you later. I just want to enjoy the peace and quiet for a while, if you don't mind."

Candy didn't mind at all. She had her own thoughts to keep her company. She had a lot to think about. As usual, her first impulse was to confide in Wes and get his thoughts on what she should do. But this time, she would work it out for herself. She would get the whole story then decide what to do. Bea had drifted off to sleep and was softly snoring and Candy smiled as she looked at her oldest child. She looked so young and innocent. She hoped that she would be able to help with whatever was bothering her and that it could be easily resolved.

They took turns driving and arrived home in record time. Auntie Mom greeted them at the door. She looked worried. "I'm so glad you're home. We've got some bad news. Nicole Knox was found dead today."

"What? No, it can't be!" Candy was incredulous. "What happened? I just saw her two days ago and she seemed fine."

"Coach went on an errand, and when he got back he thought she was taking a nap. When he took her some lunch, he couldn't wake her. He called an ambulance and when they got there, they pronounced her dead. The police are investigating now. Let's catch the news."

When they turned on the television, there was a newscaster saying, "Police are taking Mr. Knox in for questioning now." There was Wes being put in a patrol car. He looked around at the cameras in disbelief as he wiped tears from his eyes.

Candy asked, "Where is Fred?"

Auntie Mom said, "I don't know. The news didn't mention him. He might be with Markie. Markie went over to the house as soon as Fred called."

They heard the sound of footsteps on the porch, then Markie and Fred came into the living room. Markie said, "You heard? I thought Fred should stay with us. I hope you don't mind, Mom. Hi, sis," and he kissed her on the cheek.

"Of course we don't mind. You know Fred is welcome anytime. I'm so sorry to hear about your Mom, Fred." She hugged him and he slumped against her shoulder and sobbed.

When he had composed himself a little, she asked him, "Do you know what happened?"

"I was at work. Dad went shopping and came back and found her dead. I don't know what happened. But they took Dad downtown for questioning. They weren't too nice about it. They could have talked with him at home. Why did they take him downtown? Do you think they think Dad killed Mom?" And he broke down in tears again.

Aunt Maggie said, "I don't know what they think, but I know that your Dad would not hurt a hair on Nicole's head.

154

Or anyone else's either. They'll straighten it out and your Dad will be home in a little while. In the meantime, you'll stay with us. I'll call your grandma and let her know where you are. Now, if anyone is hungry, supper's ready."

No one made a move toward the kitchen. Candy said, "I'm going down to check on Wes."

Aunt Maggie said, "No, you're not. You can only make it worse for Wes. Don't you see what message that would send? Your friend the DA would jump on that like a flea on a hound dog. You know how he feels about your friendship with Wes. You just sit tight and wait to see what's going on."

Markie and Fred went up to Markie's room. Bea, Candy and Aunt Maggie went into the kitchen. Nobody was hungry, so Auntie Mom made a pot of tea. They sat at the table and sipped quietly. They didn't seem to know what to say. Then Aunt Maggie asked Bea, "So Missy, how was school? Tell us about it."

Bea replied, "It was great for the most part -- a lot harder than high school. I joined the choir and took part in a play. I had fun. I'm all registered for the Fall, and eager to start my classes."

"Okay, that covers 'the most part'," said Aunt Maggie. "Now tell us about the rest," and she chuckled.

"Well, there were these so called friends," and she proceeded to tell them about Mona and Bruce.

Candy tried to listen, but didn't comment much. She was distracted with her own thoughts. There was so much going on in her mind. Too many things had happened in a matter of two days. She was worried about Wes and about what she had discovered on her trip.

Bea was saying, "What makes people act that way?"

Auntie Mom replied, "Honey, people are like jigsaw puzzle pieces. If they don't fit, don't force it. They will fit somewhere else. Some look like they fit, but they don't complete the picture. They just don't belong. When you find the right piece, it fits, it belongs, they make the picture come together and everything works out. Your two so called 'friends', didn't belong in your picture at all. They belong to another puzzle. I hope Mona looks for some help with her obsession, but I doubt she will. She's probably had issues all her life, and it has nothing to do with you. Sounds like they're soul mates," and she laughed. "Now, if nobody is going to eat, I'll just put this food away. Candy, are you okay? You're mighty quiet."

"I'm okay, Aunt Maggie. I just feel like I should be doing something. I'll call Brandon and see what's going on."

When she finally got Brandon on the phone, she said, "Brandon? Candy. We're back. I heard what happened to Nicole Knox. What's going on? I see…. Fred is with us… We called his grandmother… That's right, Wes's mom…Oh, good. Then he knows that Fred is okay. Yes… That's good. No I'm not glad of any of this. I resent what you're saying Brandon. I'll talk with you later. Good night."

Auntie Mom said, "What is it you resent?"

156

"Oh, typical Brandon. He was being sarcastic saying now I could be Fred's mother, too. I know what he's implying."

"I told you – 'flea on a hound dog'. If the pieces don't fit, don't force it. I'm going to bed. You two could use some rest, too."

Candy said, "Good idea. See you in the morning, Bea. I doubt I'll be able to sleep, but we both need some rest."

The next morning, Candy awoke to muffled voices. Her rest had been fitful and she had slept in snatches. She put on her robe and went downstairs. Wes was talking with Aunt Maggie saying, "I can't believe what's happening. They think I killed Nicole. The DA has ordered an autopsy. I'm out on bail, and they're launching a full investigation. This is a nightmare. Where's Fred? He needs to know."

Candy said, "Oh, Wes. I'm so sorry about Nicole. I know you didn't do anything to her. This is awful. Would you like some coffee?" She wanted to throw her arms around him and console him, but she dared not touch him. She busied herself with the mugs and the coffee pot. "Fred is upstairs. He can stay with us as long as he likes, but you probably want him home. I'll go wake him."

Wes said, "No don't wake him yet. If he's able to sleep, that's the best thing for him. We're going to have some long days ahead of us. Thanks for the coffee. I need to make arrangements for Nicole. I need to talk with her family. I don't know what to do first. She was no sicker than usual. I don't know what happened. She was okay when I went shopping. When I got back, I thought she was just sleeping.

157

I don't know how long she was lying there dead..." and his voice broke into tears. He put his head down on the table and his body shook with his sobs.

Candy put her arms around his shoulders and hugged him. "Oh, Wes, I'm so sorry. I loved Nicole like a sister. She was such a nice person. I'll miss her. I know you loved her. I hope you get some answers soon. Perhaps an autopsy is the best thing. At least they'll know it wasn't anything that you did."

"Dad, what happened?" It was Fred standing in the doorway.

Aunt Maggie said, "He's out on bail. They're going to do an autopsy on your Mom to determine the cause of death. Here sit down. You want some coffee? You haven't eaten since yesterday. You're still growing. You need your strength. All of you need to eat something. I'll have your breakfast ready in no time. I know, I know. You don't feel like eating, but believe me it's the best thing in times like this. I've been through it and I know what you need. Sit, sit, sit."

In a half hour, everyone was sitting in the dining room eating Aunt Maggie's hot biscuits, eggs, bacon and grits. They had to admit, they did feel better, although no one felt like talking. After breakfast, Wes and Fred went home, and the house was quiet.

~~~~~~~~~~~~~~~~~~~~~~~~~~~~~~~

The autopsy took a week. They released the body and Wes and his family had a funeral for Nicole. Most of the town turned out – a lot of people just being nosy and wanting some excitement in their mundane lives. Wes asked Candy and her family to join his family. There were a lot of murmurs but no one said anything directly to them. Nicole's family stood behind Wes and Fred. They said they couldn't imagine Wes doing anything to hurt Nicole.

The autopsy showed an excessive amount of the painkiller that Nicole had been taking, and Wes was charged with her murder. No one believed it. Wes told the DA he had no idea how she could have gotten too much since he was always so careful about all of her medications.

The DA proceeded to build a case against Wes. He was like a dog that wouldn't let go of a bone. Candy was incensed. "Brandon, what are you trying to prove? Why are you so determined to make him guilty? Is this some personal vendetta? Why do you hate him?"

Brandon replied, "You know why. He wants you, so with his sick wife out of the picture, he thinks he can have you. Somebody gave her an overdose of those pills. I don't think the son could have done it. There was no one else in the house. You were out of town. So who could it have been, but our friend the coach?"

Candy could hardly believe what she was hearing. If she ever had doubts about Brandon's character, this proved he was not the one for her. She looked at him and saw a vindictive, small minded, well-dressed, pompous, handsome ass. There was nothing to disprove what he was saying, but he had no proof either. She started to tell him her thoughts, but she decided to keep quiet. She knew anything she would say might make things worse for Wes.

While they were waiting for trial, Wes tried to keep busy. Nicole had asked him repeatedly to paint the walls and Wes never seemed to have the time. He thought, well I've got time now. In fact I might never have the chance to paint at all if I don't do it now.

He and Fred started with the living room and decided they would work their way through the house room by room. When they got to the master bedroom, Wes found it hard to continue. Fred said, "Don't worry about it, Dad. Markie and I have this one."

Wes didn't protest. He let the young men take over. As they were moving the furniture into the middle of the room, Markie saw a brown paper bag behind the headboard. He was taking it to the trash when he looked at it more carefully then said, "Hey, Fred. There's something in this bag. Maybe it belonged to your Mom. You better look at it. Fred took the bag and peeped inside. There was an envelope and an empty pill bottle. He took them out and looked at it. The envelope had 'Wes' written on it. Fred called out to Wes, "Dad, you need to see this."

Wes came into the room saying, "What is it?"

Fred gave him the envelope, the pill bottle, and the bag. "What is this? Where did you find it?" .

Fred said, "Markie found it. It was behind the headboard."

Wes' hands were trembling as he opened the envelope. He

recognized Nicole's writing. He had tears in his eyes as he tried to read the letter.

"What does it say, Dad?"

Wes wiped his eyes. Then he gave the letter to Fred. He choked on his words, saying, "Here, it's to you, too."

Fred read the letter, then he turned to Markie and said, "Here, you found it, you need to know what it says, too. Then you can take it to the DA.

Markie read the letter, then he put it back in the envelope and put it along with the bottle back into the paper bag. He looked at the two most important men in his life and said, "I'm on my way."

When he got out to his car, Janet was standing there. "Hi, Markie. Can I have a lift if you're going my way?"

Markie said, "Sure. Where are you going?"

"I'm going wherever you're going, lover. Maybe we can stop along the way for some fun."

Markie looked at her. She looked pretty in shorts and a blouse tied in a knot under her breast, her hair up in a ponytail. Pretty as she was, Markie felt disgust. He said, "I'm going downtown on important business."

Before Markie could take off, Janet slid in the passenger's seat and said, "It just so happens that I have business downtown, too."

She picked up the bag and said, "What have we here? Is this your lunch?"

Markie grabbed the bag from her and said, "Mind your own business, Janet. Where do you want me to let you off?"

Janet said, "I can hang out with you, if that's okay."

"It's not okay, Janet. I have something very important to do and I don't need you hanging around."

"What's so important that you can't be nice to me, Markie? I bet if I was that little pickie-ninnie friend of yours who comes to stay with you, you'd have time for me. I bet you'd have lots of time for me. You'd probably have a good time with her. I hear they like it all the time."

Markie pulled the car over to the side of the road and stopped it. He turned to Janet and said, "You're not a nice person, Janet. Judy is not like you. She's just a friend. But you wouldn't know what a friend is, would you? Don't ever call her a name like that again. Now get out. I'm sure you can find a way home. Just put your thumb in the air. You're already showing your legs. Some desperate man will give you a ride home."

Janet got out of the car and slammed the door. "I'll fix you Mark Procter! Just you wait! You'll be begging me for some when that little darkie is through with you."

As Markie was driving away, he could hear her shouting, "Just you wait! I'll fix you good!"

He waved and headed down town. He wondered what he had ever seen in Janet. Pretty as she was, she was an ugly person. She made him think about Judy. Honey colored skin, big brown eyes, hair curled softly around her dimpled face – people always referred to her as 'cute', and on top of that she was kind, considerate, and thoughtful of others. He had always liked her when they were growing up and he would see her on rare occasions. He considered her a good friend. He had never thought of her as a girlfriend until now. The more he thought about it, the better he liked the idea. He thought to himself, thanks, Janet. You did me a favor.

He reflected on Judy's most recent visit. Phillis and Judy had made a special trip to come to his graduation, but graduation was not the good time they had anticipated. Fred did not feel like celebrating because of his mother's death and the threat hanging over his father's head. They had gotten through the graduation ceremony and taking pictures in their caps and gowns okay, but Fred just wanted to go home afterwards.

Amy, Fred's girlfriend, convinced him that he should try to have some fun, arguing that you only graduate from high school once. Fred relented and agreed on a trip to the drive-in. As they were piling in the car with Markie driving, Janet appeared and invited herself along, pushing Judy aside and climbing in next to Markie. Bea got in the seat next to Janet. Fred, Amy and Judy got in the back seat. While they were deciding where they could go, Janet started rubbing Markie's thigh. They went to a drive-in and ordered burgers, fries and Cokes. Fred tried to eat and join in the joking, but he couldn't swallow. He said to Markie, "I'm sorry man, but I can't do this. You guys go ahead and celebrate. I need to go home and be with my Dad."

Everyone said they understood. Bea tried to lighten up the situation by changing the subject. She mentioned the latest movie and asked what everybody thought about it. While everyone was giving their opinion, Janet whispered to Markie, "After we take everyone home, we can celebrate our way. Okay?" Markie pretended he didn't hear her. When they got to Fred's house, Markie asked if he wanted some company, and Fred said no. He thanked everyone for trying to cheer him up and they all waved to Wes who was standing in the doorway.

Markie took Amy home and then he took Janet home. He walked her to the door and she had turned to him with her face up for a kiss, and Markie kissed her on the cheek. She said, "Oh, Markie, you don't know how to treat a lady. You know what I want, lover." And she took his face in her hands and kissed him hard on the mouth. "Why don't you take them home and come back for me? We could go somewhere and celebrate, if you know what I mean."

Markie looked at her and said, "No thanks Janet, maybe some other time. Good night." When he got to the car, he said to Judy, "Why don't you join us up here so you won't have to sit by yourself in the back?" Bea got out and let Judy sit in the middle and they took off. Markie smiled at the memory. He guessed that was what had set Janet off because she was still standing on the porch watching as they drove away.

When he finally reached the courthouse and found a place to park, it was lunchtime. The DA's secretary said Markie had just missed Mr. Moore. She told Markie where he would be having lunch, and Markie headed in that direction. He entered the restaurant and felt out of place. He was wearing jeans and a tee shirt that were splattered with paint. He looked down at himself and felt embarrassed. Just as he was about to turn around and leave, Brandon saw him and came over. "Hi, Markie. What brings you here? You're not dressed for lunch."

Markie let that last remark go and said, "I have something very important to show you and it can't wait."

Brandon could see the urgency in Markie's face and said, "Come have a seat. What do you want to show me?"

Markie told him about the bag, where he had found it, and told him he needed to look inside.

One of Brandon's friends came over to the table and laughed, "You deserted us to have a brown bag lunch?"

Brandon said, "This young man thinks this is urgent. Sit down, I might need a witness. This could be interesting."

Markie was thinking, Good. A witness is just what we need. I don't actually trust Brandon. I never really liked him and don't know why. I tolerate him because of my mother.

Brandon looked in the bag and emptied the contents. When he read the letter, his face went white. His friend said, "What is it? You look like you've seen a ghost."

Brandon showed his friend the letter. After reading it, the friend said, "Well this changes everything. We need to get back to the courthouse and clear things up.

Brandon looked deflated and said in a stunned voice, "Yes, we do."

He knew the case that would put him in a favorable light with the public and give him a chance to marry Candy was kaput. He could forget about running for any public office for a while, and he would need to look for another lady to be on his arm to give him some credibility.

CHAPTER 25

Vic and Charles had settled into a routine. If either of them said, "See you at home," that meant Vic's apartment. If either said, "See you at the place." That meant Charles' studio. Vic was beginning to enjoy life again. He looked forward to their times together. They had the same interests and liked trying new adventures. They especially liked being near or in water. Sometimes they would rent a place near the beach, or head inland and rent a raft and just float down a river. They both were tanned and fit from all the outdoor activities. Life was good and Vic was happy.

Sometimes Charles would have to go out of town on a shoot. Vic missed him terribly and used the time inventing new dishes. His boss loved these times and would comment, "How long will he be gone this time?" Vic would laugh and say, "What are you talking about? How long will who be gone?"

Philip would chuckle and say, "You know what I mean. I know when Charles is out of town."

They would both laugh and Philip would say, "Show me what you've got. Impress me some more." And they would go through the same ritual to see if the new dish met with his approval. When Charles returned from his assignment, Vic would surprise him with the new dish.

When Charles worked in his studio, Vic would call him and ask the usual question, 'See you at home?' or 'See you at the place?'

Charles frequently worked with beautiful models. This was not a problem for Vic. He was not jealous or ever felt that there was a reason to be concerned. There was one model they both enjoyed hanging out with. Michele was six feet tall with thick black curly hair that she frequently wore in outlandish styles. She had high cheekbones, large dark eyes and chiseled features. She was willowy without being too thin with long legs, slim hips and generous breasts. She was always on time and very professional. Charles liked to say she was the perfect model.

One time, when they were out clubbing, she said to Vic and Charles in her husky voice, "I'm not a lesbian, I just prefer being around girls. Men are always trying to hit on me and trying to feel me up to see if they are real. I don't have to worry about you guys. I feel safe and I can relax when I'm around you two. You're fun to be with, and if anybody bothered us, I can take care of you." They all laughed.

After a while they became inseparable. Michele would sometimes spend the night when they ended up at the apartment and she had had too much to drink. She would sleep on the sofa and Vic would prepare a gourmet breakfast the next morning.

On one of those mornings when all three were hung over, Michele wrapped her hands around her mug of coffee, hunched over the table and looked at Vic and Charles with blood-shot eyes and said, "I wish I had met you guys before I had my surgery."

Vic and Charles looked at each other in wonderment and asked at the same time, "What surgery?"

She gave a wry smile, sat back in her chair and laughingly said, "My name used to be Michael. I've been Michele for five years. You mean you couldn't tell? I went overseas. They did a good job, didn't they?" and she pushed up her breast. "Now close your mouths. You look like two gold fish swimming around in a tank."

Charles recovered first and said, "Well, I'll be damned. I never would have guessed."

Michele said, "No – You be Charles, he be Vic and I be Michele." And they all laughed.

Vic said, "Tell me about the whole operation. What all did they do? Did they reconstruct it, cut it off or what? Can I see?"

Michele said, "What are you, some pervert? I'll tell you about it, but you'll keep your grubby little beady eyes off my precious body parts." And she rubbed her breasts until the nipples jutted out. "I am woman. I was born woman. I've always felt like a woman. It was just some freak of nature, some malfunction that put that appendage on me. You can't imagine what my life was like before I became who I am. Did you always know who you were?"

Charles said, "When I was in kindergarten I liked to play with the girl toys, and in elementary school, I liked to watch the boys play games, but I didn't like to join in. In Junior High, I would have to try to hide my hard-on when I saw a guy in the shower. It was awful. I finally admitted who I was and gave in to it when I went to college. What about you, Vic?"

"I don't remember exactly when I knew, I just knew I didn't feel right in the life I was living. I came to San Francisco, and now I'm free." He didn't want to tell them about the family he left behind, the intern who freed him to be himself and the sneaking around to have sex in the linen closets or any place they could find when he was supposed to be 'working late' at the hospital.

They looked at each other and Charles said, "Well, I'll be damned. Who would have thought it?"

Michele said, "No, you be Charles, he be Vic, and I be Michele." And they laughed until they cried.

Philip said, "With this rain and the wind blowing like it is, I think we'll close early. We have no reservations after five o'clock, and it's not worth our time to stay open. The wind is getting stronger, so you best try to get home as soon as you can."

Everyone was glad to hear it. Vic decided he would surprise Charles at the studio with the leftovers from the kitchen and they could stay at the studio that night. He bundled-up and put the food in containers and headed out. He called a cab and got to the building just as the rain began to come down harder.

When he went into the studio, he didn't see anyone at the usual set-up of cameras and lights. He heard noises coming from behind the partition. He put the food on the table and gasped when he saw Charles on the bed with one of his male models.

Charles jumped up and said, "Oh, Vic. This isn't what it looks like. I was just showing him how to pose for the shoot. There's nothing going on."

Vic recovered and said, "Where are the cameras? Where are the lights? Why do you have to show him on the bed? What's wrong with the usual set-up?"

Charles said, "I wanted to see if it would work in here before I moved everything. Don't get upset. There's nothing going on."

Vic didn't want to believe what his eyes were telling him. His heart was pounding in his chest and he could feel his face and neck burning. He tore off his wet coat and charged to the bed. He lifted the young man up by his jaw and threw him on the floor. The man's clothes were halfway off and he protested loudly as he tried to recover the rest of his items. He scampered away as Vic came towards him again. He was shouting, "What's wrong with you, man? I'm just doing a job. You need to get control of yourself!"

Vic screamed, "Get out! Get out!" He turned to Charles with tears in his eyes, "How long has this been going on? No wonder you want me to call before I come over. Professionalism, my ass! You just don't want to get caught. I never dreamed you could do this to me. How could you hurt me this way?" He looked out the floor-to-ceiling window and saw his reflection on the rain-streaked glass. He looked awful.

Charles came up behind him and put his head on his shoulder. "Vic, you know you're the only one. How could you think that I would want anyone else? He means nothing.

171

He's just a kid looking for a thrill. I told him that I already have the one I love in my life. He insisted on getting on the bed and I was telling him to put his clothes back on when you came in. Nothing happened. I wouldn't let it happen. You know I love you."

Vic sobbed, "This is the first time you've said that you love me. You never said it before. Why did it take this situation for you to say it? You just want to play me."

Charles said, "When I saw the fury in your eyes, I realized that you really care for me. And now I know I can never love anyone else like I love you." He kissed the side of Vic's neck and lightly bit his earlobe.

Vic half-heartedly said, "Stop Charles. You won't get out of this so easily. Stop. I don't want it. Leave me alone. I'm mad at you now."

Charles continued to woo him – nibbled his ear again and flicked his tongue in his ear. He slowly turned him around and kissed his neck. He could feel Vic's erection and he began unzipping Vic's pants. He said, "I can see you don't want to be bothered. Let me free you, poor baby." He unbuttoned Vic's pants and inched his hand down into his underwear.

Vic moaned and said, "Don't. I don't want to."

Charles said as he slowly led him toward the bed, "I know, baby. I know. Come to papa and let me fix you."

CHAPTER 26

Aunt Maggie was having a good time bustling around the kitchen fixing what she called a feast. She had said to Candy, "I don't want to call it a celebration, but I don't know what else to call it. If Markie had not found that bag, I don't know what would have happened. Here, you can mash the potatoes. Bea, you can set the table. Use the white tablecloth and the good dishes out of the china cabinet. Get the low vase out and cut some fresh flowers."

Candy said, "You're really going all out, aren't you? You're enjoying this."

"Yes, I am, my dear. Yes, I am. I just love special occasions so I can use all my good stuff. I called Wes' mom, Mabel and he will pick her up on his way."

Soon after, Wes arrived with Fred and Mabel. He greeted everyone and said, "I can't thank you enough for what you've done for my family, Maggie. I appreciate you having us over for this special occasion. I don't feel right celebrating, but it is a relief." He gave her a bottle of wine.

Maggie said, "You don't have to thank me, but I'll take the wine. Mabel, I'm so glad you could come. Come on in the kitchen and I'll give you an apron. You might want a glass of my special ice tea." She looked at Candy and winked.

Wes asked, "What's that about?"

Candy laughed and said, "I'll tell you about it one day."

Bea and Markie helped Aunt Maggie put the food on the table. Wes opened the wine and poured some in all the glasses. Candy started to object to giving the young people a glass. Then she said, "I guess they deserve a little cheer after what we've been through these last few weeks. Besides you're all young adults now. So drink up."

Wes said, "Not yet. We have to make a toast first."

Just as he was about to make the toast, the doorbell rang. Aunt Maggie said, "Hold that thought, Wes. I'll get the door."

When she opened the door, Jim Rice burst into the room with a tearful Janet following. "Where's that Mark Procter? He defiled my daughter, and I'm gonna knock the shit out of him."

Aunt Maggie said, "Hold on a minute. What are you talking about? You're in my home. You show some respect. I didn't invite you in. If you'll calm down, I'm sure we can solve whatever your problem is."

When everyone heard the ruckus, they got up from the table and came into the living room. Wes said, "What's going on, Jim? What's all the noise?"

Jim said, "I should have known you'd be here. You got rid of your wife so you could be with her. Jim pointed at Candy. "Now she had her son defile my daughter so she could be like you sinners."

Mabel broke in saying, "Stop your tirade, Jim and tell us what you're raving about. Here, sit down, calm down and stop shouting so we can understand what's going on."

Jim looked at Mabel and took a deep breath. Mabel was a no-nonsense person, and her demeanor demanded respect. He sat on the sofa and cried, "My baby was a good girl until she hooked up with Mark. Look at her. He took her out and raped her. Now she's all messed up."

Aunt Maggie said under her breath to Bea, "If anybody got raped, she raped him."

Bea tried hard not to laugh. She went over to Jim, "Mr. Rice, try to tell us what happened. What is it you think my brother did?"

Jim looked at Bea and said, "You're the smart one that went away to college, ain't you? You need to keep an eye on your brother."

Bea said, "Yes, sir. I went away to college. Now can you please tell us why you're so upset?"

Jim said, "She come home looking like that – hair all messed up, blouse torn, shorts ripped and her face all messed up, and she said Markie did it."

While everyone was focused on Jim, Markie asked Janet what was going on. She said, "I told you I would get you, Markie. I told you."

Markie said, "You fix this right now, Janet. You know I did nothing to you. You fix it, or I'll tell your daddy about

175

prom night. How you arranged everything, and you know that I was not your first."

This last revelation shocked Janet. She thought she had fooled Markie into believing that she was a virgin. She swallowed hard and cried out, "Daddy, Markie didn't do anything to me. I was so mad at him that I wasn't looking where I was going and I stumbled and fell down a hill. Everything got messed up as I was trying to climb up the hill. Some people came and helped me. I'm okay. I was still mad at Markie when I said he did it. I meant that he made me mad. You know how I get when I get mad, Daddy. I just don't think about what I say."

Jim said, "Why didn't you say something before instead of making me look like a fool? I don't believe you. I think he did something to you, and you're trying to protect him, you little hussy."

Wes spoke up, "Now, Jim. You don't have to call her names. When was this supposed to have happened?"

Jim said, "Sometime this afternoon. She come home crying about it was Markie's fault."

Wes said, "Markie couldn't have done anything to Janet this afternoon, Jim. He was at the courthouse with Fred and me talking to the DA about Nicole's death. You see we found a suicide note that Nicole had left behind the bed, and we took it down to the DA. He was with us all afternoon until now."

Janet said, "See I told you, Daddy. Markie didn't hurt me."

Red-faced, Jim said, "I'm sorry to break in on you folks like this, but you can see my dilemma. The girl comes home looking like this saying something about Markie and I just jumped to the wrong conclusion. Come on Janet, you've got some explaining to do." He turned to Wes and said, "I'm sorry about Nicole, Coach. I'm real sorry."

Candy said, "Mr. Rice, don't you owe someone else an apology?"

He turned to Markie and said, "Yeah, I guess so. Sorry Mark. I'll talk to my daughter."

Markie shook his hand and said, "Good-bye, Janet. I hope you feel better."

Janet looked back as they walked down the steps from the porch and said, "I'm sorry, Mark. I'm so sorry." She looked as if she was going to cry, but Markie was not fooled. He didn't trust her.

When they returned to the table, Aunt Maggie said, "She is some piece of work. There's no telling how far she would have taken this if Markie had not had an alibi. Okay, folks let's say grace, make a toast, and eat before it gets cold."

Wes said, "I think I should say grace. I'm the one who has the most to be grateful for. Then we'll toast our good friends."

After dinner, they sat at the table for a long time just talking and laughing. Wes felt relaxed for the first time in a long time. He looked at Fred and saw that he was enjoying himself. It felt good to be a part of this gathering.

When they were saying their good nights, Mabel took Wes' hand and Candy's hand and held them for a minute. With tears in her eyes, she said, "Wes, Candy, -- wait a sensible time, but don't wait too long. Life is too short, and time goes too fast. You have my blessings."

Wes said, "Mom, what are you talking about?"

She replied, "There are some things that don't need to be said, Wes. You and Candy know what I mean. And everybody in this room knows what I mean, and we all wish you well. You can be decent, but don't be dumb. Good night all. Come on Fred, and help your grandma to the car."

Aunt Maggie closed the door and said, "Well, that was an interesting evening, -- never a dull moment in this house. You young folk can clean up. I'm going to bed. Come on Percy. Let's read awhile. Good night." Percy meowed and tripped along after her.

CHAPTER 27

When they got in the car, Jim turned to Janet and said, "You want to tell me the truth, girl? If you fell down a hill, where's the dirt? You would have dirt or grass stains on you somewhere. All I see is torn clothes. So what happened? And don't lie to me again."

Janet started crying again and sobbed, "Please, Daddy. I don't want to talk about it. Just let's go home."

Jim said, "If you won't talk, I'll find out my way." With his jaw clinched, he started the car.

"Where are we going?" Janet cried.

Jim didn't say anything. He headed in the opposite direction from their house. Janet noticed where they were when he pulled into the parking lot at the hospital. "Daddy, there's nothing wrong with me. Please take me home. Please, Daddy."

Jim didn't say anything. He opened the passenger door and pulled Janet out. He held her arm firmly and walked her into the emergency room as she tried to pull away. "My girl's been hurt. I want somebody to look at her and tell me what's wrong."

The nurse asked how she was hurt and Jim revealed that he thought she had been raped. The nurse asked Janet, "Were you raped? How did it happen?"

Before Janet could answer, Jim said, "I want her checked out. She says she wasn't, and I say she was. I want to know. She won't say, and she lies."

The nurse said, "Okay. Fill out these forms and have a seat. We'll see you shortly."

While they were waiting, Janet cried and begged her father to take her home. "I swear to you, Daddy. Nothing happened. Let's just go home. Momma will be worried."

Jim clinched his jaw and said, "Your momma won't have to know if, as you say, nothing happened. Now, will she?"

The nurse said, "Come with me Miss. The doctor will see you now. Undress and put this gown on."

Janet felt trapped and she did as she was told. While she waited for the doctor, she recalled her afternoon. She thought, My first mistake was pissing Mark off. My second mistake was getting in Jerry's car and flirting with him. My third mistake was trying to blame Mark for this. I really fucked up this time. Why do I do things like this to myself?

As she was thinking these thoughts, the doctor came in and introduced himself. He was a young intern and Janet thought, He's cute. I could like him.

He asked Janet what was going on, and she told him that her father thought she had been raped. It was not her idea to come to the emergency room and he could just tell her father that she was okay, and they could go home and not bother the hospital any more.

"It doesn't work that way, young lady. We have to do our job. If you were not raped, did you have consensual sex with anyone within the last twelve hours?"

Janet said, in a small voice, "I think so." Then she started crying again. The doctor tried to console her as best he could. He told her to lie back and he would examine her. "Did your partner force you to have sex, or did you participate?"

Through her tears, Janet sobbed, "He didn't force me. I tore my blouse and my pants to make it look bad and to get back at my boyfriend. My daddy doesn't believe me when I tell him I haven't been raped. Could you please tell him that I wasn't raped? He doesn't have to know the rest. Please?"

The doctor finished his examination, and told Janet to get dressed. He asked her, "When was your last period?"

Janet said, "I think it was in June. I don't remember. Why? Could I be pregnant?"

The doctor said, "I suggest you make an appointment with your gynecologist soon, and you should keep better records. I'll talk with your father, but I think you need to talk with both your parents. You have some decisions to make, young lady, and you need to take better care of yourself."

Jim was waiting anxiously when Janet and the doctor came out. "What's the verdict, doc? Was she raped or not?"

"Your daughter is fine, Mr. Rice. She was not raped. I've made some follow-up suggestions to her. Have a nice evening."

"Thank you, doctor," Jim replied. "Now let's get you home, girl. What are you going to tell your mamma about your torn clothes? How are you going to explain that, huh? Your story about falling down a hill won't hold water. She'll be worried, and I want some answers."

Janet said, "Don't worry, Daddy. Momma won't even notice. And even if she does, she won't care as long as she has her Vodka. You're so busy that you don't even notice how she's always sleeping when you come home. She's not sick, she's drunk. Or don't you care anymore? You can always go to Miss Minnie's to be consoled. Yeah, you didn't think I knew, did you? I know more than you think I do. Well, I've got news for both of you."

"What news? What are you talking about, girl?"

"I'll tell you when we get home. I'll tell you both together. That is if she's sober enough to comprehend. So don't question me anymore. I'll talk when I'm good and ready."

"You talk to your daddy that way, girl? What's wrong with you? You're gonna tell me what's going on, and I mean right now!"

Janet looked at him and smiled. For some reason, she felt very calm. She was usually slightly afraid of her father. He was not an easy person to talk to – prone to over-reacting and exaggerating. She felt empowered, and it felt good. She simply smiled all the way home and never answered any of his questions.

When they reached their house, they could see the lights were on in the living room. This seldom happened unless they had company. Most of the time, they were in other parts of the house, each occupied with their own activities – seldom together for anytime. Janet said, "Looks like we might have company." Janet's mom, Flo, opened the door before they could. She wore a well-used house coat, her drab-blonde hair had not been combed, and was tangled around her flushed, bloated face. She looked at them with blood-shot eyes and slurred with a gravelly voice, "Where have you two been? I been worried sick. What you up to? What happened to you, Janet? You look awful."

Janet smiled and said, "Nice of you to notice, Mom. I'm glad you're up. Did you have a nice nap? Is dinner ready or are we on our own, as usual?"

"You being sassy, girl? Don't you git fresh with me. What you been up to, Jim? What's going on?"

Jim looked at his wife in disgust. She had a vague resemblance to the pretty girl he had married. He looked from one to the other. Would Janet end up looking harried and washed-out, too? He felt like something was slipping away from him, and he couldn't get a grip on it. "What are you doing, Flo? Let's go into the kitchen. I'll fix you a cup of coffee. You look like you could use one. Janet says she has something to tell us."

Janet and Flo sat at the table while Jim bustled around making coffee and putting mugs and fixings on the table. When they each had a mug of hot coffee, Jim sat down and said, "Okay, Janet, we're listening. Talk. What do you have to say?"

Flo looked at Janet and she began to tear-up. "What's wrong, Baby? You can talk to us. What's your problem?"

Janet looked from one parent to the other. This was the first time she could remember that they had sat at the table at the same time as a family in a long time. "The problem is your baby is not a baby any more. Your baby is going to have a baby." She sat back in her chair and smiled at their gaping mouths.

Jim stuttered, "What do you mean? Who's the boy? I'll beat him to a pulp!"

Flo started crying, "My baby's having a baby! Oh, Lord, where did I go wrong?"

Janet started laughing. "You two should see yourselves. This is the first time you've showed any concern for me in a long time. But it's not about me, is it? It's all about you. Daddy wants to beat somebody. Mama wants to crawl back into her bottle because I did her wrong. Listen, you two sit here and hash it out. You can blame each other or do what you want to do. I'm tired. I'm going to bed. You figure it out and let me know how you want to handle your shameful daughter and her bastard."

Flo reached for Jim's hand, "What are we gonna do, Jim?"

Jim looked at his wife. He felt sorry for her. "For one thing, you're going to get sober and clean-up your act. Our daughter needs us now, and we'll have to figure this out.

Janet went to bed, but not to sleep. She lay in the darkness of her room and reviewed the last few months. When was my last period? May? June? I don't remember. I need to keep it on a calendar or something. I don't think it was May. I was with Mark near the end of May. I don't think I had a period in June. Oh God, this baby has to be Mark's. It just has to be. I fixed it so it would be Mark's.

CHAPTER 28

Michele and Vic were sitting at the table sipping tea. Vic had confided his doubts about Charles. "He knows how to get to me. I love him, but I don't trust him, Michele. He makes me feel so good when he's here. But the minute he's out of my sight, I begin to worry about what he's doing and who he's doing it with. Is that crazy, or what?"

"What's that old song, 'You're not sick, you're just in love'? You're just in love, Vic. You can't help it. Love's funny, isn't it? You don't pick who you fall in love with, it just happens. I think it's a chemical thing as well as an emotional thing. How else can you explain two ugly people getting together and producing an ugly baby?"

Vic laughed in spite of himself. Michele always made him feel better in the moment.

"But seriously, Michele, what can I do? He makes me crazy. I've been a real bitch here lately. I pick a fight about nothing then I feel bad and apologize. We make-up, and that lasts for a short while, then I'm bitching about nothing again. We're in this cycle, and I can't seem to get out of it."

Michele closed one false eye-lashed eye and rubbed her chin. "I expect you like the 'making-up' part. That's why you do it. Am I right? Huh? Come on, confess. Does he do it good?"

Vic laughed again and said, "You're awful, just awful. But you're right, I do like the making-up part. He's so good. You just don't know. That's what drives me crazy. I worry about how good he is with someone else."

"No, I don't know, and I'm afraid I'll never find out," Michele laughed. "He's not my type."

"What is your type, Michele? I never see you with anybody. Is it girls or boys?"

"That's what I like about you, Vic. You go straight to the heart of the matter, no beating around the bush for you. Well, that's a good question – boy or girl. I honestly don't know. I'll see a pretty girl and it stirs something inside me and I'll wish I still had that old thing. Then I'll see a pretty boy and it stirs something inside me, and I want to do the nasty with him. I just don't know, so I take whatever suits my fancy at the moment. Is that insane, or what? I'll probably never settle down with one person. It's just not my style. But let's talk about you. You need somebody – just one steady person. You'd make a good family man. You should sit Charles down and tell him how you feel. Talk to him. Let him know how much he means to you and how he's hurt you. You need to tell him why you've been such a bitch, that you don't like being a bitch, and that you'll stop your bitchy ways, if he'll stop giving you reasons to doubt him. I'll be willing to bet a few bucks, that things will get better."

Vic laughed at her last statement, got up from the table, looked out the window, and thought to himself, She's right about the family man part. I haven't thought about my family in a long time. The kids are grown by now. I wonder what they're like, and if Candy found someone to love her as she deserved. She's right about talking to Charles, too. I'll do it when he gets back from his trip. I'll fix a beautiful dinner and we'll talk – really talk before it gets clouded with the lovemaking. With that thought, he began to get an erection.

187

Michele laughed and said, "I see you're thinking about your 'conversation' now. I suggest you talk away from the bedroom, or else you won't get to say what needs to be said."

They heard a thump in the hall and both turned towards the door to see Charles coming in. He dumped his bags and equipment and said, "Hello, my family. I'm home, and I'm going to bed."

Vic went over to him saying, "You look awful. Sit here and let me take a look at you."

Vic felt his forehead and said, "You have a fever. Maybe you have the flu. Drink some tea. You need lots of fluids and bed rest."

Charles sat and began to tremble. His clothes were wet from perspiration and his eyes were red-rimmed. He tried to pick up the mug with tea in it, and his hands began to tremble.

Vic said, "Here let me help you with that. You need to get out of these clothes and go to bed. I'll get you some aspirin to reduce your fever and we'll get you to bed."

Michele snickered, "You'll like that, won't you?"

Vic said, "Oh, hush, Michele. Can't you see he's sick?"

For once, Michele didn't have a quick comeback. She could see that Charles was in a bad way, and it frightened her. "What can I do to help, Vic? I know, I'll turn back the covers on the bed and fluff the pillows, just like they do in the movies. Maybe a shower will make you feel better, Charles, and some clean jammies will make you smell better."

They both looked at her, and she said with a wide-eyed look, "What? What did I say? I'm just trying to help. What did I say that was so wrong?" And she mumbled to herself, He does stink, whether they want to admit it or not.

The next day, Charles looked better. His fever had subsided and he was able to eat some soup. Vic was very attentive and fussed over him as if he were a child. Charles loved the attention, and Vic was able to talk with him about his fears and his trust issues. Charles assured him that he loved him and would not be unfaithful. Vic wanted to believe him and he began to feel more comfortable in the relationship again.

In the next few weeks, Charles stayed close to home. He didn't feel sick, but he didn't feel well either. He had a low-grade fever and a sore throat. Vic insisted that he see a doctor. "Maybe you have mononucleosis – you don't have much energy and you're listless. You don't have much of an appetite, and those are some of the signs."

Charles said, "How do you know all this? You sound like a doctor yourself."

Vic said, "Oh, I've been watching you and I read up on your symptoms at the library. So let's make an appointment and get you feeling better."

They made an appointment at an outpatient clinic at San Francisco General where they gave Charles a complete physical. When the doctor came to talk with Charles, Vic thought he looked familiar. Maybe he had been one of his classmates. He said nothing but watched from the background. The doctor told Charles that he had a virus. His

189

lymph nodes were swollen and he had an infection in his throat. He prescribed an antibiotic, told him to get plenty of rest and eat healthy. They made a follow-up appointment in a month, and if they found anything in the test results, the clinic would call him.

In the meantime, Vic's medical curiosity made him want to know more. He had heard about an unidentified virus that was going around, and he wanted to know more about it. He went to the hospital library and read as much as he could. He read the medical journals and anything else that would give him information. He had a sinking feeling that whatever this new illness was, Charles had it. He didn't tell Charles his fears, but he kept a close eye on him. Charles began to resent the over-protectiveness and they started having arguments again. Charles would storm out and return drunk. Vic would take care of his hangovers and fuss over him even more.

When Michele came to visit, more often than not, she would find herself in the position of arbiter. One day, as they were sampling one of Vic's new dishes, they started arguing and Michele threw down her fork, stood up and said, "Look, you two. This shit has got to stop. What's going on? You are at each other all the time. What happened to our happy little home? I can't stand it. I don't care how good your fucking food is, Vic. I'm not coming here anymore, if you can't get along long enough so I can enjoy my free food."

In spite of themselves, they had to laugh. Michele could always neutralize an unpleasant situation. She sat down and said, "Seriously, guys. What's going on?" They looked at each other, and Vic said, "I'm worried about him. I think he's sicker than he thinks he is and I want him to take care of himself. He won't listen to my advice and it bothers me."

Michele looked at Charles, and said, "Okay. That's Vic's story, now it's your turn. What the fuck is wrong with you?"

Charles said, "He treats me like a child. I get that he's concerned, but I need some space. He's not loving me, he's smothering me."

Michele said, "Now we're getting somewhere. Charles, take better care of yourself. Eat right, exercise, get plenty of rest, be faithful and don't give Vic anything to worry about. Vic, ease up with the mother hen bullshit and let Vic be a grown man. If he wants to step in front of a fucking trolley car, let him. Keep on burning your food and feeding me and we'll all be one big fat family. Problem solved. Now let's have a drink of wine and eat. Cheers!" and she toasted the air.

CHAPTER 29

Jim and Flo decided the first step would be to take Janet to a doctor to see if, in fact she was pregnant. Then they would decide what to do as a family. They would let it be Janet's decision. She could have an abortion, have the baby and put it up for adoption, or keep the baby and maybe marry the boy. That was the next question – who was he? Jim said he thought it might be Mark Procter since he was the only one he had seen Janet with. She seemed to like him a lot. But they would take it one step at a time.

When Janet came downstairs, she looked pale and tired with dark circles under her eyes. Flo began to bustle about the kitchen. "Do you want some breakfast, baby – I mean Janet? Sit right here. I'll get you a glass of milk. You look tired. Did you sleep well?"

Janet was surprised by all of the attention, and she sat with her mouth open. Her father stared at her. "Do you feel all right? Can I get you something? Your mother and I have been talking. I think first we need to take you to a doctor to see if you are, er, with child. Then we can decide what to do. It'll be your decision. What do you think, Honey?"

Janet didn't know what to make of this kindness. She expected that they would be chewing her out, calling her names and making her feel bad. She didn't know quite how to handle this treatment. She mumbled, "Okay, whatever you say."

Flo had the shakes and was dropping pans and making futile attempts at fixing bacon and eggs. Jim told her to sit down and he took over. He suggested she try to find an AA meeting to go to where she could get some support. And she agreed. Janet was again flabbergasted by this turn of events. It felt good to see her parents trying to help each other, being kind to each other and to her, too. She couldn't remember the last time they were this civil.

Flo made an appointment for Janet for the next day and she and Janet did a lot of talking about the future and her options. Janet wasn't sure what she wanted to do and spent another restless night worrying about her situation.

~~~~~~~~~~~~~~~~~~~~~~~~~~~~~~~~~

Aunt Maggie was bustling about the kitchen when she heard the doorbell. Now who could that be? Then she peeked out the window as she went to the door. Good Lord. What does that little hussy want now?

She opened the door and greeted Janet, Flo, Jim's wife, and Jim. "Come in folks. I'll get Markie for you." She shouted up the stairs, "Markie, Candy, you have company. Won't you folks come and have a seat? Can I get you something to drink?"

Janet said, "Some water, please." Jim and Flo just shook their heads.

Candy and Mark came down stairs and greeted every one. Markie was puzzled and beads of sweat showed on his upper lip. Candy said, "What can we do for you?"

Jim said, "Let's not beat around the bush. Janet's pregnant and she says Mark is the father."

Candy slumped into a chair and asked, "Markie, is this possible?"

Markie replied, "It's possible, I guess." He had a flashback to prom night. He used his own condom, but he had been told that they were not foolproof. So he had to admit that it was possible.

Janet looked at Markie in desperation, but she could not look him in the eyes. She dropped her head and concentrated on peeling the polish from her fingernails.

Candy broke the silence and said, "Well, what do you want to do, Janet?"

Before she could speak, Aunt Maggie came in from the kitchen with a glass of water. She gave it to Janet and said, "I think the young people need to talk with each other first. Let's give them some privacy. We can go into the kitchen and have some coffee or tea and let them talk. What do you think?"

Flo said, "That's a good idea. I could use a cup of coffee."

Jim helped Flo get up and they moved into the kitchen. Flo felt good with Jim supporting her. She couldn't remember when he had been so attentive. She was actually enjoying the moment of attention when most people would have been upset.

Markie said, "Okay, Janet. What's this about? Are you pregnant, and is the baby mine?"

Janet tried to look innocent, but it didn't work. She looked sneaky. She said, "Of course it's yours, Markie. You remember when we were together. It was a beautiful night. We made love."

"Yeah, I remember the night. We had sex. You tried to get me to use the condom that you gave me, but I didn't. I had my own. Yours had holes in it. What was that about, Janet? Were you trying to get pregnant? You said you loved me, so why are you trying to ruin any future I might have?"

Janet didn't know how to answer his questions. She started to cry and sobbed, "What are we going to do, Markie? Do you want to get married, and give our baby your name?"

Markie said, "Janet, we're too young to get married. I just got out of high school. I don't know how to take care of a wife and baby." He ran his fingers through his hair. "Where would we live? I don't have a full-time job, and you can't work. What could you do? Be real, Janet. Marriage is not the answer."

He sat in a chair across from her, "If you want to have the baby, you could put it up for adoption, or we could try to raise it together somehow, but marriage is out of the question."

Janet was looking down and Markie said, "Look at me, Janet. What do your parents think? Do they want you to have the baby? Do they want you to get married? Are they going to take care of you and the baby? What were you thinking when you decided you wanted to have a baby? Because that's what you did. You decided, and then you tried to trap me."

195

Markie stood and paced in front of Janet. "That's not love, Janet. That's manipulation. You used me for your little scheme. I couldn't marry someone like that. It wouldn't work. I would always resent you. Now I will give you child support, if you decide to keep the baby. I might even be a part of the baby's life, but I won't marry you. You got that?"

Janet began to sob, and it got louder. Jim came into the room. "What did you do to my little girl? Isn't it enough that you got her pregnant? Now why is she crying?"

Markie replied, "Ask *her* why she's crying? She deliberately tried to trap me. It won't work, Mr. Rice. I can't marry Janet. But I will be there for the baby, if she decides to have it."

Jim looked from Mark to Janet and back again. He had to admit to himself that this was no skinny kid he was talking to. He respected Mark for his honesty and remembered how he had had to marry Flo because she was pregnant with Janet. He loved his daughter and tried to make the marriage work, but he had never forgiven Flo for trapping him. He hadn't ever loved her, and now he felt sorry for her. He thought, I've made some mistakes but I'm not going to abandon my family. I'll do the best I can to be there for Janet and the baby if she chooses to keep it.

He turned to Markie and said, "Okay, Mark. We'll let you know what we're going to do. This is a family decision. Come on, Janet. Let's get you home. You look like you could use some rest. Go tell your momma we're going home. Mark, I'm sure you'll do the right thing. We'll be seeing you."

They said their good-byes and left. Aunt Maggie said, "That poor woman was in a bad state. She looked sick. Did you notice how she was shaking? This situation has really upset her."

Markie said, "She probably has a hang-over, Auntie Mom. Don't feel too sorry for her."

Candy said, "Markie, what are you saying? That sounds so rude and callus. How do you know this?"

"Janet talks about her mother being smashed all the time and her father running around with other women. It's not a good situation, Mom, and I don't want to get caught-up in it."

Candy replied, "You should have thought about that before you went to bed with her. Your actions have consequences. If that baby is yours, you'll be 'caught-up' in it for the rest of your life. What did you and Janet decide? You're both too young to get married, and you're not ready to raise a family."

"That's what I told her. We haven't decided anything yet. I told her I would help support the baby if she decides to have it, but I'm not marrying her. She'll have to accept that. I'm too young to get married and I don't love her. She's a little schemer and I don't trust her. Besides I've made my own plans for the future and they don't include having a wife and baby right now. If and when I decide to marry, it'll be my decision."

Aunt Maggie said, "That's my boy, uh, I mean man. I told you Candy, that little hussy was trying to get her claws

197

into Markie. Looks like she succeeded, but she didn't win. Thank God!"

~~~~~~

Markie talked with Fred and Amy about the situation. They were not surprised and suggested that if Mark wanted to take Janet out to a movie or something, that they should double date. It would be easier for Mark that way and Fred and Amy could neutralize things.

Janet was delighted when Mark called her and asked her if she wanted to go to a movie. When they got to Janet's house, she asked Amy to come upstairs with her while she got dressed. She said she was having trouble finding something to wear that wasn't too tight and needed Amy's help. As they went through Janet's wardrobe, she noticed that Janet was a little plump around the middle and she suggested that they go shopping for maternity clothes soon. Janet was glad to have someone her own age to talk with and they set a date to shop.

That Saturday, while Amy waited in the living room, she could hear Janet and Flo talking in the kitchen. Flo said, "That's a good idea, Janet. You and Amy have fun. I figured you'd be needing maternity clothes soon if the baby is due in December."

Janet said, "Shh, Mama. It's due in February, I told you. February, not December. The doctor miscounted."

"Whatever you say, honey. I guess you know your own body. You and Amy enjoy your shopping."

Amy said nothing to Janet about what she had heard, but she put two and two together and came up with nine. She concluded that she needed to talk to Fred and Markie. She also began to feel uncomfortable with Janet, and decided she didn't like her very much.

When Amy told Mark and Fred what she had overheard, Mark decided that he would wait and see how Janet chose to handle the situation. Time does not lie, and babies come when they are due. He talked with Candy, Auntie Mom, and Bea about the situation and they all agreed that it would be best to wait and see.

CHAPTER 30

Candy and Bea talked a lot about Janet's situation while they drove Bea back to college. Bea was excited about returning to school and to a new dorm. She hoped her new roommate would be friendly. She couldn't imagine being in Janet's situation. "I wonder if she knows who the father is, and just chose Markie because he has the most potential. I feel sorry for her in a way, but I don't like how she tried to trick Markie. Auntie Mom sure has her number. One day, she's going to slip and call her 'the little hussy' to her face. She never uses her name now – it's 'the little hussy is on the phone', 'the little hussy is here'. She makes me laugh when she talks about her." They both laughed about the situation.

On the way back from taking Bea to school, Candy stopped overnight at the motel where she and Markie had taken refuge from the storm. She went to the same coffee shop for breakfast. Candy was lucky and got the same waitress. There were only a few customers so they had time to talk about the pictures on the walls and the Thompson family tree. Candy took notes, writing names down quickly so she wouldn't forget them. She would need them later.

She called Aunt Maggie and told her she was going to take a detour to see Frances before she came home. She would see them in a day or two; she'd call and let them know. When she arrived in Newburn, it was late afternoon. She checked into a hotel and went to dinner. She didn't bother to call Phillis or Frances. After she ate, she went to Frances' house. When Frances opened the door, she was shocked to see Candy. "Why Candy! Why didn't you call? I'm so surprised to see you. What brings you here without notice?"

"I didn't think I needed to announce myself, Frances. I need to talk with you. Let's go into the kitchen and you can fix some tea and we can have a heart to heart." Candice felt strong and in control and Frances just nodded and went into the kitchen. She nervously began preparing the tea.

"What can I do for you, dear?" she said in a shaky voice.

"You can start by telling me the truth for once," Candy said as she put her purse in a chair and sat down. "Who are you? What's your real name and where did you come from? Who were your people? What did Bob want you to tell me as he was dying? What did I have the right to know? I'm not leaving until I get some answers." Frances began to protest and Candy put up her hand and said, "No excuses. I'll not accept your excuses any longer, Frances, if that's your name. I know some things about you, and I only need to hear your side. You have your grandchildren to think about. It's not just your secret anymore. So why don't you sit down and talk to me? I'm listening. And you know me to be a fair person. I'm in your family whether you like it or not. Mark told me that you had chosen me for him to marry, so start talking."

Frances sat down and she seemed to shrink before Candy's eyes. She suddenly looked old and frail. Her hair was in a long braid that fell over her shoulder. She had lines around her mouth and dark bags under her eyes. Her shoulders drooped and she had a frightened look in her eyes. "What do you want to know, Candice? What can I tell you?"

Candy felt sorry for her. She reached across the table and touched her hands and said, "Start at the beginning. Tell me about yourself. I've seen pictures of you when you were a little girl growing up. You fill in the blanks. I'm your friend – your daughter-in-law. You can talk to me. I don't judge, please, talk to me."

Frances' eyes began to tear. She swallowed, looked at Candy and whispered, "I'll try. Give me a minute. Shall I start at the beginning? I can remember being a happy child most of the time. I liked to play by myself. Or maybe I was by myself because I was always teased. I didn't look like my younger brothers and sister, and the children in the neighborhood teased me all the time. They pulled my hair, and said that I looked like I was white. They said I thought I was cute because I had good hair. I never knew what that meant. I thought I was ugly because nobody wanted me around. I can remember two brothers and a little sister. I wonder what ever happened to them.

"I remember feeling loved when I was with my mother, but I was afraid of my father. He was a big man with a deep voice and I learned to stay out of his way. When he was home, there was a lot of arguing. My mother would end up crying and she would come find me and hug me. I never knew why she was crying and hugging me so hard." She began twisting her blouse; she had a haunted look in her eyes and she began to sweat.

"Then one night when I was about ten, I was awakened by the noise of their shouting and I heard my mother say, 'You leave her alone! It's not her fault. Leave her alone!' I pulled the covers over my head and tried to pretend that I was

202

asleep. I felt the cool air as my father pulled the covers back. I could smell the stink of his breath, and he was mumbling something about a white man's little bastard. He pushed up my gown and put his knee between my legs. He fumbled with his pants and I was screaming and trying to punch his face. He was laughing and saying, 'This is payback, you little white bastard!' I was screaming and I could hear my mother screaming, 'Leave her alone! I'm warning you, leave her alone or I'll blow your damned head off!' Then I heard a loud blast, and my father slumped on me. I lay there pinned by his weight and felt something warm and sticky on my stomach. My mother ran out of the house screaming and two neighbors came and took him off of me. I could smell his stench and the sweet metallic odor of his blood. I felt like I was suffocating. I couldn't breathe. I was soaking wet with his blood and I tried to scream.

"I don't remember much after that except there was a tall white man who came and took me to his house. A white lady gave me a bath and an old white man gave me something bitter to drink. The next I remember, I was in a car going somewhere. The tall white man took me to a big building. He kissed me on the cheek and left me there. I had a room to myself and lots of new clothes and I went to classes every day. I learned later that it was an exclusive boarding school for rich white girls. I never saw my mother again but the white man would visit once in a while. I asked him questions about who he was and why he had brought me to that place. He tried to explain and he brought pictures and notes from my mother, but the only thing my childish mind could comprehend was that my mother had abandoned me.

"I had nightmares for years. I would wake up screaming, and there was no one to comfort me. So I decided to cut her and my family out of my life. I stayed at that place until I finished school then I met and married Bob. I told him my story and he didn't care. He loved me, he really loved me."

Tears were streaming down her face and dripping off her chin. She wiped her face with the back of her hand, and took an unsteady sip of tea before she continued. "I decided to live in his world, the white world, and never looked back. Mark never knew about my past and now you do.

"So it's up to you what you do with the information. I'm sorry if I upset you, Candy. You are generous and kind and you've done a wonderful job of raising my grandchildren all by yourself. I don't know if I would have been able to do what you have done. I depended on Bob so much because he's the only one who ever really loved me, the only one I could count on. I don't know what happened to my mother and the rest of the family. It was easier to leave that part of my life behind.

"All of a sudden, I feel very tired. Tired and relieved. Thank you, Candy. Thank you for caring." She found a tissue in her pocket and wiped her eyes and blew her nose.

Candy said, "I can fill in some of the blanks for you, if you feel like listening. I made it my business to find out all I could from talking with someone from your family."

"Oh, do tell, Candy. Tell me everything you know."

Candy fixed the tea and began to talk. "The man who took you away was your real father – Willard Graham. The lady who gave you a bath was his wife. Your mother was pregnant by Willard when he made a deal with the man you knew as your father. If he married your mother, he would always have a good-paying job in the Graham factory. This was a good thing for your father because in those days, very few black men could find work that wasn't sharecropping. When you were born, looking as white as you did, he found it hard to take. It began to erode the marriage. He started to drink, knowing he could do whatever he wanted to and not get fired from his job.

"Your mother tried to protect you as best she could. So when she killed her husband, your real father thought it best to take you out of that situation. He thought he was doing the right thing by you. Your mother never knew where he took you, but she wanted you to remember your family and that you were loved. So she sent you letters and pictures whenever your father visited. She wasn't charged with the killing of her husband. It was listed as an accident because the judge was a friend of the Graham family. Willard saw to it that your mother never wanted for anything. He thought he was protecting you, Sally Anne Thompson, when he helped you change your name to Frances Graham."

Frances sighed and said, "I wish I had kept those letters. At the time, I was so angry and afraid. I was used to being alone, so that was nothing new. But I was so afraid and lonely. I missed my mother and my siblings. I cried myself to sleep every night, and then the nightmares came. I had no friends and didn't talk much to anybody. Can you imagine how it must have been for a little girl to be torn away from her family so dramatically? I became this cold, closed-off person that few people could get to know. I'm so glad you cared enough to talk with me, Candy. Thank you." She reached out to Candy and they hugged and cried. Even though Frances was taller than Candy, she felt like she was the adult and Frances was a big child.

Candy said, "So why did you decide that I should be the one for Mark to marry?"

"You were so young and naïve, and Mark really liked you. You seemed to fit into our family, so I encouraged Mark to marry you. I didn't think you would be a problem and you and Mark would give us beautiful grandchildren."

They talked late into the night. Frances fixed omelets and they ate and talked until sunrise. Candy filled Frances in on the news about Bea and the young lady whose name was Graham. They laughed about Mona and Bruce and agreed they deserved each other. She shared the situation about Mark and Janet and Frances thought Mark had handled it well.

When Candy left Frances, they hugged, and Candy said, "Get some rest Frankie. I'm sorry I kept you up all night."

"Oh, Candy. It was one of the best nights of my life. I think I can rest now that the secret's out. I'm so grateful for you. You get some rest before you get on the road. I don't want anything to happen to you. You could stay here if you like, but you said that you were registered at the hotel. Give everyone my love."

When Candy went back to the hotel, she decided she would take a shower and a nap before she started home. As she was putting her key in the door, she looked around and there was Wes coming down the hall. He saw her and they both said at the same time, "What are you doing here?"

Once an avalanche starts it cannot be stopped. And so it was with Candy and Wes. They entered Candy's room, and without a word, they kissed. Candy began to tremble. She felt hot all over; her knees were weak and she could hardly stand. She felt an ache in the pit of her stomach, and she found it hard to breathe. Wes picked her up and took her to the bed. Before she could protest, he had his pants off and had pushed up her skirt and removed her panties. He kissed her face and pushed her skirt up further and kissed her trembling stomach. All Candy could do was moan as he entered her. As their bodies coupled, they were a perfect fit. She had never felt such exquisite ecstasy.

Wes moaned, "Oh, Candy, Candy, Candy. Oh, baby, you don't know how long I've wanted you. This is so good, so good. Oh my god, Candy!"

They cried out "Oh, my god!!" together and then lay limp in each other's arms. Tears were rolling down the corner of Candy's eyes into her ears, and they looked at each other and laughed. Wes was the first to speak. "Why did we wait so long?"

Candy said, "We had to, Wes. That makes this time even sweeter. And it was so sweet. It was so good. Oh, Wes, you don't know how long I've wanted you."

Wes rose up on one elbow and looked at her. "When did you first know?"

"The night you stayed with me in the hospital when Markie was in the accident. When did you know?"

"I think it was the same time, or soon after. You were so kind to Nicole, and so thoughtful. I admired the way you handled your life. The more I saw you, the more I thought that eventually we would be together. Don't misunderstand. I would never have done anything while Nicole was alive."

Candy placed her hand on his lips, and said, "I know you wouldn't. I would not have let you. I'll tell you a secret. Nicole asked me to take care of her boys when she was gone. Her boys – you and Fred. We both loved her, and I don't think we're being disloyal to her memory."

Wes chuckled, "You women. You have it all figured out while we men don't know which end is up. By the way, what are you doing here?"

Candy said, "I came to visit Frances. I dropped Bea off at school and decided to come here unannounced. That's why I'm staying in the hotel. What are you doing here?"

Wes replied, "I'm here for a coaches' conference. Tell me about your visit with Frances."

Candy said, "After I go to the bathroom. Let's get comfortable first. It's a long story." She went into the bathroom, and when she came out Wes had turned back the covers and was in the bed. He got up and started undressing Candy. As he unbuttoned, unzipped and pulled aside each garment, he kissed that part of her body. Candy sighed and let him do whatever he wanted to do. She held his head close to her as he kissed her breast, her stomach, and her thighs. He pulled her into the bed and whispered, "This time it will be slow and easy. This time is for you." He eased his hand between her legs. When he heard her moan they came together and began a rhythmic movement that made them reach orgasm at the same time.

They lay in each other's arms completely relaxed. Candy murmured, "Oh, Wes, I wish I could think of a word to describe how you make me feel. The only word I can think of is 'good.' You make me feel so good."

"Same here, little lady. Same here. Are you hungry?"

"Come to think of it, I am. Let's order room service and I'll tell you about my visit with Frances." She looked at him, laughed and said, "At least I will if you'll let me talk."

They ordered the food, and while Wes was in the bathroom, Candy called home and told Mark that she was staying another day to visit his grandmother. That was her reason for coming here in the first place, so it was only half a little white lie.

While they ate, Candy told Wes about her visit with Frances. Wes suggested she tell the rest of her family. She had already decided that she would. It had been a secret too long.

They made love again, took a nap, and rediscovered each other again before they ordered room service. They teased each other, made plans, talked about what ifs and supposes, and when they should get married. They slept in each other's arms and spooned when one would turn over. When morning came, Candy awakened to Wes gliding his fingertips over her body. He kissed her shoulder, her breast, her waist, the rise of her hip, down the outside of her thigh, and then the inside of her thigh. When he reached that point, she opened herself to him and they made love again.

As they lay in a lover's embrace, Candy chuckled, "You're wearing me out, Wes. Let's save some for later. What about your conference? And I need to get home. It's a long drive."

Wes said, "Yeah, I guess I should go to the meetings since I'm being paid to attend. Let's have breakfast together, then I'll send you on your way, you vixen."

CHAPTER 31

Charles seemed to be getting stronger. Vic saw to it that he ate nutritious meals and he gave him vitamins and supplements. The clinic had called with the results of his tests. They told him that he had a virus that had been labeled HIV and they wanted to make him a part of the research they were doing. Vic went with him to every appointment and talked with the staff. He wanted to know everything that was going on. Charles thought that he was just concerned about him, but Vic knew it was more than that. His medical curiosity needed to be satisfied. His years of study and practicing medicine made him want to know.

Charles started calling Vic, 'Miss Vickie', because he was always fussing over him like a mother. Vic laughed at this and it became their little private joke. Michele visited almost every day, mostly around mealtime. Vic would go to work knowing that Michele would be there to take care of Charles. She told Vic, "I just love this new diet you put us on. Look how smooth my skin is. I just look so gorgeous. And I feel so good."

Charles and Vic laughed so hard that Charles got hiccups. Michele said, "What? What did I say that was so funny?" This made them laugh harder.

After a while Michele became a regular fixture in their lives. Charles followed the doctors' orders, took the prescribed medications, and kept his regular appointments at the clinic. He felt that he was an important part of their research. Charles watched many of their friends get sick and die, and he didn't want that to happen to him. He had a persistent cough that never went away. They tried different medications, but nothing seemed to help. He had not been a smoker, so the doctors were stumped when the chest x-rays showed nothing in his lungs.

Charles was able to function and do his work for a long time, but after a few months, he began to lose weight. His hair began to fall out and he got funny-looking rashes on his face and body. They would come and go and the doctors said it was probably an allergic reaction to something. Vic became very concerned about him and suggested they investigate a clinical study that had been set up at Stanford University.

The routine at Stanford was pretty much the same as the San Francesco clinic. They looked at Charles' records and came to the same conclusions. They told Vic that so little was known about this HIV virus that they needed further study. They were grateful that Charles was willing to go through all the testing and treatments. So many young men with the virus refused to participate and it made the studies harder. They suggested Vic get tested, too.

Vic tested negative for the virus and the doctors suggested he take precautions when he had sex with anyone. They told him that his lifestyle made him vulnerable. Vic was relieved to have tested negative and told the doctors he would heed their advice.

He fixed a fabulous meal that night and of course, Michele was there to help them celebrate. Vic suggested she get tested, too. She told them, "I'm scared. I don't like needles and all that medical stuff. What if they find that I've got that HIV thang? What do I do about it? Uh, uh. Not for me. You'll keep me healthy with all this good food. You sure know how to burn, Miss Vickie. I just love giving y'all the benefit of my company."

As usual, Michele managed to lighten the subject and make them laugh. Vic told her, "I'm serious about you getting tested. With your life style, there's no telling what you might have. We know you're not monogamous – you pick up whatever you can find – so do it for us. There's nothing like knowing so you can protect yourself."

Michele said, "Okay, okay. I'll do it just to shut you up. I'll do it next week, okay? Now leave me alone and let me enjoy this food. You make me sick, always fussing over a person." She looked at Vic misty-eyed and said, "Thanks for caring. Now look what you did! You're making my mascara run. I hate you for that. You know I must always look my best for the cameras." They all laughed.

After Michele left, Charles and Vic cleaned up. As Vic was washing the dishes, Charles came up behind him, flicked his ear, nuzzled his neck and rubbed against him. Vic turned around and put soapsuds on Charles' nose. They kissed and Charles took Vic's hand and started towards the bedroom. Vic said, "Wait. I have something for you." He reached into his pocket and pulled out two condoms. "One for you, and one for me."

Charles took one and said, "I don't like this."

Vic said, "I told you what the doctors said, so, no condom, no nookie."

Charles said with a devilish look in his eyes, "Okay, we'll try it. You can help me put it on." As they walked to the bedroom, Charles put his hand down the back of Vic's pants and squeezed his buttocks.

After they made love, they both agreed that they did not like the condoms. Charles said, "It seems so contrived. I like it when we're spontaneous. I like being with only you, too. I'm not messing around anymore, and I know you're faithful to me. So let's forget the condoms, okay?"

Vic replied, "I don't know, Charles. I think we should do what the doctors say and try to protect ourselves as much as we can."

Charles was incredulous. "What do you mean, 'protect ourselves?' Have you been messing around on me? If it's just you and me, why do we need to protect ourselves? Are you afraid of me? Is that it? You don't want to make love to me anymore? You think I'm not good enough for you anymore? I'm just this person that you can fool around with, so you have to 'protect yourself' from me? You make me feel dirty. I hate you!" He began to cry and turned his back on Vic.

Vic hugged and kissed his shoulder and moved close behind him. "I'm sorry, baby. You know I love you. I just want to take care of you. I didn't mean to make you feel bad. Please forgive me. Come on. Let's try it again. Come on. Come to poppa. I've got something nice for you." He ran his hand down Charles' chest and teased his fuzzy pubic hair until he felt a response. Charles said, "No. It won't work. Leave me alone."

Vic chuckled, "But it is working, and you don't want me to leave you alone, now do you?"

Charles turned to face him and giggled, "You're so bad. You make me so mad. Show me what you've got for me. I can hardly wait. Give me your candy, daddy." They laughed, made love and slept in each other's arms.

Two days later the clinic called and said they needed Vic to come in. Vic made an appointment without telling Charles. When he got to the clinic, the doctor told him they needed to test him again. They weren't sure of the results of the first test. They thought it was a false negative, and they wanted to be sure. Vic agreed to the test.

When they called Vic with the results of the second test, Vic suspected what the results would be. He had had the suspicion when they called him to be retested. He told Charles what the results were. "You're right. If it's going to be just you and me, we don't need condoms. We both have it. We may as well enjoy each other and not worry about it. It doesn't matter who gave what to whom. Let's just love each other." He began to cry.

Charles said, "Don't worry. We'll get through this together." They hugged and cried and wiped each other's tears. They looked at each other and smiled and headed toward the bedroom. Their lovemaking was slow, compassionate, and sweet. They vowed to take care of each other and love each other for the rest of their lives. When the loving was over, Vic said, "Do you realize that we just made wedding vows?"

Charles chuckled, "You're right. We need to have a reception. Let's invite our friends and have a party."

Vic thought it was a great idea. He got Michele to help them plan. Vic took care of the menu. Michele took care of the decorating and Charles did the invitations. When Vic thought all their friends were there, he tapped the side of his glass and announced, "Attention everyone. Let me have your attention. We have an announcement to make." He took Charles' hand and they both held up their glasses. Charles said, "We'd like to propose a toast: to us, Vic and Charles. We have made a commitment to each other, sort of like a marriage. We love each other and will be together 'til death do us part." Vic and Charles clicked their glasses together and Vic said, "Till death do us part." They sipped their wine and then kissed.

The gathering cheered, "Here, here!" and people began congratulating them. Michele dabbed the corners of her eyes and said, "Oh, that's so sweet. Now I have to go fix my make-up."

CHAPTER 32

Seated holding hands around the Thanksgiving feast were Mabel, Aunt Maggie, Bea, Markie, Fred, Candy and Wes. After grace, each person told what they were thankful for. Everyone let go their hands except Candy and Wes. They looked at each other and spoke at the same time, Wes saying, "We're pregnant," and Candy saying, "We're married." They looked at each other and again, speaking at the same time, Wes said, "We're married," and Candy said, "We're pregnant."

The other people at the table looked like fish in a bowl with their mouths open. Then everyone began asking questions at the same time. Markie said, "So when you asked me if I minded if you asked my mom to marry you, you guys had pretty much made up your minds. What if I had said no?"

Fred said, "Yeah, what would you have done, Candy, if I had said no when you talked with me about my dad?"

Bea said, "So all those calls to my dorm were not to see if I was all right. You guys were just feeling me out. Sneaky, sneaky."

Mabel said, "Well, it's about time. I'm glad you didn't wait too long." She got up from her seat and went around to where Candy and Wes were seated, stood between them, and hugged them both. "Welcome to the family, Candy. I'm happy for both of you. A new grandbaby! Now I'll get to spoil this one, too."

Aunt Maggie said, "I knew something was up. You had that simple look on your face ever since you came back with the news about Frances. And all those workshops you had all of a sudden, and going to movies that lasted all night. Uh huh, I see now what you were up to. Sneaky little thing," and she laughed. "So what are your plans? Where are you two going to live? I feel like I'm talking to teenagers."

Wes said, "Let's eat and we'll tell you all about it. We plan to get our own house. Fred can stay at our house. Candy and I want to start fresh."

Aunt Maggie said, "That sounds like a good idea. In the meantime, you two won't have to sneak around anymore. It won't be as much fun, but you will save money." Everyone laughed.

When they were about to eat dessert, the phone rang. Markie answered, "Yes, this is Mark. Okay, I'll be right there."

"What's that about?" asked Candy.

Markie said, "It's about Janet. She's in the hospital. They think she's in labor. Now the truth will come out."

Candy said, "You want us to come with you?"

Markie said, "No. I'll call and let you know what's going on."

An hour later Mark called to say it was a false alarm. It was false labor and Janet was back at home.

Aunt Maggie laughed, "I bet it won't be long before she'll be in real labor. The hussy is big as a tick. When I told her she looked awfully big for almost six months, she said it was a big baby. I told her it must be twins. I don't understand how she thinks she can get away with such a lie. Anyway, her Pandora's Box will be open soon, the little hussy." And everyone laughed.

Two weeks before Christmas, Mark received a call from Jim. He and Flo were at the hospital with Janet, and this time it was real labor. Mark went to the hospital and while they were in the waiting room, he told Janet's parents that if the baby was full-term, it could not be his. He told them about the first time they had sex, and if the baby were his, it would not be born until February. Jim was surprised, but Flo was not. She told Mark that she knew all along that Janet would have the baby in December, but she thought he was the father.

Janet delivered a healthy eight pound boy. When Mark went in to see her, he said, "Janet, that baby is full-term and it has red hair. You know it cannot be mine. Do you know who the father is?"

Janet looked from her father to her mother, and then Mark. She started to cry and Mark felt sorry for her predicament. She nodded her head and sobbed, "I'm not a slut, Mark. I know who the daddy is, but I don't love him."

Mark said, "Okay, Janet. I suggest you tell him that he's a daddy. He might surprise you and step up to the plate, whoever he is. Mr. and Mrs. Rice, I wish you luck. Good-bye, Janet. I hope you can be happy. You have a fine baby boy."

When he was outside the hospital, Mark took a deep breath and looked around. The wintered trees were filigreed against a slate colored sky. He thought to himself, It looks and smells like snow. I'm glad I put the lights up before it started. It looks like we might have a white Christmas. I'll be glad to get home and call Judy and tell her everything that's going on. He liked talking with Judy. She was understanding, not condescending. She had a mind of her own and never hesitated to voice her opinion. They could disagree without arguing, and if she were wrong, Judy didn't hesitate to admit it. She also pointed out to Mark when he was wrong, without gloating. She always had something funny to share, and their conversations usually ended with laughter.

When he drove into the driveway, he could see that Auntie Mom had turned on the lights and he admired his handy work. There was a light dusting of snow on the car and the wind was getting stronger. By the time he was in the house, the snow was coming down harder and he was glad to be in for the night. He told Wes, Candy and Auntie Mom what had happened at the hospital and went to his room to call Judy.

Candy called Bea and gave her the news. Bea was relieved and said, "So I'm not an auntie yet. Now I know what I'll get baby brother for Christmas," and she told Candy her plans.

Two days later, Janet, Jim and Flo were bringing the baby home. It was a blistery day. It had stopped snowing and the wind made it seem much colder than it was. Janet held the tightly wrapped baby close to her and Flo put another blanket over the baby and Janet's shoulder. Jim helped them out of the car and cautioned Janet to walk slowly as the walkway was slippery. Before they reached the house, they heard a voice behind them. "Wait up, Janet. Let me see that baby. I heard you had a boy. Let me see him. Is he mine?"

They all turned around to see Jerry. He was wavering and unsteady. Janet could smell liquor in the mist that he breathed out. "Go away, Jerry. It's none of your business. You're drunk. Get away from us!"

Jerry reached for the blanket and pulled it back. "Let me see that baby, Janet. Let me see if he looks like me." Before Janet could get a better grip on the baby, Jerry slipped and grabbed the bundle as he was going down. The baby fell from Janet's arms, hit the cement, rolled out of his blanket and slid into the post of the mailbox. Janet screamed and quickly picked the baby up. There was blood coming out of his scalp where his head had hit the post. Jim said, "Quick, let's get him to the hospital."

They left Jerry sitting on the walkway and got into the car as fast as they could. Janet pressed the blanket tightly on the baby's head. She thought it was odd that he was not crying and she cooed and murmured until they reached the emergency room.

A nurse took Janet, Flo and the baby into a cubical while Jim filled out the paper work. When the doctor looked at the baby, he turned to Janet and said, "I'm so sorry. The baby's dead. His neck is broken."

Janet sank to the floor and started keening like a wounded animal. She rocked back and forth and sobbed and screamed. Flo tried to talk to her, and Jim tried to lift her up. She could not be consoled. She looked up and saw Jerry coming through the door. She got up and screamed as she started thrashing him with her fist, "You killed my baby! You're a monster. You're evil and I hate you. You killed my baby!"

She was scratching his face and pounding him with her fist and he just stood there with a blank look on his face whispering, "I'm so sorry. I didn't mean to. I'm so sorry."

The doctor got the story of what happened from Jim. The police were called and they arrested Jerry. He seemed dazed and went quietly with the police. Janet was hysterical and the doctor gave her a sedative.

When Jim and Flo took Janet home after making arrangements for the baby, Janet went to the room they had fixed for a nursery. She took the teddy bear that Jim had bought for the baby and sat in the rocker holding it tightly against her chest. Her breasts were swollen and the milk oozed out onto the bear. She moaned and sobbed and rocked. Flo and Jim tried to console her, but there was nothing they could say or do to help her. Finally Jim said, "Janet, we're going downstairs. Call us if you need us. We're here for you, honey. We're so sorry." He took Flo's hand and they went downstairs to the kitchen.

Jim made coffee and Flo sat at the table crying. He said, "Flo, we've come a long way. Don't let this make you backslide."

Flo nodded and said, "I'm trying, Jim. It's too bad something like this had to happen to wake us up. I appreciate you taking charge the way you do. Janet's young. She'll be okay eventually. She's got her whole life ahead of her. I was looking forward to having a baby in the house, but we'll adjust."

Jim wiped his eyes, gave Flo her coffee and said, "I think I should call that Procter boy and let him know what happened. He might be able to help Janet. He seems like a fine person."

It was almost dark when Mark got to the Rice's house. They took him upstairs to where Janet was still rocking and sobbing. She looked up and when she saw Mark she looked down and started keening again. Mark kneeled in front of her and put his arms around her. "Hush, hush, Janet, it'll be okay. I'm so sorry for your loss. I'm so sorry."

Janet tried to talk between her sobs. "No, Mark. I'm the one who should be sorry. I lied to you. I tried to trick you. It's all my fault. I'm being punished for what I tried to do to you. Please forgive me."

Mark said, "Shh, shh. It's okay, Janet. You'll be okay. I'm sorry it happened to you, but you'll be okay. You're strong and you'll bounce back in no time. There's nothing to forgive. I hope the jerk gets what's coming to him. Is he the father?"

Janet nodded, "I don't ever want to see him again. I hate him. He killed my baby!" and she started crying again.

Mark said, "I don't know what I can say or do for you, Janet. Try to get some rest. You've had a rough time. Take care of yourself and let me know if I can help. We're still friends."

Janet said, "Thanks, Mark. You're such a good person. That's why I wanted you to be the father. I'm so sorry for what I did to you. That's why I'm being punished. That's why. And Mark, tell Judy to resubmit her application. I think it got lost."

Mark asked, "What did you say? Judy's application to college got lost? I see. Thanks for telling me, Janet. I hope you feel better." He shook his head and thought, Wow! What a schemer. Maybe this will teach her a lesson, but I doubt it.

~~~~~~

There were a few people at the grave-side service for Janet's baby -- mostly family, Mark's family and a few of their classmates who were curious more than supportive. Auntie Mom talked softly to Janet, "I know this is painful, Janet, but don't let it stop you from achieving whatever you want to do with your life. I won't try to imagine how you feel. I'll just say I'm sorry this happened. Don't blame yourself, but the lesson learned is that you can't make someone love you. You are lovable without all the trickery. I know things will be all right. You're not a bad person, just misguided."

Janet burst into tears again and said, "Thank you for saying that. I worried about how you would feel about me."

"Don't worry about that, Janet. Your mother needs you now. Be the daughter she thinks you are. Help each other heal. She's had a loss, too. He was your parents' grandbaby. They both need you. Think of them and it will help you all. Now go to them. Talk with them. Help your family."

Jerry was behind a tree away from the gathering. He didn't want anyone to see him. The baby's death had been ruled an accident, and Jerry had been put on probation with a warning that if he were found intoxicated he would be put in jail. He felt guilty and vowed never to take another drink. The next week he enlisted in the Air Force.

CHAPTER 33

Candy pulled into the driveway and noticed that Wes' car was the only one there. Mark was at work, Aunt Maggie was out shopping, and Bea was coming in on the five o'clock bus. She rushed into the house, dumped her packages in the living room and went quietly up the stairs. She opened the door to the room that was now hers and Wes' and saw him putting something in the closet. She went up behind him and whispered, "What cha doing, big boy? Want to fool around while my husband is out?"

Wes laughed and turned around. Before he could say anything, Candy was unbuttoning his shirt, kissing him and undressing him. She pushed him back on the bed and proceeded to take her clothes off as fast as she could. Wes was laughing all the while. Then she got on top of him and said, "I'll give you something to laugh about." She eased onto his erection and started to ride him. Then they were both laughing. Between gasps, Wes said, "You are something else. Don't hurt the baby."

Candy said, "The baby can take care of itself. Pretty soon, I'll be too fat to do this. Enjoy it while you can." They rocked together until Wes rolled her over and they climaxed at the same time.

They lay there gasping and laughing when they heard the door downstairs. Aunt Maggie said, "Yoo-hoo. I'm home. Stop whatever you're doing and help me with these groceries. There's enough to feed an army."

Wes said, "I'll go. You need the rest after your performance," and he kissed her behind.

Mark had picked up Bea at the bus station. Fred arrived at about the same time, and they all sat down to dinner. Bea filled them in on the latest news about Mona and Bruce. They had married and Mona gave birth four months after the wedding. She had a nervous breakdown and had been sent to a psychiatric facility. Bruce was working for her father and didn't come back to school. "So that's the latest on our distant, I mean very distant, cousin."

Auntie Mom said, "So tell us what's going on with you. Any prospects in your future? Who's the lucky guy? Talk, Missy."

Bea blushed and said, "I'll tell you something when there's something to tell, nosy."

Aunt Maggie said, "Ah-ha. I knew it. You've got a sweetie. I was just fishing before. Now I know you have something to tell. So tell us. Is something wrong with him? Something you don't want us to know?"

Bea laughed and said, "I'll tell you when there's something to tell. We're just friends. We are in a couple of classes together. We study together sometimes and we're just getting to know each other. There's nothing to tell yet. When there is, I'll let you know."

Before Aunt Maggie could say anything further, the phone rang. Bea jumped up and said, "I'll get that." She rushed into the kitchen, "Hello. Oh, hello. Yes, I'm okay. The trip was not too bad. It was crowded, but I got a good seat. No, nobody bothered me. You worry too much. I appreciate that. I don't know what to say to that. Are you at home? Yes, I'm changing the subject. How is everything? Okay. It's only been one day. Yeah, I miss you, too. We'll talk later. Bye."

When she came back into the dining room, everyone pretended they were not listening. Candy said, "Can you at least tell us the name of this person you're missing? He's obviously concerned about your safety. That's saying something."

Bea giggled, "I'll tell you later. So Mark, what's new with you?" They sat and talked for a long time. Then Aunt Maggie stretched and got up saying, "Percy and I are going to turn in. Somebody can volunteer to clean up. Good night. Come on Percy. We'll see you in the morning."

Candy chuckled, "I declare, those two even walk alike. Come on Daddy, we'll do the dishes if the young folk will clear the table."

Candy was washing the dishes when Wes slipped his arms around her and placed his hands on her lower abdomen and gently rubbed. He moved his hand down lower and said, "Thank you for today, Honey. I've never been so happy. You make me feel young, and wanted, and needed, and I love you so much."

Candy leaned back against him and whispered, "I love you, too, Wes, so much. I feel the same way. We're so lucky. I hope Bea and Mark and Fred can find the same thing we have. Now, you dirty old man, leave me alone and let's get these dishes done so we can 'retire'. Is that the word I'm looking for?" and they both laughed as he picked up a dishtowel.

Early Christmas morning, Bea knocked on Mark's door. "Get up. It's late. Wake up, you two." She opened his door and stood between the twin beds and pulled the covers off at the same time and shouted, "Get up! Santa came last night. Get up! He left something for you."

Mark mumbled, "Leave me alone. Go back to bed." Fred said, "Grow up, Bea. We stopped believing in Santa years ago. Get out of here."

Bea laughed and said, "If you don't get up now, I'll pour some water on you. Now come on downstairs. It can't wait."

A few minutes later Fred and Markie came down to the Christmas tree and Markie said, "What's this all about, Bea? Why are you getting us up so early?"

Bea said, "Here's a present that Santa left that has to be opened right now."

Mark took the box and felt movement and scratching coming from inside. He lifted the lid and two beady eyes and a wet nose greeted him with a whimper. He declared, "Dang, Bea. It's a puppy! He looks like Bunny." He put the box on the floor and the puppy bounded out wagging his tail.

Fred said, "Look at the way he busted out of the box. He's ready for action. What're you going to call him?"

Mark had tears in his eyes as the puppy started licking his face. "Wow, I don't know. Thanks, Bea, Mrs. Clause.

This is great -- just what I needed." The puppy went over to the tree and knocked one of the ornaments off the tree. It hit the floor with a soft ting and shattered into pieces.

Fred said, "How about calling him 'Buster' since he's busting up the place?"

Mark said, "Yeah that suits him. Buster, come here boy." Buster came waddling over to Mark and licked his face again.

Bea said, "I think you need to take him out to pee. He's started sniffing the tree and I don't think Auntie Mom would like that."

When Mark came back inside, Buster started barking. Aunt Maggie and Percy came in to see what all the noise was about. Percy looked at Buster and sniffed him. Buster started jumping around Percy and Percy reared up on his hind legs, slapped him twice and hissed. Buster yelped and ran to Mark. "I guess he knows who's in charge now," Aunt Maggie said. Percy trotted after her into the kitchen.

Bea said, "He might be hungry. There's some puppy food in a container in the box." Mark put the food in Bunny's old dish and Buster gobbled it down. Then he investigated the packages under the tree, finally settled down and went to sleep. Percy crept close to him, sniffed him all over, then nestled up next to him and went to sleep, too.

Candy and Wes came down and saw the two. "Ah, how sweet. I'll have to get a picture of this," Candy commented. They all exchanged gifts, then had breakfast.

CHAPTER 34

Vic woke up feeling cold and damp. Charles was shivering next to him. The bed was soaking wet and so was Charles who was sweating profusely and moaning in his sleep. Vic woke him, took his temperature, changed the sheets and gave him clean pajamas. He gave him the medicines the doctors had prescribed and made breakfast.

The night sweats had been going on almost nightly for the past three or four months. Charles continued to have a low-grade fever. His glands were swollen and he was losing weight because he found it difficult to swallow. He had white patches of thrush in his mouth. He could no longer work because he had no energy. Vic was taking him to the clinic weekly. The doctors were tracking his progress, or lack thereof, and trying different medications. His chest x-rays, instead of being dark, were beginning to cloud over and he was diagnosed with Pneumocystis carinii pneumonia. The doctors attributed this to a new acquired cellular immunodeficiency syndrome they were calling AIDS that was occurring in people with HIV.

When Vic took Charles to the clinic for his weekly visit, the attending physician called in another doctor to look at Charles. They both agreed that he should be hospitalized. He had the beginning of lesions attributed to Kaposi's sarcoma. Vic knew what this meant. He refused to let them hospitalize Charles. He told them, "I'll take care of him at home. He's my responsibility." He conferred with them about medications and his treatment then they went home.

Michele was waiting for them. "What did the doctors say? Is he going to be all right? What can they do for him?"

Vic replied, "Let's get you to bed, Charles. You look tired." Charles just nodded, too weak to talk.

After Vic got Charles settled, he gave him something to help with the pain and make him sleep. He told Michele what was going on. "He's not contagious. You can only get this disease from body fluids, not from touching someone. If you can stay with him while I'm at work, I'd appreciate it. Just give him his meds and keep him company. Can you do that for me?"

For once, Michele had no snappy comeback. She simply nodded. Then she whispered, "Is he going to die, Vic? I don't want him to die on my watch. I don't know what to do with dead people."

Vic shook his head and said, "We're all going to die eventually, Michele, but I don't think Charles will die any time soon."

~~~~~~

Charles was wasting away. The blotches from Karposi's Sarcoma were getting larger. Vic held him close trying to keep him warm when he shivered. He felt like a sack of bones in his arms. They cried together and Vic tended to him as best he could. Michele stayed with him when Vic was at work. She read to him, played music, danced and sang to try to cheer him up. Sometimes it worked and she could get him to smile.

Vic put up Christmas decorations over the entire apartment. He put the tree in the bedroom so Charles could see it. Michele came Christmas Eve with her arms loaded with gifts. She and Vic had a bottle of wine with the feast that Vic prepared and they sang carols and exchanged gifts. Charles sat up in bed, sipped eggnog through a straw and seemed to enjoy the gathering. In his frail voice he said, "Vic, look on the shelf in the closet. Your gift is there. I didn't get to wrap it for Christmas."

Vic looked in the closet and found a brown paper package. He took it down and opened it. There were beautiful pictures of sunsets and sunrises and he recognized the places he and Charles had stayed when they first became lovers. They exchanged meaningful looks and wept together.

Michele went over to Charles, and for the first time since she got the news of how grave his illness was, she hugged him, and all three cried. Then she said, "Okay. That's enough. This is a celebration. Let's have a toast – Merry Christmas. Here's to us!" They clicked glasses.

The next morning Michele stretched and got up from the couch. On her way back from the bathroom, she looked into the bedroom and saw Vic sitting on the side of the bed crying. She said, "What's wrong, Vic?"

He looked up and said, "He's gone, Michele. He's gone. It must have happened during the night. When I woke, he was cold. He's dead." He began to sob loudly and took heaving breaths.

Michele went to him and they hugged and cried together. Michele amazed herself as she took over and made

234

all the necessary calls and arrangements. Vic had Charles cremated. Vic and Michele scattered his ashes over the lake where they had loved to stay.

They had a memorial get together at the apartment. Some of the people who were at the commitment gathering were no longer there. It was noticed by everyone. There was an air of foreboding. They told anecdotes about Charles and had a few laughs, but even Michele could not lighten the atmosphere.

After everyone left, Michele said, "Do you want me to stay with you?"

Vic shook his head. "Thanks, Michele, for everything. I'll be okay. I'll have to get used to being alone sooner or later. Philip gave me the week off, but I think I'll go back to work. It helps to keep busy." He kissed her on the cheek and said, "Thanks again. We can still hang out, okay?"

She replied, "Okay. If that's the way you want it. You know how to find me if you need anything. Love you."

Vic walked through the apartment deciding where he would hang the pictures Charles had given him. Then he thought, they are too beautiful not to share. Maybe I'll have copies made and put them in a book. I'll dedicate it to Charles. He would have loved that. He was so talented. I miss him so much. Vic fell onto the bed, curled up with Charles' pillow and sobbed.

CHAPTER 35

Candy and Wes bought a house in February. While walking through debating what they would do in each room, Candy stopped short and gasped, "Oh, Wes!" She grabbed her stomach and laughed.

Wes said, "What is it? You okay? What's the matter?"

Candy took his hand and held it to her stomach. "Feel. No, right there. Wait a second." Wes' hand bounced off as if it were on fire. Then he laughed and gently touched her stomach again. "Wow! He can really kick! I mean, he or she," and they both laughed. He kissed her quickly and said, "Let's finish our tour." She grabbed his hand and said, "Slow down. This can be the nursery. I think a nice soft green for the walls. What do you think? Let's christen it." She put her arms around his waist. They kissed slowly and sank to the carpet. They made love slowly and then lay there talking about the house and the changes they would make.

Candy said, "Wes, I can truly say this is the happiest I've ever been in my life. You make me feel complete."

Wes mocked, "Aw, shucks, Ma'am. I just do my best to please." They laughed and continued their tour into the back yard. They talked about the changes they would make and where the swing set should go.

~~~~~~~~~~~~~~~~~~~~~~~~~~~~~~~~~~~~

Joseph Jr., or Jay-Jay, as he was called, greeted Mark at the door with a manly handshake and a shoulder bump.

They had both outgrown the boyish hugs they used to give each other. "Come on in brother. I can call you that now and mean it." They both laughed. "Judy is almost ready. Have a seat."

Joseph Sr., or Joe as everyone called him, came into the room and hugged Markie. "Good to see you, Markie." They were deep into a discussion about baseball when Judy and Phillis said, "Ahem."

All three looked up and then stood. Jay-Jay said, "Wow, sis. You washed your face. You look good!"

Judy curtseyed and said, "Of course. I always look good."

Phillis said, "You can close your mouth now, Markie, and stop drooling."

Mark said, "Yeah. Judy, you're beautiful!"

Judy appeared to float down the stairs. She seemed to glow. Her dress was a soft yellow – a perfect complement to her honey colored skin and her make-up was just enough to enhance her features. When she saw the look on Mark's face, she felt beautiful and it showed in her manner.

Markie gave Phillis the flowers to pin on Judy's dress. The exchange between the two youngsters was not missed by Joe. He was a tall man, brown skinned with regular features, graying at the temples. He cleared his throat and said, "Come here, Markie while the ladies finish." He took Mark into the living room and quietly said, "Markie, you bring her back the same way you took her. You understand me?"

Mark stammered, "Oh, yes sir. I would never dream of doing anything to hurt Judy. I cherish her. Er, I mean I respect her. Um, she's not like any girl I've ever met. That is, I've known her all my life – like a sister. We wouldn't um, you know. It's not like that."

Joe said, "Okay, just keep that in mind and have her back here by twelve. Now have a good time."

Back in the entry, Joe kissed Judy on the cheek and said, "You're gorgeous, honey. Have a good time. Markie will have you back here by twelve."

Judy said, "Thanks, Daddy. How about one?" Joe shook his head and she said, "Twelve-thirty?" He shook his head again.

Phillis said, "I think you better stop there, Judy, unless you want it to be eleven." Everybody laughed.

Mark helped Judy with her coat and they exited after Phillis took pictures. "I'll send copies to your mother and aunt. Have a good time." They waved good-bye to the couple as Phillis dabbed her eyes. She looked at Joe and said, "Did you see what I saw? Don't be surprised if he becomes your son-in-law." Joe hugged her around the shoulders and said, "I won't be surprised at all. He 'cherishes' her – his words. I just hope they keep a lid on until he can support her. We had a little talk. He's a nice young man. She could do worse. She could hook-up with some no good engineer who just got a promotion and is making big bucks like her brother." He punched Jay-Jay on the arm and gave him a hug and all three laughed.

When they walked into the gym, all eyes turned toward Judy and her date. There were whispers and a couple of Judy's girlfriends came over to be introduced. Her closest friend Joan whispered, "No wonder you didn't tell anybody who your date was. He's cute, and you hardly notice the limp." Judy replied, "I don't notice it at all. Let's dance, Markie."

They glided onto the dance floor with eyes only for each other. Markie danced smoothly despite his bad leg. It was just a little shorter than the other one and didn't keep him from doing anything he wanted to do.

During a break, Markie went to the bathroom. There were guys talking and he overheard one say, "That's who she invited, man. I can't do anything about that. I asked her to come with me and she said she already had a date." He looked up and saw Markie. "How long you been knowing Judy, man?"

Mark replied, "All my life. We grew up together. I live in Millerton."

"You mean you came here just to take Judy to the prom?"

"Well, my grandmother lives here, too. I'm Mark, by the way."

"Doug. Nice to meet you, man."

As Mark was leaving, he heard Doug say, "Why she want to date a white boy?" Mark just smiled to himself and thought, if you only knew.

Mark found Judy with her girlfriends. She took his hand and introduced him to the ones he hadn't met, they were all cordial. When they walked onto the dance floor, they could hear them whispering. They could only imagine what the conversation was. Mark said, "I met your friend Doug. Seems nice enough. He wanted to take you to the prom. Why didn't you go with him?"

Judy replied, "You sound jealous, Mark. He's only one of many who wanted to take me. Who did I invite to take me? So what's your problem?"

"I guess I am jealous. They get to see you all the time. I only get to talk to you on the phone. I don't want other guys sniffing around my girl."

"Am I your girl, Mark? Is that how you feel?"

Mark looked down at her, "Yeah, that's how I feel. I tell you stuff that I don't share with anybody else. I really like you a lot." He pulled her closer to him. She laid her head on his shoulder and they swayed to a slow dance. He thought about his prom the year before with Janet and how she had tried to manipulate him. Being here, dancing with Judy, seemed so right. He thought, I want to hold her like this forever. She feels good in my arms. She smells good. I want to protect her, not just make love to her. Is this the love that they talk about? He pulled away and looked down at her again. She looked up at him and he wanted to kiss her. She took a deep breath, their eyes locked, and she whispered, "Mark, I don't know what to say."

Mark felt himself get aroused. He pushed her back and said, "Let's take a break. I could use some punch. How about you? I'll go get some."

Judy found a table and sat there waiting for Mark to bring the drinks. On his way to the table where Judy was waiting he was bumped several times. He didn't respond because he knew it was "accidently on purpose". When he got to the table, Joan was sitting there with Judy. Mark said, "Would you like some punch, Joan?" She replied, "No thanks, nice of you to ask. My boyfriend is bringing me some. Why don't you guys come with us after the prom for something to eat?"

Mark said, "Sounds like a good idea. What do you think, Jude?" Judy replied, "That would be fine, as long as I'm home by twelve."

Mark was glad for the company. He dreaded being alone with Judy because he felt he would have a hard time controlling himself. As he looked at her sipping her drink, he wanted her in the worst way. He excused himself and went to the bathroom.

They had a good time eating burgers and shakes. He got along well with Joan and her date, Kurt. They laughed and joked a lot. Mark and Kurt had a lot in common. Joan was impressed that he had a radio show, and they talked about their futures. Joan was going to college in Millerton and hoped she and Judy could be roommates. Kurt was going to school there in town. They talked easily together and Mark looked at his watch. "Much as I hate to break this up, I have to get Judy home by twelve before she turns into a witch. It's a quarter to. I don't want your daddy on my case."

They drove to Judy's house in silence each taking turns glimpsing at each other. When Mark drove into the driveway, he jumped out of the car and hurried to the passenger's side and opened the door. Judy got out, looked up at him and said, "Are you mad at me or something? You've hardly said a word since we left the diner. Did I sa....." Before she could finish her sentence, Mark kissed her long and hard. He held her close, looked down at her and kissed her again. In a husky voice, he whispered, "You didn't do or say anything. I've wanted to do that all night – from the time I saw you on the stairs. I find it hard to control myself around you, Jude. I don't know what this feeling is, but I just want to hold you and be with you. I respect you too much to do anything, but I want you."

Judy gasped, "I know. I feel the same way, Mark. I've never - you know. But I have these feelings when I'm near you. I don't know what to do or say when I'm with you like this. I better go inside before we get into trouble."

They walked to the porch. Judy unlocked the door and turned to Mark. "Good night, Mark. Thanks for a wonderful time. It was magical. Maybe we'll feel differently in the morning. Will I see you tomorrow before you leave?"

Mark said, "Yes, Miss Roberts. I'll see you tomorrow. Good-night, my dear." He kissed her on the forehead, then the cheek, then on her lips. She sighed and slipped through the door. He stood there for a minute with his hand on the door trying to get himself together, waiting for his erection to subside. Judy was leaning on the door on the other side.

While Mark was driving home the next afternoon, he thought about his visit. He loved being with Judy and, to his surprise, he enjoyed his stay with Frances. She seemed more relaxed and he enjoyed talking with her. She had fixed a large breakfast for him and pulled out a lot of old family pictures. She told him stories about his father; he wished he could have stayed longer.

No matter what thoughts he had, his mind always drifted back to Judy. He couldn't stop thinking about her. It had been hard to keep his eyes off her when he went to their house before he started the drive home. He didn't dare sit next to her, and he was pretty sure that everyone picked up on the tension between them. Most of the conversation centered on Linda, Judy's older sister, and her career. Phillis remarked, "I can't believe that all my children are grown. That includes you too, Markie. I remember when all of you were running around getting into trouble. Do you remember the time …" and she would drift off into details he would rather forget. It was late afternoon before Mark could tear himself away from Judy's side. Which meant it would be very late when he got home, but he didn't mind.

He could hear Buster barking before he opened the door. Buster jumped up and down wagging all over and licking him. Percy looked him up and down and sauntered into the bedroom. Auntie Mom greeted him with the news about Candy. She told him that Candy was in the hospital. "Now don't get upset. She'll be all right. It's just a precaution. They want her to have complete bed rest until she delivers the baby. You know she's no spring chicken and it gets harder as you get older. She's got what they call pre-eclampsia, which could put her and the baby in jeopardy. They have her on medication to lower her blood pressure and keep her calm. I'm sure she'll be all right. You can go see her tomorrow. So how was your trip, and how is old lady Procter?"

"The trip was good, but I'm worried about Mom. Are you sure she's okay? Is Coach with her, or at home? I'll call him. Does Bea know?"

Mark dialed Wes' number. "Hello, Coach. Auntie Mom told me about Mom. How is she? Okay…Okay… Well what happened? Oh, that's good. Are you sure? Have you talked with Bea? Yeah. Okay, I'll see her tomorrow. Oh it was good. I'll tell you about it later. Oh, yeah, a real good time. Okay. Good night."

When Mark went to Candy's room the next day, she was napping. He stood by her bed and marveled at how big she was. She looked pretty and relaxed, but her body was huge. She sensed his presence, opened her eyes and whispered, "My baby is here. How was your trip? I'm so glad to see you, honey."

Mark leaned over and kissed her on the cheek. "Are you okay, Mom? How long are you going to be here? Since I saw you last week, you've gotten really big."

Candy chuckled, "You know how to make a lady feel good. This is what you get when you eat too much watermelon. I have to stay here until the baby is born. I'm getting excellent care so don't worry. This is just a

244

precaution, and it will only be three or four weeks before I can pop it out. I have a favor to ask. If you can get the time off, can you drive up to get Bea next week. I told her it didn't make sense to come home now when she's in the midst of finals, and then have to go back to get her stuff. Now tell me about your trip."

"Okay. I'll talk with her and we'll work it out. Don't you worry, just take it easy and rest. The trip was wonderful," and he proceeded to tell her everything about his stay with Frances, the prom and the Roberts family.

"Now, you've conveniently avoided the subject of Judy. How did that go? I want all the details. What color was her dress, and how did she look?"

"She wore this creamy-yellow thing that made her just glow. Mom, I don't know about Judy. I think about her all the time. She's constantly on my mind. She's behind every thought. She is so beautiful – not the little tom boy I played with. I just want to be with her all the time. I can talk with her about anything. She was the prettiest girl at the prom, and I just wanted to protect her from all those guys leering at her."

Candy reached out to him and he hugged her. "Markie, you're in love, baby. Is this the first time you've felt this way about a girl? Did you feel this way about Janet?"

"I felt no where nearly like this about Janet. She did all the chasing and seduction. I only wanted to protect myself against her. I didn't think I had to protect her at all. With Judy, I just want the best for her. I want to be able to provide for her. I guess you could call it love. In fact, I've got to call her and tell her you're all right. I'll come back to see you this evening after work." He kissed her on the cheek, and on his way out, Wes was coming into the room. They talked for a minute and Mark left.

Wes gave Candy flowers and kissed her. As he looked around the room he noticed a very large arrangement on the windowsill. "Where did all the flowers come from?"

Candy replied, "I'll give you one guess. Who do you know who is that ostentatious?"

Together they said, "Brandon!" and laughed.

Candy reached her arms out to Wes and said, "My knight in shining armor, thank you, darling. Sit down, and I'll fill you in on the latest about Mark."

CHAPTER 36

The waiting room was filled to capacity with expectant fathers and other relatives. Wes, Mabel, Mark, Bea, Fred, and Aunt Maggie helped increase the crowd. "Waiting is the hardest thing to do when someone else is doing all the work. I guess that's one of the reasons it's called labor," said Maggie, trying to lighten the moment. There were no comments from anyone else. Each person had their own thoughts, and they were all worried, but afraid to voice it.

"Is anyone here for the Knox family?" asked the nurse. When all six people stood up, she said, "Wow, I should say so. Who's the father?"

Wes raised his hand, "Right here. Is she all right? What's wrong? Did she deliver yet?"

"Mr. Knox everybody is fine. You can see your wife in a few minutes. I'll come and get you."

Bea said, "Is the baby okay? Boy or girl?"

The nurse replied, "Yes." She smiled and walked away. Bea looked at the others and said, "What does she mean?"

Wes ran his fingers through his hair and laughingly said, "It's two of them – twins, evidently one of each – a boy and a girl."

Maggie said, "You knew all along? Why didn't you or Candy tell us? No wonder she was so big. You scalawag, you!"

"We wanted to surprise you, and I guess we did. Let's go see Candy and the babies."

Candy's eyes fluttered open when Wes kissed her on the cheek. "Hey, Daddy, have you seen the babies yet?" She looked tired but happy.

Two nurses came into the room each holding a baby. Everyone ooed and aahed, and the babies were passed around for each person to hold. Aunt Maggie asked, "What are you going to name them?"

Candy replied, "Nicole, after Fred's mother, and Evan after my father."

Mark asked, "Did you know there would be one of each when you were thinking of names?"

Wes answered, "No, we just had several choices just in case it would be two boys or two girls. This made it easy."

Dr. Levy, Candy's obstetrician, entered the room, "Congratulations Mr. and Mrs. Knox. You have two beautiful babies. Is this the rest of the family?" He was the same doctor who had treated Janet in the emergency room and had delivered Janet's baby. He recognized Mark and greeted him. Mark introduced him to the others in the room. The doctor couldn't keep his eyes off Bea, but no one seemed to notice. They were focused on the babies. He told Wes that

Candy would have to stay in the hospital until her pressure was stabilized, but everything seemed to be fine.

The next day, when Bea went to visit Candy, she saw Dr. Levy in the hall and spoke to him on her way to Candy's room. He stopped her and said, "Miss Procter, after you visit your mother, would you have a cup of coffee with me? I'd like to talk to you about her condition."

Bea said, "Of course. Where will you be?"

He replied, "I'll wait for you in the cafeteria. I'll be on break. Just look for me."

"Okay." Bea wasn't sure, but she thought she saw him blush. She didn't mention it to Candy as she didn't want to worry her. She cut her visit short because she was worried about what Dr. Levy would say.

When she entered the cafeteria, she saw him stand up at a table in the corner. He held a chair for her and said, "How do you like your coffee?"

Bea replied, "Actually, I would rather have tea, if you don't mind." She watched him as he walked away and thought to herself, he's kind of cute. I wonder how old he is. He looks young, but it's hard to tell with some people. Whatever it is he has to tell me, I hope it's not bad news. She studied him as he walked back to the table. Not bad looking at all. I wonder if he's married.

"Dr. Levy, what about my mother, is it serious?"

"No. She'll be fine. She just needs bed rest for a while until her blood pressure stabilizes. She had a rough time, but she'll be okay. Please call me Kenneth."

"Oh, that's a relief. You sounded so serious. I thought something was wrong."

"I'm sorry if I worried you. I really just wanted to get to know you better. May I call you Bea?"

Bea could feel her face getting hot, "Of course. Is this how you get to know the daughters of your patients, by scaring them?"

Kenneth chuckled, "No, just the pretty ones. Tell me about yourself."

Bea replied, "You first. Where are you from?"

They talked until they heard over the loud speaker. "Dr. Levy, Dr. Kenneth Levy to emergency, please, Dr. Kenneth Levy to emergency."

Kenneth stood up, "I'm sorry, Bea. I have to go. Can I take you to dinner tonight? I'd like to get to know you better."

"So you said." Bea said. She paused a moment then put him out of his misery. "Yes, I'd like that."

"I'll pick you up at seven. See you then."

Before Bea could give him the address, he was gone. She shrugged her shoulders and smiled. Interesting, very interesting. We'll see where this leads.

Aunt Maggie said, "Who's the lucky guy?" when Bea told her she would be going out for dinner.

"Dr. Levy. He's picking me up at seven. How do I look?"

"You look gorgeous. He's a lucky fellow. So maybe we'll have a doctor in the house? Maybe I can get some freebies," Aunt Maggie chuckled.

"Oh, for heaven's sake, it's just a dinner. Don't start making plans yet. We don't even know each other."

"But you will. I saw the way he looked at you in your momma's room. Nobody else noticed, but I saw he couldn't keep his eyes off you. He looked like he wanted to eat you up. Be careful. He could be a wolf in scrubs."

"Auntie Mom, you're so funny. I'll keep my guard up, okay?"

The bell rang and Bea answered the door. "Hi, Kenneth, come in. I'll just get a jacket. You remember Aunt Maggie? How did you know where to come? I didn't give you my address."

Kenneth said, "Of course I remember your aunt. Good evening, Ma'am. Your address was easy. I just talked with your mother. I'm resourceful that way."

Bea replied, "I'll remember that. See you later, Auntie Mom. Don't wait up." Aunt Maggie winked and chuckled as they went out the door.

Aunt Maggie addressed Percy, "Well, well, well, Percy, here we go again. Let's go to bed. You're slowing down, old fellow." Percy sauntered after her and gave Buster a passing rub. Now that Buster had outgrown his puppy stage, Percy tolerated him better and spent more time sleeping with him and even played with him once in a while.

Kenneth sat in his car in Bea's driveway for a long time after he walked Bea to her door. He had wanted to kiss her in the worst way, but he just said, "Thanks for a wonderful time, Bea. I'll call you." They had done a lot of talking and not much eating at dinner. He began to feel the faint pangs of hunger as he reviewed every minute of their date. What would life be like if he could come home to Bea every night?

He thought to himself, ho, boy. Wait up. You haven't even kissed her yet. She might not feel the same way. She has her own plans and they might not include you. She probably already has a fellow – but she didn't mention one. That doesn't mean anything. I didn't mention the nurses I've dated either. What are you thinking? One date and you're planning a future? Slow down. Take it slow. Get to know her better. But you already know her, his inner self argued back. You never felt this way about a girl before. It was like you knew she was the one the moment you saw her at the hospital. Maybe this is what mom meant when she said, 'Son, you'll know her when you see her.' Wow, could Bea be the one? I wonder what kind of kids we'll have. There you go again. Stop that and go home. Stop thinking about her!

He drove slowly to his apartment all the while fantasizing about a wedding and introducing Bea to his parents. How would they receive her? Would they like her?

252

Of course they would. How could they not, if he loved her? Did he love her? After only one date, how could he know? Back at his apartment, he surveyed it from what he thought would be Bea's perspective. What would Bea think of his place? He would have to neaten it up a bit and maybe he could get her to help with some decorating ideas. He thought, Oh, man. You've got it bad. You never thought about living with a woman before, or taking her to meet your folks. This must be it. He drank a glass of milk, got ready for bed and had a fitful night's sleep with dreams of Bea and his mother laughing and talking about him.

~~~~~~

Bea closed the door and locked it. She wondered why Kenneth had not tried to kiss her. She wanted him to, but he was such a gentleman. He had said he would call her, so maybe they'd have a second date.

He had been so easy to talk to. But she liked talking with George, too. George was more like a good friend though. She knew George was attracted to her, but did she like him in the same way? She wasn't sure about her feelings for either man.

She thought to herself, we've only had one date. I'll just wait and see. If he calls and we have a second date, I'll know more about my feelings. Idly, she wondered, would Kenneth make a good husband? I've heard being a doctor's wife is a lonely life. Would it be that way with us? If he were a ditch digger, would you feel the same way? Could he be the one that everyone says, 'You'll know when you meet him?' Oh, stop it Bea, she admonished herself. You don't even know the man.

Bea went up to her room and, when she adjusted the drapes, saw Kenneth's car still in the driveway. She watched from her window until the car move slowly down the street. What was that about, she wondered. He was just sitting there. I thought he might be having car trouble at first. I wonder what he was thinking. Could he be having the same thoughts about me? He's an interesting man. I want to know more about him – a lot more. She giggled to herself and tried to imagine him in her bed. What would it be like to kiss him? Would she want to make love to him? Would he be gentle? Bea had never made love with anybody, not even George, though it wasn't for a lack of trying on his part. She had left him frustrated many times. It made her feel powerful that she could turn him on so easily, but she never thought of him in that way. Why was she thinking about Ken that way? Could he be the one? Wow! Bea had begun to think that something was wrong with her when the other girls would talk about their affairs, but she had never felt that way about a guy. She got ready for bed then went down to the kitchen and had a glass of milk, remembering that they had not done much eating, just a lot of talking.

Sleep did not come right away for Bea. She lay awake fantasizing about Kenneth. She practiced calling him 'Ken' and fell asleep thinking about him. She dreamed she was wearing a long white gown and when she turned sideways she had a huge belly.

CHAPTER 37

Vic took his idea for a book of Charles' pictures to the publisher of the cookbook where his work had appeared; Franko Forbes was delighted with the idea. He had a catalogue of Charles' work and they collaborated on the best way to present the book. They worked many months and this kept Vic busy. He and Michele spent many hours poring over books of quotations and or poetry, trying to find ones that would fit each picture. They had decided to make a coffee table sized book that would do justice to the pictures. Vic was given the assignment for the text, and he had a hard time writing what he thought would reflect the essence of each picture. Michele had suggested that he try to find words that had already been written. They spent many nights drinking wine and reading poems and writings. They discovered that they worked well together and were comfortable with each other.

"Michele, I love you like the sister I never had," Vic said one night when they had consumed a bottle of wine. Michele looked at him and replied, "That's just the wine talking, but I love you, too. I've been thinking, I spend more time here at your place than I do at mine. Why don't I move in here? We could share the rent and split everything down the middle. I could clean and you could cook."

Vic thought it was a good plan. Vic laughingly said, "First we'll have to get twin beds. The couch won't do for you and you're not going to sleep with me. You can have the big closet. Most of my stuff will fit in the small one. You decide what you want to bring and I'll help you move it in. This will be fun. I really don't like living alone."

It was a good arrangement and the work on the book seemed to go faster. It took over two years to complete the book and print it. The publisher was pleased with the outcome and wanted to present it in the best way. It was decided that they would have a presentation of Charles' pictures in an art museum and have the books for sale at the museum. After the showing, they could have the books available at bookstores.

The exhibit's reception was a big success. They nearly sold out and had to have a second printing. Vic was pleased with himself, and felt good for the first time since Charles' death. Michele was in great form and as flamboyant at ever – making jokes and greeting everyone.

Franco, the publisher hired them to collaborate on other projects and they settled into a profitable arrangement. Their circle of friends expanded and they began hobnobbing with a more intellectual crowd. At one of the gatherings, Vic met a young writer named Jerrod who seemed to want to be around him all the time. He followed him everywhere and it was clear he was interested in Vic. Vic took no notice of him until Michele whispered, "He wants to get in your pants."

Vic said, "Oh, hush, Michele. You should be ashamed of yourself."

Vic introduced himself to Jerrod and started to talk with him and found that the young man was very intelligent and seemed smitten with him. This made Vic think of things he had not thought about since Charles' death. He decided that he wanted to get to know this young man better. They made a date to meet for lunch the next day and Vic felt excited with anticipation.

Jerrod Munson had moved to San Francisco from a small Oregon town. He had never fit in there so he moved to San Francisco where he thought he would be more accepted. Had it not been for the allowance his parents sent him every month, he would have starved because he was not selling any of his writing. He even applied for a job as an office boy for several publishing company, but he blew every interview because he was too shy to sell himself. He was drawn to Vic because Vic seemed so sure of himself. He didn't know what he was feeling, but he wanted to be near this man more than anything. He had gathered all his nerve to come to the party and try to mingle with the people there but no one would talk with him. When Vic finally took notice of him, he was so nervous he almost wet his pants. He tried to calm himself and found that talking with Vic was easier than he expected. He could hardly wait for lunch the next day. They had agreed to meet at a restaurant near the publisher's building.

~~~~~~

The following day, Vic had not thought much about the young man until he felt the rumblings of hunger around eleven thirty and remembered he was supposed to meet Jerrod at noon. He neatened his desk and walked to the restaurant. He saw Jerrod pacing in front of the building, mumbling to himself. Vic chuckled to himself and thought, He's nervous. I never thought I could affect someone like that. He's not a bad looking kid, a little skinny, but not bad looking. Well, well, let's see where this leads.

Jerrod was jittery all during lunch. Vic tried to put him at ease with small talk,

"So, Jerrod, where are you working?"

Jerrod admitted, "I haven't found a job yet. If I don't get one soon, I'll have to move back home to Oregon. I don't want to do that. I've been looking for work every day."

"I might be able to help you out. I'll ask around. Give me your number, and I'll let you know if I come up with anything. How old are you?"

Jerrod was so excited that he could hardly contain himself. He spilled his drink and nervously wiped it up with his napkin.

Vic thought, he's young enough to be my son. I'll try to help him and mentor him, but that's all. He considered two possibilities. Jerrod could help in the kitchen at Phillipe's or be a gofer at the publishing company.

During lunch he watched Jerrod with more interest than he wanted to. He looked at his lips. They were sensuous. His eyelashes were long and his eyebrows perfectly arched. He wondered if Jerrod knew just how attractive he was. With a little more meat on his bones, he could be a handsome man, not a skinny little kid. He acted and looked much younger than his twenty-four years.

That evening at Phillipe's, Vic looked around the kitchen and tried to picture Jerrod working there. He nixed that idea. He decided he would not want to see him every day because of the thoughts he was having.

He would talk with Frank, the publisher, and see if there was something for him at the publishing company.

Frank and Vic's relationship had grown over the years into a strong friendship. They respected each other's life styles. Frank was fascinated with Michele, but she would have nothing to do with him when she found out he was married. When Vic asked him about a position for Jerrod, Frank said he could find something for him in the mailroom. "Return the favor; can you get me a date with Michele?"

Vic replied, "I don't do match making. You're on your own with Michele. She has a mind of her own and I have no influence over her at all. You can keep trying if you don't mind getting your feelings hurt," and he laughed.

When Vic told Jerrod about the job he thought Jerrod would jump through the phone. "Oh, man! That's so great! Can you meet me for drinks?"

Vic consented and when he arrived at the agreed upon place with Michele, Jerrod seemed disappointed. He had wanted Vic to himself.

When Jerrod went to the men's room, Michele said, "I haven't been the third wheel in a long time. That little boy wants you, and he wants me gone. Go for it, Vic. You haven't had any action for a long time. I can disappear whenever you like."

Vic replied, "Don't you dare. He's too young for me. I'm old enough to be his father, for Chris-sake. Besides, I'm too old for any drama, and I'm not ready for any romance. That's why I wanted you to come with me."

"There doesn't have to be any drama, just a roll in the hay once in a while. Let him know up front that you don't want any entanglements. He might not want any either. He acts shy, but I'll bet he's no innocent."

Before Vic could respond, Jerrod returned to the table. Michele broke the tension, "So Jerrod, Vic tells me you're a writer. What kind of stuff do you write?"

Jerrod was relieved and glad to be talking about his writing. He told them the gist of some of his stories, and asked if they wanted to read some of his work. Michele said, "Sure. When can we see some of them? We'll be glad to read them." She nudged Vic's knee under the table. "Won't we, Vic?"

Vic snapped back, "Yeah, sure. We'd like to see your work."

Jerrod said, "I don't live far from here. If you don't mind a mess, we could go to my place now, and I could show you."

Before Vic could object, Michele said, "Okay. Let's go. We don't mind messes, do we Vic?"

On their way out of the bar, Vic whispered to Michele, "What are you trying to do? You know you don't give a shit about this boy's work."

"I'm just curious about him. He's got the hots for you, and I want to see how you handle it. Besides I'm interested in how he lives, I want to see if he's good enough for you. I have to look out for you, you know."

Vic laughed and they walked the three blocks to Jerrod's place. It was a large room in a Victorian house. He had his own private bath, and all in all it was not a bad arrangement for a young man just starting out. The landlady was a friend of his family and was motherly toward him, so he was not entirely alone.

When they entered the foyer of the house, the landlady was sitting in the parlor. "Is that you, Jerrod?"

He replied, "Yes, ma'am. I have some company with me -- friends from work. I hope you don't mind." He wanted her to know that he had a job.

"I don't mind at all. Just don't get rowdy."

Michele giggled, "I can't remember the last time I was rowdy."

They went upstairs to his room where the only mess they could see was papers piled on a large desk. Michele said, "You call this a mess. You should see our place. Now that's a mess."

Vic said, "Why don't you give us each a copy of two different stories. We can critique them and give them back to you. How does that sound?"

Jerrod said, "That'd be great. Let me see what I would like for you to read." He brushed past Vic, a little too close.

Michele said, "I just remembered, I have an early shoot tomorrow. I'll just leave you two alone and you can bring the stories home with you, Vic." She headed for the door.

Vic said, "That's okay, Michele, I need to turn in early, too. We'll go home together. Just wait a minute."

Jerrod looked disappointed and gave them each a manuscript. "I look forward to hearing from you. Thanks for everything."

They said their goodnights, and when they were out on the street, Vic said, "What were you trying to do? I don't want to get mixed-up with that boy."

Michele laughed, "It's not nice to mess with Mother Nature, Vic. I could see the sparks between you two. You're in denial. You can have a love life, you know. Just be careful, protect yourself – your heart and your other parts."

Vic said, "What about you? I don't see you panting behind anyone. Why not give Franko a chance? He has the hots for you. He might even leave his wife."

"Now, now, Vic, let's not get carried away. I don't need any drama either. His wife will never give him a divorce. She controls him and the company. It's been in her family for years. He's not going to give up his cushy life for me or any of his other bimbos."

"How do you know all this, Michele?" Vic was incredulous.

"I have my sources, and I've done my research. I always check out anybody I might get involved with. I was very attracted to him at one point, but decided against it. You see, I can control my urges, unlike some people I know."

"Are you saying I can't?"

"Well, I'm just saying. You're the type to get 'involved'. You have to have a 'love affair'," she made quotation marks in the air. "You have to love somebody before you make love with somebody. This boy might be good for you. I don't think he would hurt you. He admires you, and I don't think he's sophisticated enough to play you like Charles did. If anything, you might end up hurting him."

"Oh, Michele, I don't want to hurt anybody or get involved with him right now. I like my life the way it is. So let's change the subject. What's this shoot you have to go on so early?"

"I don't have a shoot. I just wanted to leave you two alone and see what would happen."

"Give it up, Michele. If I decide to have an affair, I'll make the plans, okay? Hands off my love life, and I'll be hands off on yours, deal?"

They high-fived and Michele replied, "Deal. So when will you see him again?"

Vic punched her on the arm. They laughed and hugged each other as they walked home.

CHAPTER 38

Auntie Mom and Bea were eating breakfast when Bea asked, "Where's Percy? I haven't seen him this morning."

"I left him sleeping on my bed. He's slowing down, and I've noticed that he's lost a lot of weight. I think I'll make an appointment with the vet. He's due for a checkup. We're both getting on up there in age slowing down."

"You're not slowing down. You're just as feisty as ever, and just as nosy. But I'm worried about Percy, too. I'll go with you to the vet, if you want me to. Just let me know when. I can take some time off from my summer job."

"Oh, that's so sweet of you, dear. You're just like your mother – always thinking of other people's needs. What about your own? How are things going with the doctor? And how are things going with George? Can you make up your mind? When it comes to love affairs, it's either feast or famine," she chuckled.

Bea laughed, "There you go, being nosy again. Would you like another cup of coffee?"

"Yes, I would, and don't try to change the subject. What's happening in your life besides work and school?"

Bea poured fresh coffee, "Well, Auntie Mom, I'm confused right now. I like George as a friend. He's easy to talk with and we have a lot in common. We hardly ever disagree and he's comfortable to be with. He wants to get married after we graduate next year."

264

Aunt Maggie said, "But …. Go on finish it, but what about Kenneth?"

"I don't know about Kenneth. I don't know how I feel about him. I like being with him. I look forward to seeing him, but there's this tension between us. I'm not sure of what I'm feeling. I have these 'impure thoughts' about him," she made quotation marks in the air and giggled.

"You're blushing! Have you ever had 'impure thoughts' about George?" and she made quotation marks in the air, too.

"No, I can't say that I have. But Kenneth makes me mad sometimes. I think he does it on purpose, just to see if he can get a rise out of me. We don't agree on everything. And then there are religious issues. You know that he's Jewish, and there are some things that I don't understand. He's modern in his thinking and doesn't adhere to some of the traditional things, and he says his family is open-minded."

"I think you know your own mind. Regardless of the religious thing, you're in love with Kenneth. There's a spark there, and that's what it takes to keep a relationship going. You don't have to agree on everything. You can be your own person, disagree, and still love each other. Respect – that's the most important thing. How does he handle an argument? Can you agree to disagree and still have a civilized conversation?"

"Oh, yes. Sometimes we have long discussions. We respect each other's point of view. I've never seen him pout or get angry because I don't agree with him. Auntie Mom, you always know just what to say. You're so wise. How come you never got married?"

"I couldn't find a man smart enough for me," she laughed. "You're grown now, and I can talk with you like a grown-up." She told Bea about her relationships. "I sometimes wish I had married my high school sweetheart. But I don't think it would have turned out too good. Don't you let this opportunity slip away from you. When you act on your 'impure thoughts', and you will, protect yourself. Girls don't have to get pregnant nowadays, unless they want to. There are ways to prevent that. You need to have this talk with your mother -- twins indeed. They were really going at it, weren't they?" and she laughed. "That was all that pent-up frustration through the years. I must say they were decent about it, though. I admire their strength. Go talk with your doctor about protecting yourself. Don't rely on Kenneth to do it. He may be a doctor, but he's still a man, and when they stop thinking, the other head takes over."

"Auntie Mom! You say the most outrageous things, but I'm glad we had this talk. I don't know if I could have talked with Mom like this. Thanks. Let me know what you want to do about Percy. I'm going to get dressed now, or I'll be late for work."

When Bea came down stairs, Mark was in the kitchen. He was holding Aunt Maggie and consoling her. "What's wrong? What's going on?"

Markie looked at her with tears in his eyes. "It's Percy. He's gone. I went to check on him and he was just

266

lying there. I thought he was asleep, but he must have died during the night. Just like Bunny."

"Oh, Auntie Mom, I'm so sorry. He had a good life, better than some people. He was well loved, but we were just talking about how frail he was. I'm so sorry. I'll call in sick."

Aunt Maggie said, "You don't have to do that, Bea. I'll be alright. You go on to work. In fact, I need to be alone. Markie said he'll bury him under the tree with Bunny. I'll be all right."

Bea called Candy and Wes and told them what had happened. Wes said he would come right over. Wes and Markie dug the grave – Buster helped dig the hole – and they had a quiet ceremony for Percy. Aunt Maggie took his collar and put it in her keepsake box. Bea ordered flowers from work, and when she told Kenneth about it, he sent flowers too.

Markie said, "Buster thinks we're playing with him. He's getting a mixed message, since I'm always telling him not to dig." Buster acted like he was enjoying himself until Markie brought Percy's body out to place in the hole. Buster sniffed at the towel, poked at it and tried to pull it off Percy's body. He started barking and whining and tried to dig Percy back up after they buried him. Markie talked to him and he seemed to understand. Then he lay down by the grave and whined.

Wes said, "Aunt Maggie, I'm so sorry. How would you like to come over and see the twins for a while? I know Candy would love for you to spend the day."

"Okay, Wes. That would be a good distraction. It would do me good to get out of the house and be around your lively little rug rats. Let's go."

That Saturday night, when Kenneth came to get Bea for their dinner date, Aunt Maggie thanked him for the flowers. As they were leaving, she said to Bea, "Time flies. Don't wait too long."

Bea rolled her eyes and said, "Good night, Auntie Mom, you old busy body."

Auntie Mom replied, "I won't wait up."

Kenneth said, "What was that all about?"

"Just a private joke. I'll tell you about it one day."

During dinner, they made small talk, then Kenneth reached across the table as they were eating dessert, took her hands, and said, "Bea, I think you know how I feel. I think about us all the time and I'm distracted from my work. I just want to be with you, and I love our discussions. You stimulate my mind and, ahem, other body parts. I love you. I've never said that to any girl before. I want to make love to you. I want you in my bed and in my life. Give us a chance. Let me make love to you tonight."

Bea blushed and stammered, "Ken, I don't know what to say. I … You … We … I've thought about it. I've thought about it a lot, too much, in fact. I think I love you, too. I love being with you, and when we kiss, I have to make myself pull away. I want it to go on forever. But Ken, I don't know what to do. What I mean is, I've never, you know, um … never been with a man in that way. I mean I want to … with you, but I don't know how to … I wouldn't know what to do, or how to …" her voice trailed off and she had tears in her eyes.

Kenneth leaned across the table and said, "Oh, Bea. Don't be afraid of me. I'll be gentle. I knew you were special, but I didn't know how special. I won't do anything you don't want me to do. I promise I won't hurt you. I just love you so much and I want you so much. I feel we were meant to be."

Bea took a deep breath and said, "I know, Ken. I feel like I'm ready to join the grown-up world. I've talked with my doctor about birth control and I want to make love with you. Or try to make love with you. I don't know what I'm saying." She took another deep breath, and in a shaky voice said, "Ken, I think I'm ready to love you the way a woman loves a man."

Ken chuckled and said, "You sound like you've rehearsed that speech."

She laughed and said, "I did." They both laughed, and Ken said, "Relax. I think we're both ready. Let's go to my place if you don't mind a mess. I've never taken a woman to my place before."

On the way to Ken's apartment, they said very little. Bea sat demurely in the passenger's seat holding her hands in her lap. Ken reached over and gently squeezed her hands, "Don't be nervous. I'll take care of you. I love you, Bea."

Bea self-consciously looked around Ken's apartment and said, "It's not messy at all. You're very neat."

Ken took her coat and said, "Make yourself at home. Would you like a glass of wine, or something?"

Bea took a deep breath and said, "I'd love a glass of wine." She took a sip and Ken took her in his arms. He put her glass on the table, kissed her, her forehead, each cheek, her ears, and said, "I love your chin." He nipped her chin, kissed her throat and then her lips.

Bea sighed and leaned into him. She kissed him back – this time she did not pull away. She relaxed in his arms. He steered her towards the bedroom. He began to undress and she said she wanted to use the bathroom. When she came out, he had removed his pants and shirt. He took her in his arms and very slowly began to undress her. When he got down to her bra and panties, he moved back and looked at her with admiration and said, "My god, you're beautiful. How did I get so lucky?"

Bea giggled nervously and he kissed her and led her to the bed. As they moved, he deftly unfastened her bra and slipped it off her arms. He kissed her throat and then each breast. He gently nipped each nipple, kissed her stomach, her thighs and slowly removed her panties. In the process, he managed to remove his own underwear. He kissed her on the lips and whispered, "Are you okay?"

She nodded and he continued to caress her breast and her thighs. When he caressed her inner thigh, she stiffened and he whispered, "Do you want me to stop?"

Bea replied in a small voice, "No, I don't. I'll be all right."

He continued to lovingly caress her and slowly moved his hand until he could feel her clitoris. He rubbed it gently and when he felt her become wet, he eased himself inside her. She gasped and squeezed his back tightly. He very slowly moved in and out, in and out until she began to relax and move with him. She moaned, and when he could no longer control himself, he came, and lay on top of her, spent. She held him close and ran her fingers through his curly hair. She whispered, "Oh, Ken. I love you so."

He rolled over, took her into his arms and asked, "Did I hurt you? I don't ever want to hurt you. It will get better, I promise. It won't always hurt. You'll see. I want to make you happy. It only hurts for the first couple of times."

Bea said as she wiped tears from the corners of her eyes, "It hurt at first. But it got better. I'm hurting a little now. I don't know much about sex, but are you larger than some men? I've heard girls talk, and I've got nothing to compare it with, but you seem big to me."

Ken laughed and said, "Uh, yeah. I've been told I'm generously endowed. You dear, sweet girl -- so innocent, so gentle and kind. When can we get married? I want to wake-up with you every morning and go to bed with you every night."

Bea said, "I don't know, Ken. I want to finish school before I get married. I want to meet your family and get to know them and get to know you better. Marriage is a big step. We have plenty of time. Let's take it slow for a while."

Ken said, "You're right. I'll slow down, but remember, you belong to me. You are woman – I am man." He rose up on his knees and beat his chest.

They both laughed and for the first time Bea saw him nude. Her eyes grew wide and she thought, I'm going to the library and have a look at the male anatomy. It looks big to me.

Bea didn't realize just how sore she was until she started walking to the bathroom. She took a shower and got dressed. Ken had dressed in the meantime and was in the kitchen. He made omelets and had the table set for two. When Bea came into the room, he kissed her and said, "I wish you would stay the night. I don't want to take you to your aunt's house. I want you to think of this as home."

Bea replied, "I don't think I should. I hurt, and I'm bleeding. Maybe I'll stay some other time. I just feel like I should be home tonight. I need to think about tonight without any distractions. You are a distraction, you know. The answer to your unasked question is yes. Yes I'll marry you. If I ever had any doubts before, now I know I am in love with you, Dr. Kenneth Levy. We'll have many nights together, I promise."

"Okay. Good enough. I'm so sorry I hurt you. Next time will be better. Now eat. You didn't eat much at dinner. I'll take you to your other home, but I won't like it."

On Sunday, Aunt Maggie cooked dinner for the family including Wes, Candy, Mabel, Fred and Amy. Bea asked Ken to join them. When everybody was at the table and the twins were asleep, Ken said, "I have something to say." He stood up and surveyed the table. "I've gotten to know this family over the past few months and I'm thankful that you have welcomed me at your table and into your lives. I hope to become a permanent part of this family." He took a ring box out of his coat pocket, got on one knee, gave Bea the box and said, "Beatrice Procter, with all my flaws, and everything I am, I love you. Will you make me the happiest man on earth? Will you marry me?"

Bea giggled, opened the box and marveled at the beautiful ring. Coyly she said, "I don't know. What flaws are we talking about?" Everyone laughed. "Of course I'll marry you. I love you. Now get up and eat your dinner."

Everyone congratulated them both and Markie made a toast. Aunt Maggie said, "It's about time. Cheers."

Mark watched Bea and Ken and wished that Judy could be with him. He could hardly wait to talk with her and tell her the news.

~~~~~~~~~~~~~~~~~~~~~~~~~~~~~~~~~~

The following Friday Bea told Aunt Maggie that Ken was cooking dinner for her and she wouldn't be home. When Bea left the house she told Aunt Maggie not to wait up, and she said, "I hadn't planned to. I'll see you when I see you. Have a good time playing house, hee, hee, hee." Bea laughed and kissed her on the cheek.

The table was set, flowers in a vase, and a bottle of wine chilling when Bea arrived. He had dinner all ready and there was a tiny box tied with a ribbon on Bea's plate.

"What's this? It's not my birthday."

"Just a little something for my fiancée. Open it," he smiled.

Bea took the bow off and lifted the lid. There was a key. She looked at Ken with a questioning expression.

He kissed her and said, "To my heart and to my home. I want you to come here anytime you want. We'll have to work out something for when you go back to school. I hope you'll come home as often as you can. I'll come to the school whenever I can get away from the hospital, and maybe sometimes we can meet half way. We'll have to work out something somehow. I've missed you terribly all week. Are you still hurting? I'm sorry. I didn't mean to ask that. Let's eat before dinner gets cold."

Bea kissed his cheek and said, "Thank you, darling. You make me feel so loved. You can ask me anything you want. As far as hurting, we'll have to find out, won't we? Yum, that smells delicious. Let's eat, I'm starved."

Ken poured the wine and they began to nibble at the food. Bea drained her glass and Ken filled it again. They began to relax and Bea slipped out of her shoes. She said, "I'm getting sleepy. How about you? I brought my toothbrush and my nightie. I plan to stay the night, if that's all right with you."

Ken chuckled, "More than all right. Let's finish dinner. We've got all night to go to bed." After dinner Ken turned on the stereo. They drank more wine and danced. They glided toward the bedroom to some sultry music. Bea whirled around and without missing a beat, took her nightie out of her bag and continued dancing into the bedroom. They swayed to the music, kissed and undressed each other. Bea forgot about the nightie when they got in the bed. They continued touching and kissing and this time when Ken tried to enter her, Bea stiffened only slightly. Then she relaxed and it only hurt a little. He was very gentle with her and went until she reached a climax. Then he found his own release, and then lay on her exhausted.

Bea whispered, "Now I know what all the fuss is about. You were right. It does get better. I think I could learn to like this, Dr. Levy."

Ken chuckled and rolled over on his back. Bea snuggled up beside him. He kissed her on the forehead and hugged her close. "I'm glad I can please you, Bea. I want you to love me as much as I love you. Let's get some sleep."

~~~~~~~~~~~~~~~~~~~~~~~~~~~~~~~~~~~

Bea opened her eyes and didn't know where she was at first. She quietly got out of bed, stepped on her nightie, picked it up and went to the bathroom. She tried to get back in the bed without waking Ken. She could barely make out his features in the dim morning light. She looked at the clock on his nightstand. It showed 3:15. She thought, maybe I can go back to sleep without waking him. She slid under the covers and Ken turned over, wrapped his arms around her and said, "What are you doing with this garment on? Don't you know it gets in the way?"

She laughed and said, "I thought you were asleep. I didn't want to wake you. If it gets in your way, you know what to do, don't you?"

He laughed and said, "Naughty, naughty. Let's see about this contraption," and he proceeded to slip her gown off her shoulders and moved it down her body until it was off. Then he kissed her breast and they made love again.

CHAPTER 39

"We need to have a serious talk Judy. You'll be going off to college in a few weeks. I wish you would stay home and go to school here. " Phillis and Judy were sitting in their back yard. "I'm going to worry about you living so close to Markie. I've seen the way you two act when you're with each other. You probably won't spend your time studying, I'll bet. I'm afraid you won't be able to control yourselves."

"Aw, Mom, I don't know what you're talking about," Judy said defensively.

"I'm not accusing you of anything, child. I'm just talking about reality as I see it. Your father and I have noticed your attachment to Markie, and we know human nature. So we need to be open and talk realistically about your situation. How are you going to handle your feelings for Markie? If you find it too hard to resist him, you need to be prepared. I'd rather you would wait, but if you can't, you need to be able to take care of yourself. Markie's a nice young man, but a woman has to take care of herself. Don't depend on a man to do it."

"Moooom! You're embarrassing me. Markie and I have never discussed what you're talking about," Judy moaned.

"Maybe you haven't, but you should. That is, if you're feeling the way I think you're feeling. I've seen how he looks at you, and how you look at him. I don't know what you talk about for hours on the phone, but you always seem to have a lot to say. So, all I'm saying is I want you to talk with our

277

doctor and get all the information you need so you'll be prepared if, or when you decide to be intimate with Markie, or anyone else for that matter."

"Oh, Mom, there could never be anyone else but Mark!"

"Uh huh, you just answered all my questions, and your own, too. So we'll see the doctor before you go away to college. I love you, baby, and I want the best for you. I want you to reach all the goals you have for yourself without any mishaps along the way. I love Markie, too, but just remember, you're your own person. Don't do anything just to please someone else. Be sure it's what you want, too."

Judy shyly dropped her head and said, "Thanks, Mom. I'm glad we had this talk. I didn't know how to start the conversation. But you know me better than I know myself. Does Daddy know you are talking to me about this?"

"Of course he does. In fact he suggested that I do it, or he would have. I felt you would rather talk to me, though. Your father is a realist. You know he loves all his children, and wants the best for you. Don't be embarrassed. Joe and I know what it's like to be young and in love. Believe it or not, we once felt the way you and Markie feel. How do you think we got three children? Phillis laughed. "And we didn't plan a one of you. – So be careful."

~~~~~~~~~~~~~~~~~~~~~~~~~~~~~~~~~~~~~~

Judy quickly settled into her dorm room. Her friend Joan had the room across the hall. She found that she liked dormitory life, and rarely felt homesick.

She didn't get to see Mark much. Judy was trying to make the track team. The coach said she showed great promise as a runner. Between their full academic schedules, Mark's radio job, and her extracurricular activities, they only saw each other on weekends. They tried to study together. He helped her with math, and she helped him with writing compositions and research. She had dinner with the family almost every Sunday. When she told Phillis that she hardly ever saw Mark, Phillis heaved a sigh of relief. Judy went home for Thanksgiving and Bea went with Ken to meet his family. Mark missed Judy being at the table. He missed her husky voice and her silly jokes. She and Auntie Mom got along well, and Judy helped her cook sometimes. Aunt Maggie said to Mark, "I like that little girl. You do right by her, you hear?"

Mark replied, "I intend to, old lady. You'll see. I've got it all planned out."

"Who're you calling 'old', boy?" and she popped him with a dishtowel.

Bea and Ken got back to town in time for Sunday dinner. Mark went to get Judy at the bus station so she could join the family for dinner, also. When she got off the bus and saw him, her face lit up. Mark thought she had the prettiest smile. He didn't realize it, but he, too was grinning from ear to ear. He swooped her up, spun her around and kissed her. She laughingly said, "I think you missed me. I was only gone a week."

He said, "I didn't realize it, but I did. Sunday dinner won't be the same without you. Will you come? Everyone will be there. Bea and Ken are coming, too. I can get you to your dorm on time."

"Sure, the food is good, and most of the company," and she poked him in the ribs.

"How is everybody in your family?"

"Everybody's fine. They all said to tell you hello. My sister is engaged and my brother is going steady. So things are moving along. Mom and Dad are the same. You know what? I missed you, too. We don't get to see each other as often as I would like. But that's okay. I think it's better this way, don't you?"

"Mmm, maybe. I don't know. Why do you say better?"

"I just think less is better because we're not too tempted. We get to be glad to see each other when we can, and we're not arousing those feelings. Know what I mean?"

Mark stopped walking and looked at her. "Are you saying that I arouse feelings in you – feelings of a carnal nature? I didn't know little girls felt those things."

Judy laughed and punched him on the arm, "You know what I mean. Why do you have to make it so hard for me, Mark?"

Mark spun her around and kissed her nose. "Your nose is cold. Get inside and get warm." He opened his overcoat and wrapped her inside. "There, isn't that better?"

"Oh, Mark, much better." She looked up at him and they kissed and her hat fell off. "I think you'd better feed me before we get into trouble."

Mark took a deep breath and said in a husky voice, "I'd love to get into trouble with you, but you're right. Let's go eat. You can call home from my house and let them know that you got here safely. I'm sure Mom will want to talk with your mom."

Dinner was noisy and fun. The twins were the center of attention. Everybody wanted to hold them, and they gladly went from arm to arm. They squealed and giggled at Buster.

Candy pulled Bea aside and said to her, "I don't get to see you enough. How are things going with you and Ken? Have you set a date yet, or made any plans? How's school, and how did George take your engagement?"

"Oh, Mom, I miss our chats, too. George was shocked when I showed him the ring. He said something like, 'How can you marry someone you hardly know? I thought we were going to get married. You've known me for a long time and we get along. Why can't you marry me?' I felt badly for him, and I tried to explain to him that my feelings for him were friend to friend, but my feelings for Ken were something else. He seemed shocked, and said he didn't think I would feel that way with anyone but him. It was all I could do to keep from laughing, because I've never felt that way about George. It was all on his part, and he just assumed that because he wanted me, I would want him. Anyway, he wished me good luck and said he would always be my friend and if Ken didn't work out, he would be in the wings waiting to pick me up. I thanked him and said I appreciated it. I kind of felt sorry for him. We haven't set a date yet. I want it to be after I graduate. We'll look at a calendar and decide soon. It will depend on when Ken can get away – maybe sometime next summer. How are things going with you? You look happy, but tired."

"I am happy. The twins are great, but a lot of work. I don't get much sleep. I'll be glad when they sleep longer at night. They're getting better, but I swear I believe they take turns keeping us up. It's like they play tag. One starts and then the other one takes up where he or she left off. We laugh a lot. It's that or we'll go crazy. They're getting better, though. I hope they get tired out tonight so we can get some sleep."

When Judy told them that Linda was engaged, Bea said she would call her to see what Linda's plans were so they didn't set their wedding date for the same time.

After the Thanksgiving break, things got back to normal. The hustle and bustle of the Christmas holidays began – decorating, shopping, making plans for Christmas Eve and Christmas day. Bea reminded everyone that they had to include plans for Hanukkah, and it was decided that Ken could decide what, if anything he wanted to do with the family. Bea and Ken decided they would spend Hanukkah with his family, and Christmas Eve and Christmas Day with her family.

One day during the week after Thanksgiving, as Wes was leaving his office, the phone rang. "Hello. Candy? What's wrong? Okay, I'll get my assistant to handle practice. I'll be right there. Can you tell me what's wrong? Okay, I'm on my way." He hung up the phone and asked his assistant to take over. "There's some emergency at home. I'll see you later."

When he got home, the house seemed dark even though it was just after noon. He noticed the blinds were drawn and the lamp on the table in the entry was on low. There was a note in the dish where he always put his keys. He read, "Follow the petals and do as you are told." He chuckled and thought, must be one of Candy's tricks.

He looked on the floor and there were rose petals leading to the kitchen. On the counter was a bottle of wine, two glasses and another note. "Open the wine. Follow the petals. Bring the wine and glasses with you. Be very quiet."

He did as instructed and when he reached the bedroom, there was Candy in a pink negligee propped up on pillows. The blinds were drawn and the only light came from several candles. Candy said in a husky voice, "You follow instructions well. Now pour the wine and get over here before my husband comes home."

Wes laughed out loud, "Where are the babies? When did you do all this? I thought there was something wrong with you or one of the twins. You said you needed me. I thought it was an emergency."

"I gave them to a band of gypsies in exchange for this ten dollar bottle of wine. They won't bother us again. I didn't say it was an emergency. I said I needed you. And I do. So stop talking and get on over here. Don't worry about making more babies. I took care of that. Now we have to get busy before my husband finds out about us."

Wes said, "I have a confession to make. I took care of the baby factory, too. I had a vasectomy while you were laid-up in the hospital waiting for the babies. I thought about everything you were going through, and I decided it was the least I could do. So I'm like Buster. I've been fixed."

They both laughed and Candy said, "You should have told me. That should have been something we decided together. But I forgive you. Now that makes it easier for us to fool around whenever we get the chance. So let's get started before the gypsies bring them back. Fred and Amy took them for the afternoon. Wasn't that sweet of them?"

Wes started taking off his clothes and he said, "I've missed this. I've missed you. It will be good not to have to listen for sounds from the nursery. Come here, woman. We're not too old yet." He grabbed her and started kissing her all over. They giggled and caressed each other and made love for a long time. Then they both went to sleep. They were awakened by the sound of Fred's car in the driveway. They jumped out of bed and got dressed. Wes answered the doorbell while Candy put out the candles and started scooping up the petals. She turned on the kitchen light and was putting the petals in the trash when Fred and Amy came into the kitchen with the babies. Candy whispered to Wes as she passed him to greet the babies, "Back to the real world, Daddy."

She and Wes put the babies in their cribs and she asked Fred and Amy if they wanted to stay for dinner. Fred replied, "No, thanks. We have something to discuss with you." Wes said, "Okay. Want some juice? Shoot, what's it about?"

Fred looked at Amy, took a deep breath and said, "Amy and I are married. We went to a Justice of the Peace last weekend. We just told Amy's folks, now you guys are the second to know."

Candy said, "Why did you do that? We could have given you a nice wedding. How do your folks feel about it, Amy?"

Amy replied, "They're okay with it. They could never afford a fancy wedding. With everything going on – the babies, Bea's graduation and wedding coming up, we just thought it would be easier this way."

Candy said, "Is that all, Amy? Is there something else you want to tell us? Why the rush? Are you pregnant?"

Fred put his hand up in protest, "Wait a minute. We're didn't get married because we're pregnant – we are, but we got married because we love each other."

Wes said, "Well, looks like I'm going to be a grandpa. Congratulations twice." He looked at Candy, "Are you ready to be a grandma?"

Candy chuckled, "Ready or not, it looks like we will be grandparents. Can we give you a reception? It doesn't have to be big and elaborate -- just family and a few of your close friends. I'm thinking – how about New Year's Eve? What do you think, Wes?"

Wes said, "It's okay with me. You women take care of it. I wouldn't know what to do anyway. Come on Fred, we men have things to talk about."

CHAPTER 40

"Are you sure you want to move out?" Vic asked Michele. "You need to think it over before you make such a commitment. What if it doesn't work out with Frank?"

Michele answered, "There are no guarantees in life. You should know that. Sometimes you just have to take a chance and hope for the best. I've never felt this way about a person before. I've been completely open and honest with him. He knows everything. He's even seen me without my wigs, and he still wants me. Can you believe that? He must be crazy or crazy in love. I love him, Vic, I think mostly because he loves me. I never had anyone love me just because. Well, maybe my mother, but I don't remember her. I know we'll never be together the way most couples are, but I've decided to take what I can get. I'll be the 'other woman' if I have to, just to be with him. I've never been promiscuous."

She put up her hand as if to stop Vic from saying something. "I know, I know, I talk a lot of shit and I flirt and carry-on, but it's a front. Now only two people know the real me – you and Frank. I've only been with two people like that. The first when I thought I was gay and the second after the operation. I didn't like it. He didn't want to make love, he just wanted nookie. I vowed I would never be used again. Until now, I've been celibate.

I play a role every day, but Frank has seen the real me. And he likes me. Can you believe that shit? He likes me. I can be myself around him. We enjoy each other. It's not just about sex – even though that's good. We just like to be with each other. We enjoy playing house. That's what it is, you know, playing house. He's with me more than he's at home."

Vic smiled and said, "I want you to be happy. I hope it lasts, but what if it doesn't? What about his wife? What if she's one of those crazy women who'll come to your door with a gun? What are you going to do?"

"Vic, I don't think she cares enough to cause a ruckus. She doesn't give a fuck. She just wants the façade -- the intact family, seen by the public. She doesn't care about him. He says the last time they had sex was ten years ago. She won't give him a divorce, but she doesn't want him. If he gets a divorce, he'll end up with nothing. He signed a prenup. He thinks she has a lover on the side. He hardly ever sees the children. They all go their separate ways. So he set me up in this fabulous apartment. It's in my name, but he pays the rent and all the other bills. He doesn't mind that I work, so I'm not a kept woman. I'm saving my money, so if, or when, the shit hits the fan, I'll be okay. I hate leaving you like this, but I've got to fly away and be with my man." She flapped her arms pretending they were wings, and they both laughed. "What about you? How are things going with your writer friend?"

"They're not going. I don't want to get involved with anyone. I like my solitude. I guess I'm a hermit at heart. I love working with the books – it stimulates my mind. And you know I love making new dishes at Phillipe's. So my life is full. I don't have time for anyone. I'm concentrating on my health now. I'm still in the research study, and I'm on new meds that seem to be keeping me healthy. Besides, he's too young for me. He's not much more than a boy. I try to avoid him as much as possible. He probably thinks I don't like him. I could like him, but I won't give him a chance. So there, you satisfied?"

"No. Not a whit. I don't believe you want to be alone. I know you pretty well. You'll come around sooner or later. I've seen the way he looks at you. He puts your mail at the bottom of the pile so when he gets to your office, he has time to linger. He thinks I don't see all that, but I've been watching him. He's like a school kid smitten with his teacher. I feel sorry for him, poor baby. He's pining for you, and you won't throw him a crumb. Shame on you," and she laughed.

Vic helped Michele carry the last of her belongings down to the waiting limo. They hugged and kissed and he felt a lump in his throat. "I'll miss you."

"Ah, man, don't make me mess up my mascara. We'll see each other at the office. I'm not moving to Mars, you know – just across town. We can visit each other, and I'll even let you cook for us. Frank loves your cooking. Maybe I'll get domestic and let you teach me a few things besides boiling water and making toast. Love you, ta-ta."

Vic stood on the sidewalk and watched the limo drive down the hill. He felt lonely all of a sudden and didn't really want to go back to his empty apartment. It was a pleasant evening so he decided to take a walk. He wandered down to the corner bar and decided to have a beer. When his eyes adjusted to the gloom, he looked around, recognized a few regulars and waved or nodded to them, but he didn't talk with anyone. Over in a corner, he spotted Jerrod sitting by himself. At first he was annoyed. Of all the people in the world, Jerrod was the last one he wanted to see. Jerrod waved eagerly. He looked so young and vulnerable. Vic mumbled to himself, "Shit. I can't ignore him. He knows I've seen him. It would be rude, and I don't want to hurt his feelings."

He took his beer and walked over to the table where Jerrod was sitting. "Hi, young fellow. You here by yourself? What are you doing in this neighborhood? This is a long way from where you live, isn't it?"

Jerrod nervously replied. "I was visiting a friend a couple of blocks from here and just thought I'd stop in here on my way home."

Vic could see that he was lying, but he let it pass. He didn't want to get into a big discussion with him. He didn't have the energy. He surmised that Jerrod was stalking him, in a way. He decided he'd put an end to it once and for all. He didn't want to lead him on.

He spoke matter-of-factly, "Jerrod, what do you want from me? Where do you think our relationship is going? We can only be co-workers, so stop following me around, okay?"

The second the words were out of his mouth, he wanted to take them back. He knew he had hurt the young man's feelings, but he didn't know what else to say.

Jerrod looked at him with tears in his eyes and stammered, "I... I don't... I don't know what I want. I... I... just ... I just like you, I guess. I mean, you've been so good to me – helping me get this job and all. And your friend Ms. Tate has been so good to me. I didn't mean any harm. I'm sorry if I bothered you."

Vic said, "It's all right, Jerrod. I didn't mean to be so cross with you. I'm in a bad mood this evening. Ms. Tate, Michele, was my roommate and she moved out today. I guess I'm just missing her and I took it out on you. I'm sorry." He touched Jerrod's hand and he thought Jerrod would faint.

They sipped their beers in silence. Then Vic got up and said, "Well, Jerrod, I'll see you back at the office. Good night."

Jerrod said, "Okay, Mr. Newman. See you back at the office."

Vic walked out of the bar and didn't look back. He didn't want to see the look on Jerrod's face. He convinced himself that he didn't want anything to do with him. He wished Jerrod would leave him alone so he wouldn't have to deal with his feelings. If Jerrod had stayed out of his way – if he hadn't seen him - he wouldn't be having these thoughts about him.

He thought of a hymn he used to hear when his mother took him to church. "Yield not to temptation, for yielding is sin. Each victory will help you, some other to win." He started humming to himself and he smiled. I haven't thought of my mother in years. That's strange. I wonder why now? She might not even be alive.

I wonder what my life would have been if I had stayed with Candy and the children. I can't think of that now. I can't change a thing. It's too late. I chose to stay away, so to them, I'm dead. Oh, Charles, I miss you so. For the second time that evening, he wiped tears from his eyes.

The following week, Vic knocked on Frank's office door, and without waiting for an answer, he opened it. There was Michele on Frank's lap and they were giggling. Vic said, "Oh, excuse me. Don't you guys care if you get caught or not?"

Michele hopped up and straightened her clothes. Frank said, "Most people wait to be acknowledged before they enter."

Vic replied, "Fix your wig, Michele. I just came to invite you guys to my place on Saturday. I'm having a few friends over to try out some new ideas I have for appetizers. I'll have a variety of wines, too, and I'd love to have you."

At that moment, Jerrod appeared at the door with a handful of mail. "Excuse me. Mr. Forbes, here's your mail." He turned to go and Michele said, "Maybe Jerrod would like to try your appetizers, too."

Jerrod said, "That's all right. I wasn't invited."

Vic replied, "Of course you're invited. I'm having several people over. Bring a friend -- the more, the merrier. Come around eight, Saturday evening." He turned his back and made a fist at Michele.

Michele, facing Jerrod, grinned and said, "Yeah, bring a friend. It'll be a ball. Vic is known for his food, honey."

Jerrod said, "Okay. Do I bring anything?"

Michele replied, "Just yourself, sugar. Just yourself, um and your friend, of course."

When Jerrod left, Michele started laughing. Frank said, "That was not nice, Michele." Vic said, "You ought to be ashamed of yourself."

They all laughed and Michele said, "I know, but this should be fun. Don't you think, Vic?"

That Saturday, Vic spent most of the day preparing for his party. He was excited and a little nervous. He wanted everything to be just so. He had invited Philip, some of the workers at the restaurant, and a few co-workers from the office. People started drifting in a little before eight o'clock, and by eight fifteen, his apartment was quite full. Everyone was chatting and giving their opinions about his dishes and drinking lots of wine. By ten o'clock, it was quite noisy. By twelve, the crowd was beginning to thin out.

Michele spoke to Vic as she started picking up dirty dishes and glasses, "I'd say your little gathering was a success. Everybody seemed full and happy. The food was delicious, by the way. I especially liked the little salmon puffs. There isn't much left to clean up. I didn't see much of your little friend. Where is he?"

Vic said, "I don't know where he disappeared to. Maybe he went home early. Thanks Michele, you don't have to bother with the mess. I'll take care of it. I'm glad you and Frank had a good time."

Frank shook Vic's hand. "It was wonderful, my man. Food was delicious. This little lady is becoming quite a good cook with your tutelage. Between the two of you, I've got to watch my weight." He hugged Michele around the waist and she blushed.

Vic finished picking up and decided to wash the dishes the next morning. He was very tired. He locked the door, turned out the lights and went into the bedroom. As he was taking off his clothes, he noticed Jerrod sprawled on one of the beds. He was out cold. Vic just shook his head. He took Jerrod's shoes off, pushed his limp body to a more comfortable angle, and threw a blanket over him. He stood and looked at him. Damned kid, doesn't even know when to stop drinking. I just hope he doesn't throw-up. I don't feel like cleaning up vomit. Shit. I'm going to strangle Michele.

As he looked at Jerrod, Vic thought, he's a handsome young man. I really could go for him, but he's so young and naïve. I don't want to hurt him. He'll have to go. I'll do it in the morning.

The next morning, Vic woke to gasping and vomiting coming from the bathroom. He had a flashback to when Charles was sick. Then he remembered Jerrod. – Well, he made it to the bathroom at least, thank goodness.

Jerrod came into the bedroom looking sheepish and wiping his face with a washcloth. "I'm so sorry. I guess I had too much to drink. I borrowed a cloth. It was a good party. Thanks for inviting me. This is so embarrassing. I don't usually act this way. I've never passed out before." He paused, twisting the washcloth in his hands. "It was a good party, thanks for inviting me. I'll just put my shoes on and leave. I'm so sorry."

He bent down to pick up his shoes and a wave of nausea hit him , and he rushed to the bathroom. When he came out, he was white as a ghost. Vic steered him to the bed and helped him lay down. "You need to sleep it off. You can leave when you feel better. Don't worry about it, I've had my share of hangovers, too."

Jerrod nodded gratefully and was soon fast asleep again. Vic went into the kitchen and began washing the dishes. He was drinking coffee and reading the paper when Jerrod finally came into the kitchen. Vic looked up, "Well, look what the buzzards drug in. You look awful; sit down and I'll get you some coffee."

Jerrod smiled wanly and said, "I apologize for being such a poor guest. I'll just leave. I don't want to impose on you anymore."

Vic said, "Nonsense, Jerrod, sit down. You need something on your stomach. You're not imposing on me. Sit down. How do you like your coffee? How about some eggs and toast? That should make you feel better."

Jerrod sat down with his head in his hands. He looked so pitiful, Vic felt sorry for him. He gave him a cup of coffee, put his hand on his shoulder and said, "How do you want your eggs?"

Jerrod put his hand on top of Vic's and looked up at him with watery eyes. Vic pulled away and got out the frying pan. Jerrod whispered, "Scrambled will be fine."

Vic sat and watched him eat then he said, "Look, Jerrod. I like you. I like you a lot, but we can't have a relationship. I'm too old for you. You need someone your own age, and besides there are things you need to know about me. I'm only going to tell you this for your own good and I want you to respect me enough not to reveal to anyone what I'm about to tell you. I'm HIV positive and I don't want to give it to you. Do you understand? I don't want to infect you with this virus. I watched my true love die from AIDS, and I can't go through that again. I just can't. That's why I've been less than friendly with you. You see, you have awakened feelings in me that I thought were dead. It's me, not you. So you'd better run for your life, and I mean that literally."

Jerrod said, "I'm glad you told me. I was beginning to think you didn't like me at all. I really like you. I don't know why, but I do. Now I know why you've been so cold to me. If you're ever inclined, I'd be willing to chance it.

I'm not a virgin, Vic. We could use protection if that's what you're worried about. I've always played it safe. I don't mess around a lot. My first lover was when I was in high school. I've only had two since then. I can't be casual like some guys, so you wouldn't have to worry about me cheating on you. But since you've made up your mind, I won't bother you anymore." He got up to leave. "I feel better now, so I'll be going. Thanks for your hospitality. And just so you know, I won't tell anyone."

Vic thought to himself, shit. I know I'm going to regret this, but here goes. "You don't have to leave right away. Let's have another cup of coffee and you can tell me about yourself."

They talked for a long time, then they took a walk, had lunch at a sidewalk café, stopped at a drug store and went back to the apartment. Jerrod bought a toothbrush and other

295

items, and he stayed the night. The next day Vic got rid of the twin beds and he bought a double bed.

CHAPTER 41

Bea said she would be happy to decorate Candy's house for Fred and Amy's reception when she came home for the holidays. Candy, Mabel, Aunt Maggie, Amy and Amy's mom met in Candy's kitchen to make plans. Everyone would be tired out from cooking for the holidays so they decided to have it catered. Amy made out her guest list with Fred's input. She wanted to invite Janet, who seemed to be friendless these days. Amy felt sorry for her.

Fred asked Markie if he minded if Janet came to the reception. Markie said it wouldn't bother him at all.

Christmas Eve was as fun-filled as usual. Aunt Maggie fixed a light supper and everyone was there when Bea and Ken gave her a Christmas present. She said, "I thought we opened our presents on Christmas morning."

Bea said, "We can still do that, but you realize we're not all living in the same house anymore. So Ken and I wanted you to have our present tonight. Tomorrow might be too busy. Here, open it quick."

Aunt Maggie chuckled, "I know what it is by the sound. I just don't know what color it is." She took the ribbon off, and inside the big box was a brown and white kitten wearing a big red bow, yowling its head off. In the box were some food, a litter box, some litter, a kitty toy and a blanket.

"Ah, Bea, you did it again. Last Christmas it was Buster. Now what do we call this one?" Aunt Maggie grinned.

The kitten tumbled out of the box and waddled over to Aunt Maggie meowing loudly. She leaned down to the kitten singing, "Here comes Susie, Susie, Susie. Here comes Susie, Susie now." She picked the kitten up. "You walk like you're drunk. If you were a boy cat, I'd call you Drunkard. But lucky for you, you're a girl, so I'll call you Susie."

~~~~~~

Christmas day was the twin's first Christmas. They got toys from everyone. Candy and Wes decided they would put most of them away until they were old enough to play with them, then take out only a few at a time. Amy remarked to Candy, "You and Wes seem to agree on almost everything. Do you ever fight? I mean, how is it you get along so well?"

Candy told her, "Basically, we respect each other. We disagree sometimes, but we never let that get in the way of our love and respect for the other person. You can have different opinions without arguing or fighting. Besides, most of the time, I'm right," she laughed and gave Amy a high-five.

Markie couldn't wait to talk with Judy. He told her everything and asked her to come back to school early so she could come to the reception – besides he wanted to bring in the New Year with her. She assured him that she would convince her parents to let her come back to school early. The dorms would be practically deserted, but there would be a few people there, not everyone went home for the holidays.

~~~~~~

Linda asked Judy, "So what's going on with you and Markie? Did you get it on yet?"

Judy blushed, "Of course not. We're not like that. He wants to, but I'm not ready."

"What are you waiting for? It's obvious he loves you and you love him. Don't wait too long. You might lose him."

"Have you and Harvey – uh, you know?"

"Of course we have. That's a big part of marriage. You want to know if you're compatible if you're going to be living together until ye part by death or divorce. Seriously, I'm not saying you should or shouldn't. It's up to you. But Harvey and I have a good relationship in the bedroom and outside the bedroom. If we don't make it, it won't be because we didn't try in every way. And I mean every way. We're still getting to know each other, but at least we know that sex won't be a problem. We're not living in Victorian times, you know. Be real. Think about it, little sister. You're old enough, just don't be careless. There are ways to be safe. Do you need some information?"

Judy stuttered, "No, no. I talked with Mom before I went away to school and I talked with our doctor. I think I know how to take care of myself, if the time ever comes. Did Mom ever talk to you? How did you know what to do?"

"Oh, the time will come, alright. Yeah, Mom and I talked before I went away to college, too. So when I knew that Harvey was the one, I was not naïve. I was scared, of course, but Harvey was so sweet and understanding. I have to tell you, the first time was not fun. Mama didn't tell me that it would hurt. So I'm telling you, don't expect it to be great the first time, but if you love him, it will get better. Oh, boy, will it get better," she laughed. "I can't wait to march down the aisle to my man. We can go look for your dress before you go back to school. It goes without saying that you'll be my maid-of-honor. When do you go back?"

"Mark wants me there for his best friend's reception on New Year's Eve. It so happens, that he's also his step-brother since Mark's mom married Fred's dad. Anyway, Fred and Amy went to a Justice of the Peace without telling anybody, so they're giving them a reception. I need you to help me convince Mom and Dad to let me go back to school early so I can be with Mark on New Year's Eve. Um, I mean so I can go to Fred and Amy's reception since they're such good friends of mine. Okay?"

Linda snickered, "Oh, I see where this is going. Okay, I'll bring it up at dinner."

It was just beginning to get dark when Mark picked up Judy at the bus station. He took her to the dorm so she could change her clothes for the New Year's Eve celebration. She came downstairs to the receiving room looking radiant. She wore a navy velvet skirt and a silver sweater set that sparkled every time she moved. Mark said, "Wow, you look gorgeous!" She twirled around and said, "I'm ready."

When they got in the car, she moved close to Mark and in a small voice said, "I mean I'm ready, Mark."

Mark looked at her, stepped on the brakes, and said, "You mean tonight? You won't stop us this time? Are you sure?"

Judy said, "Stop talking, Mark. Let's go to the reception and have a good time. We can talk later."

They hardly recognized Wes and Candy's house. Bea had done a wonderful job decorating. The furniture had been moved to make room for a dance floor; platters of finger foods covered all the tables. They had hired a disc jockey so there was continuous music. Everyone seemed to be having a good time. Wes made a speech. Markie made a toast to the happy couple, and everyone danced, drank and ate with abandon since it was, after all, New Year's Eve.

Ken was called to the hospital and asked Mark if he could see that Bea got home okay. Mark laughed and asked, "Which home?" Ken chuckled and said, "Let her decide."

With a slow song playing, Mark and Judy danced together and he asked her, "Do you mind if I ask Janet to dance? She hasn't moved from that chair since she came in. She looks so lost and alone."

Judy pulled away and looked up at him and said, "Should I mind? Should you feel sorry for her after what she tried to pull on you? Dance with her if you want, I can't stop you. You're a free man. I don't care."

Mark pulled her back close to him and said, "Don't start acting jealous. You have nothing to worry about. In fact, Janet helped me see that I loved you. You should thank her."

Judy looked up at him, "What do you mean?" Mark told her about the night of graduation when Janet suggested that he liked Judy. They laughed and Judy said, "By all means, go dance with her. Tell her I can't thank her enough."

The crowd started thinning out and Mark found Bea and asked if she was ready to go home. She said she should stay awhile and help clean up. Candy insisted that she leave. "Wes and I can handle this mess. Besides, we hired a caterer, remember? That's their job. We'll see you later."

Mark said, "Where to Ma'am? Your new home, or your old home?"

Bea laughed, "Choices, choices. I'll go to my new home, thank you very much."

Mark walked Bea to Ken's door and kissed her on the cheek. "Good night, sis. It's good to have you home. Love you."

Bea said, "Love you, too, little brother. Be good to her."

Instead of driving towards the college, Mark headed in the opposite direction. He pulled into a motel and before he went in to register, he turned to Judy and asked, "Are you sure?" She nodded, and he went inside.

He unlocked the door and pushed it open. Before Judy could walk through, he picked her up and carried her inside. She giggled. "You make me feel like a bride. You can put me down now."

"I want you to think of yourself as my bride." Mark set her on her feet, but didn't let go. He put one hand under her chin, lifted her face up and kissed her very tenderly. She began to tremble and he held her close and whispered, "Don't be nervous. You can change your mind any time you want to. I won't get mad. Well maybe I will get mad, but you don't have to do anything you don't want to do, okay?"

She whispered, "Okay. Can I have some water, please?"

"All right. I'll go get some ice. Be right back."

When he came back into the room, he didn't see Judy. He called, "Jude, where are you?"

She opened the bathroom door and peeped out. "Here I am. Turn the lights out. I don't want you to see me."

He chuckled, "Okay. You're going to be shy, are you? Should I leave the room?"

She laughed nervously, "No, silly. Turn your back."

He took his coat off, turned around and soon he felt her arms around his waist. He turned towards her. He ran his fingers through her curls, kissed her on the forehead, the nose, the chin, the neck, the hollow of her throat, and then on the lips. She shuddered and put her arms around his neck. He picked her up and carried her towards the bed while they continued to kiss. He said in a husky voice, "Do you still want that water?" She shook her head and said, "Don't stop."

Mark said, "Do you mind if I stop long enough to take my clothes off? I see you're wearing some little flimsy thing. Can I get comfortable, too?"

303

She giggled nervously, "Of course. I want you to be comfortable. I'll fix both of us some water. Maybe it should be wine. Maybe that's what we need – some wine for this special occasion. They say wine is good for your digestion and your circulation. I read this article in a health magazine...."

As she chattered on and on, Mark went into the bathroom and came out with nothing on but his shorts. He took the water glasses out of her hands and put them on the table and said, "Did anyone ever tell you, you talk too much? Come here, woman." He grabbed her and kissed her hard. She sank into his embrace and he maneuvered her to the bed. She lifted her arms over her head and Mark pushed her gown up and over her arms. He put her under the covers and took his shorts off. He rested his head on her chest and she ran her fingers through his hair. She started to say something, but Mark stopped her with his kiss. "Shh, don't talk, just relax. We'll take our time. I don't want to rush you."

"Okay, Markie, it's just that I'm nervous. You know it's my first time, don't you, and I'm scared I'll disappoint you, or you'll hu…"

Again, Mark stopped her chatter with a kiss. He lovingly caressed her breasts and ran his fingers down the small of her back, onto her hips then down her thighs. He kissed her shoulders, her neck, and throat and ran his tongue around her erect nipples, down her stomach and into her navel. He kissed her inner thighs and felt her stiffen when his hand reached her mound. He twisted her pubic hair around his finger and eased his middle finger between her legs and onto her clitoris. She grabbed his hair and pulled him close to her chest. He opened her legs and tried to enter her, but she was too tight. He whispered coarsely, "Jude, I'm so sorry. I don't want to hurt you. If I try harder it will be like rape. I can't get into you without hurting you. Let's stop. I'm sorry."

Judy protested, "No, Markie, I'm the one who's sorry. Wait a minute. My sister gave me something she said I should use the first time to make it easier. Let me get my purse." She hopped out of bed, reached inside her purse and brought out a tube. Judy gave the tube to Mark and said, "I don't know what to do with it. You take it."

In the illumination provided by the bathroom nightlight, Mark could barely make out the words 'lubricant'. Judy climbed back in beside him and kissed him, then said, "Let's continue where we left off."

Mark chuckled and said, "Okay. We'll try again. If at any time you want me to stop, just let me know."

He began kissing her all over. Her nipples were harder than before and when he put his hand between her legs, he put the lubricant in her and on himself. He rubbed her clitoris until she opened her legs. This time he entered her slowly and she cried out. "Oh, my god! It hurts, Mark. Stop! No, don't stop. Stop! No, just go slow, real slow. I had no idea something could hurt and feel good at the same time. Oh, Markie, Markie, Markie. Oh, my goodness. I know, I talk too much. Oh Mark, don't stop. Oh, Markie, I'm sorry I'm such a baby."

Mark reached his climax and slumped on her chest. She kissed his forehead and ran her fingers through his hair.

He kissed her and wiped the tears from her cheeks with his thumb. "I'm sorry I hurt you. I didn't know how to make it easier for you. At a certain point, it's impossible for a man to stop. I couldn't have stopped once I was inside you. I'm sorry, baby."

Judy sniffed through her tears, "I didn't want you to stop, Markie. I want to make love to you. Linda says it gets better. We'll have to find out, won't we? I hope I didn't disturb the neighbors," she giggled.

CHAPTER 42

Linda's wedding was during spring break. Markie drove with Aunt Maggie riding shotgun. They talked almost all the way, and she gave him some good advice. He told her his plans for the future, and she said she admired his good common sense. She said, "You take after your mother that way. She was always very practical."

Mark asked, "What do you remember about my dad? Was he practical, or did he rush into things without thinking?"

"As I remember, he was a nice boy – very thoughtful. You remind me of him when he was a little older than you. He liked being around Candy and the family a lot. I didn't see much of him after his graduation when he and your momma moved away. I only saw him when Bea was born, and then when you came along. Too bad he died so young. I wish you could have gotten to know him. But you turned out all right. Your momma did a good job raising you two. I'm glad she's found a good man now. I bet she wasn't counting on raising two more kids, though," she chuckled.

Mark said, "I'm glad for her, too, but she didn't raise us all by herself. You were there every step of the way, and don't you forget it"

~~~~~~

Wes and Candy reached Frances' house just a few minutes before Mark and Aunt Maggie did. Frances had insisted they stay with her for Linda's wedding. She had it all figured out and even borrowed a crib from one of her neighbors. She told Candy, "I think of them as my grandchildren, even though technically, they're not. I put the crib in my bedroom where you and Wes can sleep. Maggie can sleep in the guest room and Markie can sleep in Mark's old room. I'll sleep on the daybed in the sunroom, and I'll not hear another word about it. It's settled."

Candy was pleased that Frances seemed so relaxed and really enjoyed having them. She played with the babies and had Cora cook special meals for everyone. She was like a different person. Her hair was streaked with gray, and she still wore it straight back in a severe bun, but she seemed softer. She even told jokes and surprisingly, knew a lot about football, baseball, basketball, and who was on what teams. She enjoyed talking with Wes about sports and everyone seemed to enjoy her. She told Maggie, "I finally figured out what your secret ingredient is, and I have one of my own. Would you like a glass of tea, my dear?"

Maggie stammered, "Well, I guess I would."

Frances poured some tea over a little bit of ice and said, "Here, taste it. The trick is not to put too much ice. It dilutes it too much. Tell me what you think, then I'll show you my secret ingredient."

Maggie tasted it, smacked her lips, took another sip and said, "By Jove, that's good. What did you do to it?"

Frances took her over to the sink, opened the bottom cabinet, moved a few cleaning containers and brought out a fifth of bourbon. They both laughed until they cried. Then they put some glasses with a little ice in each one and took them into the living room with the pitcher of tea. They poured a glass for everyone but the babies and Frances said, "Here's to family, friendship, and love. Drink up, everybody."

Cora said, "Did you put in your secret ingredient?"

Frances and Maggie said at the same time, "We sure did," and they laughed harder.

The wedding ceremony and the reception afterwards went off without a flaw. Phillis wore a beautiful gold brocade evening suit. The bridesmaids wore deep red tea-length dresses that could be worn again after the wedding without looking like a foo-fooey bridesmaid's dress. All the men wore tuxedos. Ken and Bea got there just in time for the ceremony. Ken had had to work the night before. Mark was Bea's partner, and Candy got tears in her eyes when she saw how handsome he was and how beautiful she was. She thought, my babies, they've turned-out okay. Ken leaned over and whispered, "Isn't she gorgeous? I can't wait until it's our turn." Candy squeezed his hand.

At the reception, Mark and Judy could not keep their hands off each other. They danced every dance except when Joe, Jay-Jay, Wes or Ken danced with Judy. During one of the slow dances, Mark whispered, "Judy, you're so beautiful. That color really becomes you. I wish we could go somewhere."

Judy looked into his eyes and said, "I know. I want to, too. You look so good in a tux. I want you all to myself. I'll be glad when we can tie the knot."

"I will, too. We'll have to figure something out. This is too painful. I want to be with you tonight. I wanted to get a motel room, but my grandmother insisted that we all stay with her. She's actually been a lot of fun, but I'd rather be with my favorite girl. I can't dance a slow dance with you anymore. You do something to me that's embarrassing, so don't look at me like that." He pulled her close and whispered, "I love you." Then he twirled her around and they danced apart.

~~~~~~~~~~~~~~~~~~~~~~~~~~~~~~~~~~~~~~~

Bea and Ken chose a June wedding in Aunt Maggie's back yard. They would rent all the furniture they needed, erect a dance floor and a chuppah, and hire a live band. Ken's parents, Freda and Max, would take care of the catering. They decided to have a minister and a rabbi. They would incorporate both religions. This pleased Ken's parents.

The wedding took place on a beautiful Saturday afternoon. Aunt Maggie and Candy helped Bea get dressed in her room. Linda, Judy, Amy and her girlfriend Alice, were bridesmaids, with Linda the matron-of-honor. Bea had put no restrictions on the dresses except that they had to be baby blue. She knew that one design would not work for all because her friend was chubby, Amy was very much pregnant, Linda was tall, and Judy was petite. When she saw the four of them together in the dresses they had chosen, she was pleased. "You're all so gorgeous. Thanks, girls."

Aunt Maggie said, "You make a beautiful bride. I'm so glad you could fit into your mother's dress. It's perfect. You have something old – the dress; something new – your headdress; something borrowed – the earrings that my first sweetheart gave me-- they only have sentimental value, and now we need something blue."

Linda spoke up saying, "I have that. Here's your garter. Make him work for it, put it up high." Everybody laughed.

Mark knocked on the door, "Are you ready? It's time." Bea opened the door and Mark let out a long low whistle. "Wow, you look wonderful. If I were not taken, I'd marry you myself. Let's go ladies, show time."

Kenneth's best man was his older brother. His younger brother walked with Judy, a cousin walked with Bea's friend, Fred and Amy walked together, and Mark escorted his sister down the aisle to the chuppah in the lower part of the yard. Bea, Aunt Maggie and Wes sat on one side and Ken's family sat on the other. Candy sniffed and wiped away tears during the entire ceremony. Wes patted her hand and Aunt Maggie dabbed at her own eyes. Ken stomped on the glass and everyone cheered and shouted "Mozel Tov!"

Frances and Cora looked after the twins. The band played and everyone seemed to have a wonderful time dancing, eating, and drinking. Aunt Maggie joined Frances and Cora and asked, "Would you ladies like some ice tea – my own special blend?" The three of them giggled and went in the house to the kitchen. They put the twins down for a nap and sat in the living room sipping their tea, gossiping and giggling. Frances seemed to really enjoy herself.

When Judy was dancing the jitter-bug with Harvey, he spun her out, pulled her back and Judy thought he made a gesture toward her crotch. She decided it couldn't be and they

311

continued to dance. He spun her out and pulled her back again and when he made the same gesture, she stopped dancing and looked at him. He raised one eyebrow and winked at her. She looked around, not wanting to make a scene and got close to his ear. She whispered through clenched teeth, "If you ever come-on to me like that again, I'll knock the shit out of you and I'll tell Linda. I think you've had too much to drink. You need to sit down." She flounced off and went to look for Jay-Jay.

She found him talking with a group of people. She went over to him and said, "Excuse me, folks. I need to dance with my brother. I don't get to see him often enough."

Jay-Jay said, "Okay, let's go. Let's see what you've got."

They moved toward the dance platform and Judy said, "I don't want to dance. I need to talk with you. How well do you know Harvey?"

"I don't know him that much. Linda met him at school. We've talked a little but we haven't spent much time together. Why do you ask?'

Judy hesitated and then she blurted out, "The son-of-a-bitch made a pass at me. At first I thought I misunderstood, but he did it a second time, leaving no doubt. I put him in his place, but I think you need to keep an eye on him. Maybe he has a problem with alcohol. I won't say anything to Linda, but I think we need to stay close to her. I think she's going to need us down the road. Now close your mouth, and be cool. I might have over-reacted."

Jay-Jay said, "Okay. It's your call, but I'll watch him. I hope you're wrong. I'd hate to see Linda get hurt. They've only been married a few months. I'm glad you gave me a head's-up. Now let's dance. This is a party, you know."

The next tune was a slow dance and Markie touched Jay-Jay on the shoulder, "May I cut in?"

Jay-Jay grinned and said, "By all means." He winked at Judy and went searching for Linda and Harvey.

Markie held Judy close and they swayed to the music. He said, "I saw you leave Harvey during the dance, and then I saw you talking with Jay-Jay. You looked upset. Can you tell me what that was about?"

Judy said, "Well, I wasn't going to say anything to anybody but Jay-Jay. But I'll tell you if you promise not to get upset or over-react. You promise?"

Markie nodded, "Okay, what is it?"

Judy told Markie what had happened and her suspicions. "You don't need to worry. I put him in his place. I don't think he'll bother me again, but I'm worried about Linda. I hope I'm wrong."

Markie asked, "How did you put him in his place? What did you say?"

When Judy told him what she had said, Markie threw his head back and laughed. "I bet that sobered him up. I could just see you popping him. You're something else, you know that?"

Judy chuckled and made a fist and pretended to punch Markie. He took her fist and kissed it and hugged her close. Markie held Judy close while they swayed to a slow dance. "God, I love you so much." She whispered, "Me, too. Let's slip away."

"You sure?" he asked. She nodded, "I'm sure."

Markie looked around and said, "I think we need to mingle first, and I have to make a toast to the bride and groom. Let's go and talk with my new in-laws. I haven't met some of them yet, and I want to show you off. Then we can make our get-away. I don't think anybody will miss us, okay?"

She nodded and moved in closer to him. "I just want to be with you. I guess that tux turns me on, you handsome devil."

Mark laughed, twirled her around and dipped her. He brought her back to her feet and said, "Let's mingle. The sooner we get this over with the better."

CHAPTER 43

Jerrod visited with Vic two or three nights a week. Then it increased to three or four nights. The signal was usually Jerrod asking Vic, "See you tonight?" always with a question in his voice. Vic either nodded or shook his head. Jerrod became increasingly more skeptical of his place in Vic's life and he felt very insecure.

Then one Monday morning as Jerrod was leaving for work, Vic said, "I won't be into the office today. I have some business to take care of. See you tonight."

Jerrod's eyes lit up. It was the first time Vic had used the phrase and it was not a question. He replied, "Yeah, sure, see you tonight. Can I bring anything?"

Vic chuckled, patted him on the butt and said, "Just yourself, unless you think you might need a change of clothes."

Jerrod could hardly contain himself and nervously watched the clock all day. While waiting for the bus, he was so excited he felt like bouncing. He couldn't imagine what lay ahead. Vic had never showed much affection before. He, Jerrod, was always the pursuer. When he knocked on the door, Vic opened it and hugged him. He walked into the apartment and was stunned at what he saw.

The furniture in the living room had been rearranged and over by the window was a big beautiful desk with a typewriter and a stack of paper on top. Vic said, "Welcome home, Jerrod. That is if you want to move in."

Jerrod's hands went to his face and he blinked his eyes as if he could not believe what he was looking at. "Oh my! Oh my. Do you mean it, Vic? Oh, this is so wonderful. Oh, nobody ever did anything like this for me before." He went to the desk and rubbed the surface, repeating, "Oh my" over and over again. Then he went to Vic and hugged him, and kissed him on the neck. "Oh thank you Vic. I can't thank you enough. I'll go get my stuff."

Vic said, "Can't it wait 'til tomorrow? You might want to think about it. Besides dinner is ready and we have the whole night ahead of us. There are things I want to show you -- things I learned from Charles that we haven't tried yet. You're in for an exciting evening."

Jerrod giggled and said, "I can hardly wait."

Vic told Michele that Jerrod had moved in and she was delighted. "It's about time you relaxed into the relationship. I told you the boy was crazy for you. I hope you'll be as happy as I am."

Before Vic could reply, Michele's phone rang. "Yes.... Thank you. Tell him I'll be right there." She hung-up the phone, "Mr. Forbes wants to see me right away. His secretary said it's urgent." She giggled and said, "He probably wants a quickie."

Vic laughed, "Talk with you later," and waved as he left her office. He had just settled at his desk when Michele came in with tears streaming down her face. "It's awful, just awful!"

Vic got up and hugged her heaving shoulders, "What is it? What's wrong?"

"It's Frank's son. He's dead. His car was found wrapped around a tree this morning. No one knows exactly when the accident happened. Rigor mortis had already set in. Frank is really torn up about it. He has gone to be with his family and I can't be there to console him. Oh, Vic, I feel so helpless. Poor baby, and my mascara is running all over the place."

Vic gave her a tissue, "I'm sorry Michele. We'll just have to wait and see what we can do after Frank lets us know what's going on."

Evidence showed that Frank's son was speeding and failed to negotiate a curve, went over an embankment, and was stopped by a tree. It was just luck that the car didn't explode. Some driver saw the lights when the fog began to lift the next morning. No one else was involved in the wreck.

Weeks later the results of the autopsy showed an excessive amount of drugs and alcohol in the son's system. Frank blamed himself for not being more involved in his son's life and he was very remorseful.

Michele, Vic and Jerrod attended the funeral along with other people from Frank's office. When they moved through the line of mourners, Michele hugged Frank and whispered, "When can I see you?"

Frank looked at her with sadness and an emptiness she had never seen before. He didn't answer. Vic shook his hand, gave him a hug, and expressed his condolences. He took

317

Michele's elbow and steered her on through the line as she began to sob. Most of the people from Frank's office knew about Michele and Frank's relationship and they felt as sorry for Michele as they did for Frank.

~~~~~~

One Saturday night Michele sat at Vic's table dabbing her eyes with a tissue and sipping a glass of wine. "It's been two months since I've seen him, Vic. He won't call me and he won't answer my messages. I know he needs to be with his family now, but it's as if he's closed the door on our relationship. I don't know what to do. I have never felt so lonely in my life. I wish I had never met him. Damn it, I haven't done anything wrong, so why is he closing me out?"

Vic said, "He probably feels he neglected his family to be with you and he's ashamed." He reached over and took her hands in his. "It will take time, Michele, have patience. When things settle down at home, he'll start missing you and he'll be back. Just wait and see. He might not know what to do right now. Things will get better when he comes back to work. You'll see."

"I hope you're right, Vic. I don't want to live without him. Maybe I'll just kill myself. Then he'll be sorry and he'll be back."

Vic laughed, "Do you realize what you just said? It must be the wine talking. Have another glass. You're staying here tonight. I'm not letting you out of my sight. Things will get better, Michele, I promise. Even if he never comes back, you'll find a way to keep on going and make a life for yourself."

"I guess you're right. You got along after Charles and he's not coming back ever. Oh, I'm sorry, that was so insensitive of me. But you're stronger than me, Vic, you always manage to do things right. I should take a lesson from you. I'll just have to be patient."

Vic thought, if only you knew, Michele. If only you knew.

The next morning while Vic cooked breakfast, Jerrod took a shower and Michele was just beginning to stretch on the sofa when they heard a knock on Vic's door. Vic peeped out mumbling to himself, "Now who can that be this early in the morning?"

He turned to Michele and whispered, "It's Frank. You want me to let him in?"

Michele grabbed her wig from the coffee table and said, "Of course. Just give me a minute." She threw the wig on her head and began straightening her clothes. The wig landed sideways and she nodded, "Let him in."

Frank hugged Vic and said, "Have you seen Michele? I went to the apartment and she wasn't there. The only place I could think she might be was here. Is she all right? Have you seen her?"

Vic stepped back and without a word, waved Frank into the apartment. Michele was getting up off the sofa and Frank said, "Thank goodness, you're here. I was worried. Are you okay, baby?"

Michele stood there looking at Frank with blood-shot eyes as if she couldn't believe it was him. Her clothes were askew and the wig had slipped to one side. She said, "Oh, Frank, you came. I must look a mess."

Frank said, "You look fine, just fine. Come here." He took the wig off, held her face in his hands and tenderly kissed her.

She said, "I think I'm going to faint. Are you okay?"

Frank said, "I've done a lot of soul searching. Let's sit down and I'll tell you all about it."

Vic said, "Do you want some privacy? I can go in the other room."

Frank said, "It's all right, Vic. Do you have some coffee? I want you to hear what I have to say, too."

Vic poured coffee for everyone including Jerrod. Frank motioned for him to join them. He took Michele's hand and held it as he began. "This tragedy woke me up. Life is too short not to be with the ones you love. I regret not being closer to my son, but I can't change that. It wasn't entirely my fault. Jennifer and I grew apart when the children were little. I think it would have been better for them if we had divorced when they were young. Jennifer could have found someone to love her and I could have, too. Then maybe the children could have seen how normal people live instead of having to experience all the tension and hostility in our house. I've grown closer to my daughter, Cathy, since my son, Brian's death and I really like her. She wants to work with me and that makes me feel good. I told Jennifer that I want a divorce; and if I have to leave the business, so be it. If I have to start over, I know enough about the publishing world that I can make it without her family's money, and everything that goes with it. She surprised me by saying she wants a divorce, too, and that we can work something out. She said I can have the business as part of a settlement and everything else is up for negotiation. The biggest surprise of all? She tore-up the prenup and burned it."

He turned to Michele and said, "I'm sorry I've ignored you, but I needed this time to work things out. As soon as the divorce is final, will you marry me?"

Michele started laughing and crying at the same time. She hugged Frank around the neck and spilled her coffee on the table. Vic jumped up and got a dishcloth to wipe up the mess. Through her tears sobbing she said, "Of course I'll marry you. Oh my god, I must look a mess." She grabbed the dishcloth from Vic and began wiping her face. Everybody laughed and Vic squeezed Jerrod's knee under the table.

Frank and Michele were married on a sunny Sunday afternoon in the courtyard at Phillipe's. They closed the restaurant for the day and had the reception there. Cathy and a few of their close friends attended. Cathy and Michele were getting to know and like each other. They had shopped for their dresses together. Phillip gifted the champagne and the food was delicious, of course. Vic had supervised everything and Jerrod and Michele had decorated. Michele looked radiant in an ivory satin gown that flattered her figure. She wore a very tasteful headdress and carried a bouquet of calla lilies. Frank wore a black silk suit with an ivory shirt and tie. He beamed with pride as he took Michele's hand and tucked her arm under his as they walked to the judge. He whispered, "You look gorgeous."

She looked at him lovingly and said, "You do, too. Don't worry I'm wearing smudge-proof mascara." They giggled and faced the judge.

During the exchange of the vows, Jerrod timidly touched Vic's hand. Vic took his hand and squeezed it. Jerrod thought, I've died and gone to heaven.

CHAPTER 44

The crowd was on its feet screaming and shouting. It was the last race of the track meet. Judy started as scheduled – the last runner on the last lap of the relay race. She reminded herself to concentrate and do just as they had done in practice. When she felt the baton slapped in her left hand, she gathered speed and pumped her legs like pistons, caught up to the runner in front and passed her. She ignored the pain in her left side, gritted her teeth and gave the race all she had. She crossed the finish line about twenty seconds before the next runner – a clear win. Her team mates ran and picked her up off the ground. Everybody was laughing, jumping up and down and hugging her. Nobody noticed that she was in pain. Tears were streaming down her cheeks. When they let her go, she sank to the ground holding her side. It was obvious that she was in agony.

Markie told the announcer next to him to take over and he dashed out of the reporting booth and ran to the track. By the time he reached Judy, the coach had picked her up and was carrying her over to the side. Markie could hear the siren and saw the ambulance coming on to the track. When he reached her, Judy seemed to have fainted. He took her hand, "Judy, baby, what is it? Speak to me. What's wrong? Jude! Jude, wake up!"

Markie could vaguely hear what was being said over the loud speakers as they picked her up. There was no room for him in the ambulance, so he sprinted to the parking lot, jumped into his car and headed for the hospital.

The emergency room was not too crowded and he raced to the reception desk to see what he could find out. They couldn't tell him anything. When he looked around, he saw Wes, Candy, Phillis, Joe and the twins coming through the door. Phillis and Joe talked with the nurse, but there was nothing she could tell them.

"As soon as we know something, we'll call you. In the meantime there is some paperwork to fill out," the nurse said.

Joe was ready to say something to the nurse when Phillis said, "It's all right, Joe. I'll take care of it. She's just doing her job."

A little while later a resident came looking for Judy's parents.

"Judy has internal bleeding and needs surgery," she said. "I have some release forms that need to be signed." Phillis asked, "What's wrong? Why does she need surgery? What are you looking for? Is it her appendix?"

The doctor replied, "It's not her appendix. The problem is on the left side and we won't know until we get in there and find out what's wrong. We're prepping her for surgery now. We'll let you know what's going on as soon as we know. Try not to worry. Our best surgeon is scrubbing up now."

Phillis relayed what the doctor had told her to the others. All they could do was wait. The twins got restless so Wes took them home. He told Candy to call him when she knew something. He patted Markie on the back and said, "Try not to worry. I'm sure she'll be all right."

Waiting was hard. No one knew what to say or do. Candy had a flashback to when she was in the same waiting room after Markie's accident. They tried to make small talk. Candy said, "I'm so glad that you two are here. Think how awful it would be if you were home and heard the news."

Joe said, "Yeah that would be worse."

Markie said, "Mr. Roberts, can take a walk?"

Joe looked at Phillis and shrugged, "Okay, Markie. Let's go."

The sun was making long shadows as they walked outside the building. Joe spoke first, "Markie, what do you want to talk about?"

Markie cleared his throat. He was as tall as Joe, but much slimmer. He still wore a size twenty-eight waist pants. He hitched-up his pants and said, "Mr. Roberts, I guess you know how I feel about Judy. I've never felt so helpless in my life with her laying up there in surgery and me not knowing what's going on. What I mean is I want to take care of her. She means everything to me. I know we talked about waiting until we finished college to get married, but I don't want to wait any longer. I make a living at the radio station and I feel I can take care of her. What I'm trying to say is, with your permission, when she's better, I want to marry your daughter. I feel I have to talk with you about it now so you and Phil... er Mrs. Roberts can discuss it and let me know how you feel before I ask Judy. I know she's going to be all right. I feel it in my gut. She just has to be okay. I don't know what I'd do without her." He sniffed and wiped his eyes with the back of his hand.

Joe took a deep breath, cleared his throat and said, "I'm sure she's going to be okay, er -- Mark. I can't call you 'Markie' any more. I appreciate you coming to me like a man. We'll go talk with the ladies now and hope for the best. By the way, I think getting married is Judy's call. You know she has a mind of her own. I don't think she would approve of us making plans for her life without her knowledge. She might not want to get married now, you know."

Mark replied, "We've talked about getting married one day. But, no I haven't asked her specifically. I guess I should, huh?"

Joe smiled and said, "That would be my plan, er… son. I think you should call me Joe, or Pops, or something less formal than Mr. Roberts, okay? I wish my other son-in-law was as decent a fellow as you. I thought he was an okay guy when Linda first brought him home. He's from a good family and has a promising career, but I have my doubts about his character. There's something about him that I just don't like. Anyway it's Linda's problem. I just hope she doesn't get hurt in the process. Let's go talk with the ladies." He put his arm on Mark's shoulder and they walked back to the emergency room.

As they were going through the doors, Joe was saying, "What about your dream of becoming a doctor? I don't think you should give up your dream. Judy wouldn't want you to, and you might grow to resent it."

Mark replied, "I have no intention of giving it up. I'm sure we can work it out. I graduate in June and I've been accepted at the medical school here. Judy can finish her last year while I start Medical school. I've already talked with Auntie Mom and she wants us to live with her. So I think it will be okay. I just need Jude to say yes. I haven't run my plan by her yet, so I guess I'm jumping the gun. I talked with Auntie Mom about it when we came up to Linda's wedding. I just hadn't planned on doing it now. This episode scared me so much I figured we'd better do it now. I don't want to wait. I hope Judy feels the same way."

Joe looked at Mark with his mouth open, "You mean to say you were planning to marry Judy way back then?"

Mark chuckled, "Even before that. Remember when I came up to take her to her prom? When I saw her in that yellow dress, I knew then. So this is my wake-up call. If Judy will have me, maybe we can have a summer wedding."

Joe said, "Yeah I remember you said that you cherished her. I'd never heard that term used before. I'd say you've got it bad." He paused. "I hope we hear something soon. This waiting is getting on my nerves. I'm not a patient man."

"What were you two talking about?" Phillis asked.

Joe said, "You want to tell her, or do you want me to?"

Mark said, "Mom, Mrs. Roberts, I asked Joe if he minded if I asked Judy to marry me."

Phillis and Candy looked at each other and Candy smiled and said, "I told you that was what Mark had in mind."

Phillis said, "Well, Joe, what did you tell him?"

Joe said, "I have to admit I wasn't surprised. But he hasn't asked her yet. He's just taking for granted that because they've talked about it, she's okay with it. I told him, knowing our daughter, he'd better ask her before he makes any plans. She's always been independent and I don't think she would want us making plans for her without her being in the middle of it all."

Candy said, "What made you want to do it now, Mark?"

Mark said, "This scare woke me up. It made me realize you can't always go by a plan. You have to grab happiness when you can. So as soon as she comes out of this, I'll ask her. I know she'll be alright. She just has to be. Have they told you anything yet?"

"No, honey, we'll just have to wait." They started recounting different events that they had shared through the years and that helped the time seem to pass faster.

Three hours later the surgeon came to see them. "Your daughter is being taken to recovery. You'll be able to see her one person at a time in about a half hour. We'll come and get you."

Phillis said, "What's wrong with her? Why did you have to operate?"

The doctor looked from one to the other and said, "She had a tubal pregnancy and it burst. She's young and in good health. She'll be able to have more children. We managed to repair the fallopian tube, and with proper care she'll be good as new. If there are no complications, she should be able to go home in about a week."

In a threatening tone Joe said, "Mark, did you know she was pregnant? If you love her the way you say you do, why did you do this to her?"

Phillis said, "Now Joe. You know it takes two. I'm sure he didn't force her. They've been going together for a long time. What did you think they were doing? I'm sure you haven't forgotten how we were at their age. And besides, she probably didn't know she was pregnant herself since it was a tubal pregnancy. You can't blame Mark, things happen for a reason. Now they can go on with their lives. A minute ago you were all for Mark's plans and now you're blowing smoke out of your nose. Calm down. Everything will be okay."

Joe said, "Yeah, I guess you're right. I'm glad she's okay. Is anyone else hungry? I'm starved now that the wait is over. I'll go get some sandwiches."

Phillis went in to see Judy first. When she saw her with tubes everywhere and monitors going, she started to cry. For the first time since Judy collapsed Phillis let herself give in to her emotions. "Oh, baby. How do you feel? Are you in pain? I'm here. Mommy's here."

329

Judy's eyes fluttered open. "Momma, what happened?" She reached for Phillis' hand. "I don't remember what happened. Did we win?"

"Yes, baby. You won in more ways than one. Did you know you were pregnant?"

Judy looked shocked, "No, I didn't know. Oh, Mom, I'm so sorry."

"You have nothing to be sorry about. It happens no matter how careful you are. It was a tubal pregnancy that ruptured. The doctor said you'll be fine, they were able to repair things and you'll be able to have more babies. In a way, it could be a good thing. I don't think you were ready for a baby now anyway. Were you?"

"No. We didn't plan on it. Does Pop know? He must be so disappointed in me. What can I say to him?"

"Yes, Joe knows. You don't have to worry, he loves you no matter what. You'll always be his baby. Now I'll let him come in to see you. They only let one person at a time. So I'll let him come in now, okay?" She kissed her on the cheek and said, "See you later."

Joe came in, took her free hand and kissed her on the forehead. He had tears in his eyes. "How you doing, baby? We were so worried about you. I'm so glad you're okay. How do you feel?"

Judy started sobbing, "Oh, Daddy, I'm so sorry I disappointed you. I didn't mean for it to happen. You must be ashamed of me."

Joe wiped his eyes and said, "Shh, don't talk like that. You were the fastest runner out there. You won the race. Don't you know they always save the best for last?" He put his finger on her lips to stop her protest. "I know you're not talking about the race, but that doesn't bother me either. You're a good girl and I know you and Mark love each other. I'm just glad you're okay. Doctor said you're healthy and will make a full recovery. You can have more babies when the time is right. Now there's someone else who can't wait to see you. I'll send him in."

Judy sobbed, "Thank you, Daddy. The last thing I want to do is disappoint you."

Joe said, "You haven't, and you won't. You know I love you no matter what."

When Mark saw Judy he bit his lower lip and his chin quivered. He was fighting back tears. Judy reached out to him with her free hand and he went to her and put his head on her chest. "Jude, I'm so sorry. Did they tell you what happened? Are you all right?"

Judy rubbed his head, "Mom told me. I lost the baby. I'm so sorry, Markie. I didn't even know I was pregnant. I thought we were being so careful. I hate I did this to you."

Mark raised up and looked at her, "What do you mean? You didn't do anything to me. I'm the one who's sorry I got you in this fix. The doctor said we could have more babies, so don't worry about it. Judy, I know we've talked about getting married someday, but I want to do it now. I want to take care of you, Jude. You scared me, and I don't want to

331

take a chance of losing you. So I'm asking you, Judith Roberts, will you marry me?"

Judy sniffed and said, "Are you asking me because I was pregnant? Why now, when I'm laid up half-drunk with a sedative? Maybe you think while I'm vulnerable and weak that I'll do what you say. You never asked me right out before. It's always been 'when we get married'. It's never been 'will you marry me' before. Why now w…"

Mark stopped her speech with a kiss, "I've always said you talk too much. Be quiet, woman. I'll ask you again tomorrow when you're sober. Now get some rest. You've got to get well so we can go on with our lives." He put his finger to her lips and said, "Get some rest, and I'll do the same. You're not strong enough to be so bossy."

Judy lay back and whispered, "Okay. But seriously, Markie, did you ask me just because I got pregnant?"

Mark took her hand and said, "No. I told your father that I wanted to marry you before we even knew what was wrong. I knew in my gut that you were going to be all right. I prayed that you would be and decided that I wanted you as my wife, no matter what. We can work out the details as we go. Let's not put it on hold any longer."

"You talked with Daddy? Was he okay with it? Oh, Markie ask me again."

Mark chuckled, "Tomorrow. I'll ask you again tomorrow when you're fully awake. Now get some rest and I'll see you in the morning." He kissed her on the cheek, the forehead and the lips. "Good night, love."

CHAPTER 45

Phillis and Linda were helping Judy get dressed. Phillis was fixing Judy's hair and headdress when Judy said, "Linda, are you alright? You don't look happy to me. You can talk to me and Mom, you know. What's wrong?"

Linda replied, "I'm okay. I just get choked-up at weddings."

Phillis said, "It's not the wedding, Linda. I've seen it for some time now. I'm glad Judy brought it up. We need to talk. Since when did you start to wear so much make-up? Come here and let me have a look at you."

"It's nothing, Mother. I'm a grown woman and I can wear any kind of make-up I want to."

Judy turned to her and said, "Now I know something is wrong. Since when did you start getting smart with Mom? You know you can talk with us, and it won't go past these walls. Tell us what's going on. We're your family and we love you."

Phillis pulled Linda over to the window, lifted her chin and turned her face towards the window. "You did a good job hiding that bruise. How long has this been going on? How many times has he hit you, and why? Talk to us, Linda, or do I get Joe to ask Harvey about it?"

Linda put her hand up in protest, "Please, Mom. Don't tell Daddy. He'll go after Harvey and then he'll be in trouble."

Judy said, "How long are you going to put up with it? You need to leave that jerk. You're young, beautiful, talented, with your own career. You don't need him. You have no children and he's a scum bucket. He drinks too much and then uses that as an excuse to hit on women. He even made a pass at me. I told him he better not try it again or I'd tell Jay-Jay. And I said a few other choice words, too."

Linda started crying and tried to defend him until she realized the more she talked, what Judy had said was true. She said, "Okay. I'll talk to Jay-Jay and he can help me move out tomorrow. Can I come home for a little while, Mom, just until I can find my own place?"

Phillis said, "You don't even have to ask. I'll talk to Joe and keep him calm. Don't you worry about a thing. I think he'll be pleased to have you back home again. And just so you know, Joe doesn't like Harvey anyway. He says he doesn't trust him. So dry your eyes, fix your make-up, we've got a wedding to attend. Look at your sister. She makes a beautiful bride."

Linda hugged Phillis and Judy and said, "I hope you'll be happy Jude. I know Markie loves you and you love him. You've been together since you were kids. You know each other very well. I just know you'll be happy."

Judy said, "Okay, ladies, show time. Let's get going. We don't want to be late."

At the church, Joe kissed Judy on the cheek and tucked her hand under his arm. He whispered, "Here goes, baby. I hope you'll be very happy."

Judy whispered, "Thank you, Daddy. I'm sure I will be."

When the music began, she looked towards the altar and even though Linda and Fred were in attendance, she only saw Mark. She took a deep breath and thought, he looks so handsome. I'm the luckiest girl in the world. In a few minutes I'll be Mrs. Judith Procter. We've waited long enough. I'm glad Mark didn't want to wait any longer. It'll be rough for a while, but we'll make it. I just know we will.

Fred could hear Mark as he sucked in his breath and whispered as he breathed out, "Wow!" when he saw Judy coming down the aisle. He patted Mark on the back and whispered, "It's okay, Buddy."

Mark thought, "She's gorgeous. She looks just like she did when I took her to the prom. I hope I can be a good husband to her. We'll be okay. It'll be tight for a while, but we'll make it. I love her so much."

When Joe reached the altar with Judy, he handed her over to Mark and whispered to him, "Cherish her."

Mark smiled and winked at him and murmured, "I already do."

Judy whispered, "What was that?"

Mark said, "Shh. I'll tell you later. It's a private joke between your Dad and me."

Judy whispered a little louder, "You have a private joke with my Dad and I ..." The minister said, "Ahem. Shall we begin?"

The reception was decorated in yellow and white. Everything went smoothly. Amy asked Candy to watch Fred Junior while she danced with Fred. Aunt Maggie commented that she was glad to see Amy relax a little after the scare she had with Little Fred. Frances didn't know what they were talking about, and Candy and Aunt Maggie filled her in.

Aunt Maggie told her she was driving home from the grocers when she saw Janet hurrying down the street clutching a bundle in her arms. As she looked closer she recognized the blanket she, Aunt Maggie, had crocheted for little Fred. She pulled over and got out of her car and spoke to Janet and asked her where she was going. Janet just stared at her as if she didn't know who she was. Aunt Maggie's intuition kicked in. She gently took the baby from Janet, and asked her if she could give her a ride home. Janet shook her head and ran off. Aunt Maggie took little Fred back to Amy and Fred's house. The front door was open and Amy was lying on the floor in the living room. After checking to see if Amy was alright, she called Fred at work. By the time he got home, Amy was awake. She didn't know what had happened. The last thing she remembered she and Janet were drinking tea. They called the police and discovered that Janet had drugged Amy and taken the baby.

Frances said, "That poor girl. I hope Janet's getting some help. No wonder Amy is so protective of her baby. I hope Amy gets some help, too. Otherwise, she'll make that little boy afraid of his own shadow."

Jay-Jay and Joe were keeping their eyes on Harvey. They decided as the evening went on that they didn't want Linda to wait until the next day to leave. Jay-Jay told her he would keep Harvey busy while she and Joe went to get some of her things.

The cake was cut, they had the champagne toast, and everyone was dancing and having a grand time. Mark and Judy were showered with rose petals as they ran to their car. They would spend the night at a hotel in town and then leave the next day for a honeymoon in Hawaii.

Candy said to Frances, "That is so generous of you to give them a trip to Hawaii. As tight as things are going to be for them, they probably could use the money."

Frances chuckled, "Oh, Candy. I wish I could have done it for you and Mark. Every couple deserves a lovely honeymoon. Besides, I have nothing else to do with my money but to spend it on my grandchildren. I've helped Bea and Kenneth and I'll continue to help Mark and Judy, so none of your talk about pinching pennies."

~~~~~~~~~~~~~~~~~~~~~~~~~~~~~~~~~~~~~~

Mark picked Judy up and carried her into their room. They kissed and he said, "Hello, Mrs. Procter."

Judy said, "Hello yourself, Mr. Procter. Shall we get ready for bed? I'm very tired. We've had a long day."

Mark replied, "Yes, Ma'am. By all means, let's get ready for bed," and they giggled.

When Mark came out of the bathroom, Judy was standing by the window in a yellow gown. He came up behind her, wrapped his arms around her waist and slid his hand down to her mound. He could feel her pubic hair through the silky material and he rubbed gently. She turned toward him and crossed her arms lowering the straps of her gown. She pulled her arms out of the straps and the gown hung precariously on her nipples. Mark picked her up and before they could reach the bed, the gown fell to the floor.

~~~~~~

Harvey stumbled home later that night shouting, "Linda, where are you? Come here woman. Your man is home. Linda? Come here, sugar. You hiding from your husband?"

He went into the bedroom and saw the closet doors open and drawers pulled out. There was a note on his pillow. He picked it up and had a hard time focusing his eyes and read out loud, "Harvey, I deserve better. I'm leaving you. Linda."

He spoke to the empty room, "She say she leaving me. She leaving me. How she gone leave me? I'mma bring her ass home." He turned around, his foot caught on the bed skirt and he fell on the bed and was out like a light.

The next day Harvey went to Joe and Phillis' house and banged on the door. Then he entered without waiting for anyone to open it. "Where's Linda? Where's my wife?" He was stopped by Jay-Jay as he started up the stairs.

Linda was at the top of the stairs. "Go away, Harvey. I've left you and I'm not coming back. Now go and get sober so you can sign the divorce papers."

Harvey stumbled on the steps, "You can't divorce me. What will people think? Come on back home, baby. You know I love you. We can work this out. Come on home."

Jay-Jay said, "Is that how you show you love someone? You hit them and you get drunk? She said she's left you. Now go on home, Harvey."

"I didn't hit her. Tell them, Linda. I'd never hit her. She bumps into the walls sometimes. Don't you, baby? Tell them."

Linda screamed, "Get out, Harvey! Get out and leave me alone. You'll hear from my lawyer. Now leave!"

Joe came out of his bedroom and stood by Linda and in his very deep voice loudly said, "Harvey, I think you'd better leave. Linda has spoken and we back her up one hundred percent. We don't want any trouble out of you. But if you insist, we can give you lots of trouble. Now leave before I come downstairs and put you out." He stepped down two steps.

Harvey said, "Okay, okay, I'm going. This ain't right, Linda. You shouldn't be leaving me."

Jay-Jay took him by the elbow and pushed him out the door as he was shouting profanities. Linda turned to Joe and cried. Joe patted her on the back and said, "It's okay, honey. It's okay. You've got us and you'll be okay."

CHAPTER 46

It was just a cold, Vic thought. He took the medicines the doctors suggested, but couldn't seem to shake the cough and low-grade fever that left him feeling tired. There were days when he didn't even want to get out of bed. Jerrod attended to his needs as best he could and Vic seemed to get better.

When he returned to the restaurant, Phillip said, "You don't look so hot. Are you okay? Your cold seems to be lasting a long time. Do you need some time off?"

Vic replied, "I'm better now, thanks for asking, Phil. I'll be fine. I need to work to keep my mind busy. I've got all kinds of ideas for adding more vegetable dishes to the menu. I've been scouring the farmers' markets looking for different kinds of vegetables and fixing them in different ways, you know, to make the menu healthier. Are you up to sampling some veggies?"

Phillip laughed and rubbed his stomach, "You know I love my meat. But if you make a vegetable taste as good as you do your meat dishes, I'll try it. I got nothing to lose except my chippies' playground, know what I mean?"

They both laughed and Vic said, "I could use some time off in a few weeks. I haven't had a vacation for over five years. I might take you up on the offer. I'll let you know."

That night, Vic broached the subject of going away on a trip with Jerrod. Jerrod was delighted. He had never been further than San Francisco and he agreed to any suggestion

Vic made. Vic laughed, "I can see you're not going to be any help. I'll decide when and where we're going and let you know so you can get the time off. You're about due for a vacation. You haven't had one since you've been with the company. You've been working very hard and Frank's pleased with the job you're doing. Where we're going will be a surprise."

Jerrod hopped up and down and clapped his hands in delight. Vic thought, he's like a kid. You'd think I'd said we're going to Disneyland. Now there's an idea. Maybe we'll do just that. It'll do us both good.

Vic made the arrangements and a month later they hopped on a plane and went to Disneyland. Jerrod acted like a twelve year old, and Vic delighted in his child-like pleasure. After three days, they got on another plane and when Jerrod realized they were not going back to San Francisco his eyes were huge with wonderment. They arrived at the Honolulu airport around ten the next morning. Vic had rented a cottage on the beach. When Jerrod saw it, he jumped up and down and ran to Vic and hugged him and kissed him and squealed with delight. The cab driver just shook his head, put the bags down and left.

When they returned to San Francisco, Vic looked tan and rested. They had spent most of their time sunning on the beach, resting and reading. Vic slept a lot and Jerrod could see him getting stronger. He had been very worried before they left. Now he felt relieved.

Jerrod invited Michele and Frank to dinner as a surprise for Vic. He had prepared Vic's favorite dish and had his favorite wine chilled. When Vic came home, the three of them shouted, "Surprise!"

Vic laughed, "It's not my birthday. What's the big deal?"

"We're just glad to see you looking so good, big guy," teased Michele.

A month later, Vic woke with a sore throat. He thought he had another virus and he fixed a warm cup of salt water to gargle with. He opened his mouth and looked in the mirror. He was disturbed to see the tell-tale white blotches on the inside of his cheeks. He remembered seeing them in Charles' mouth. All of a sudden he had a chill and broke-out in a sweat. Is this it? Is this the beginning of the end? He asked himself. Is it finally catching up with me? I've been so careful. I've followed the doctor's orders. I eat healthy and I only sleep with Jerrod. Oh, God, please don't let it be!

That night he told Jerrod, "Sit down. We have to talk. There's something you should know. I'm getting sicker. You need to know what to expect so you can bail out now if you don't want to deal with it. I think I'm dying or AIDS. I have some literature for you to read and I'll tell you how I handled taking care of Charles. It's better you know what to expect because I don't think it will get any better. I'll understand if you decide to leave – no hard feelings. Not many people would sign-up for this duty. That's one of the reasons I was reluctant to start an affair with you."

Jerrod swallowed hard and, with tears in his eyes, said, "Vic, you're the first person who's acted like you like me just because I'm me. I love you. I guess I haven't said it often

342

enough or you wouldn't be asking me to leave. I could never leave you; – sick or well. I'm in for the long haul – whatever that is. You can't get rid of me that easily. Now let's go to bed, you need your rest. What can I get you before we turn-in?"

Vic whispered, "Thanks, Jerrod. I don't need anything – just you. I love you, too. You're a good man."

Jerrod's chest swelled with pride. Vic usually referred to him as a boy.

The next day Jerrod invited Michele to lunch and told her what Vic had said. She shook her head, "Oh, man. I was hoping it wouldn't happen to him. I went through it with Vic when Charles was sick. It's not pretty. Are you sure you're up to this?"

Jerrod nodded, "I'm in. I love him."

Michele said, "Okay. You know I love Vic, and I'll help as much as I can. You keep me posted on his progress. He'll try to hide things from me. I know him. Don't worry. It's not going to happen overnight, it'll be a slow process. You might have a few more years. And remember, I'm here for you."

Jerrod sniffed, "Thanks, Michele. I knew I could count on you. I won't tell him I've said anything to you, okay?"

343

CHAPTER 47

Aunt Maggie said, "Judy, you're a treasure. My house has never been so clean. You're an excellent housekeeper and, I must admit, a pretty good cook. I don't know where you get all your energy. I guess that's youth for you."

Judy chuckled, "It's easy if you stay on top of it. That is, I mean, him, if you know what I mean. You know who the messy one in this household is, and I don't mean Buster." They both laughed. "I can't believe the time has gone so fast. Did Mark tell you he's been accepted at San Francisco General for his internship? Oops, I talk too much. He wanted to tell everybody at once. Please pretend you didn't hear it from me. He's always telling me I talk too much."

Aunt Maggie hugged her around the waist, "I didn't hear a thing. Don't worry. I'm going to miss you. You're the best thing that's happened to Mark. You two have filled this old house with life. I hope someday you'll come back here to live. Maybe Mark could set up his practice here, and I know the high school can always use you. It's something to think about."

"I'm going to miss you, too." She knelt down so Aunt Maggie wouldn't see the tears in her eyes, "I'm gonna miss Buster and Miss Susie, too." Buster wagged over and licked her cheek, and Susie bumped against her leg.

The phone rang and Aunt Maggie answered, "Hello. Oh, hi, sweetie. My goodness, yes. You don't even have to ask. Well, let's just make it dinner. I know it's short notice, but I'll try to get everyone over. See you around six or six-thirty." To Judy, she said, "That was Bea. She and Ken want to come over tonight and tell us something. I bet she's pregnant. Anyway, I'll get on the horn and let the others know. Let's see, what can we have?"

Judy said, "Good. We'll have everyone here and Mark can share his news. I'll help with dinner. Let's put our heads together and I'll run to the store."

While they were peeling and chopping Aunt Maggie asked, "How's your sister? What do you hear from her?"

"Oh, Linda's okay, I guess. She's having trouble with relationships. I think she's afraid to trust anybody, and I don't much blame her after that clown, Harvey. He still calls her and tries to make-up with her. I think she needs to move away where he can't find her. Then maybe she can break those ties."

Aunt Maggie shook her head, "Too bad. Some people have a hard time breaking with the past and moving on. She's such a pretty girl and so smart. There's not much you can do for her. She has to do it herself. I just hope she doesn't become bitter and cut herself off from a healthy relationship."

Judy said, "I've talked with her about that but I don't think I got too far. Anyway, I guess I'm the lucky one. When other women talk about their relationships, I realize how lucky I am. Mark is so special. I can't even join in their conversations. I have no complaints."

"Hey, luck has nothing to do with it. I've seen how you two treat each other. You both work on your marriage.

I've seen your little tiffs, but they don't last long and you seem to be able to talk things out."

Judy laughed, "Yeah, it's usually me doing the fussing. But I like the making up part."

Aunt Maggie laughed, too, "I just bet you do."

By six-forty-five, dinner was ready and all the adults were seated around the dining room table. The children were at the kitchen table including Fred and Amy's two-year-old daughter who was in a high chair. Their plates had been served and they were eating and teasing each other.

After grace was said, Aunt Maggie said, "Okay, Mrs. Levy. Spill the beans. Why did you want this gathering? Are you pregnant?"

Everybody laughed and Bea said, "No, not yet. . We're still trying to get it right. Ken why don't you tell everyone your news?"

Ken said, "Well, I've decided that I want to specialize in radiology. I've been interested for a long time. The field is wide open and a school in New York has accepted me. Bea has been accepted into a doctoral program there, too. She'll be teaching math at the community college while she studies. It's going to be challenging for a while, but we're eager to get started. We'll be leaving next month."

Candy said, "I'm going to miss you two. I love having you so close, but you have to do what you have to do. At least it will give us a reason to visit New York."

346

Wes squeezed her hand. "We'll make it a point to visit and of course you'll be coming home for visits, too. It won't be so bad."

Mark cleared his throat, "I may as well share my news, too. I've been accepted for my internship at San Francisco General. We'll be leaving in a few months, too."

Aunt Maggie wiped her eyes with her napkin, "Seems like everyone is leaving. This old house won't be the same."

At that moment they heard squabbling coming from the kitchen. Evan was saying, "Stop that, Nicole," and Nicole was saying, "Make me!" Fred Jr. was saying "Shut up, both of you!" Little Heather was squealing and banging a spoon on the high chair tray, and Buster was barking.

Bea said, "I don't think you'll have to worry about it being too quiet, Auntie Mom."

Candy said, "We'll just have to get together as often as we can. The time goes by so fast. I found a gray hair this morning, and I don't want to even think about it."

Judy said, "Mark, you're awfully quiet."

Mark replied, "Yeah, I'm just thinking. It will be strange. This is the only home I've ever known. My roots are here. I'll miss it, but most of all, I'll miss you," and he took Aunt Maggie's hand and kissed it.

She dabbed her eyes again and said, "Now see what you've done? Stop this carrying on and let's eat."

CHAPTER 48

Mark and Judy were settled in their small apartment in San Francisco. Judy had a part-time job while Mark was doing his internship. They talked with the folks back home often.

Judy and Candy had managed to keep their plans a secret from Mark. After he left for San Francisco General, Judy went to the airport hoping the plane would be on time. If it were late, her surprise might not work. .She couldn't have asked for things to be any better. The plane was on time and all the luggage arrived intact. In the car on the way back from the airport, the twins were so excited, they got the giggles and Candy didn't even try to calm them down. She and Wes were excited, too.

Judy got them settled back at the apartment and then they had lunch. After lunch they went to the hospital. The plan was to have Mark paged to come to the emergency room. Judy knew his schedule and that it would not be unusual for him to be called to the emergency. They would be in the waiting area and surprise him there.

Candy took Nicole to the restroom. There were three people ahead of her. She commented, "Always a line for the ladies." Everyone chuckled. The woman in front of her was tall and striking, fashionably dressed with an air of assurance. Candy thought, "She must be a model. Nobody dresses like that to come to the hospital."

The lady turned around and said, "It's always this way isn't it? That color is just perfect for you. It brings out the color in your beautiful eyes."

Candy stuttered, "Why, thank you. It's my favorite color. Now I know why."

On their way back to the waiting area, she saw the elegant lady sitting with two men. There was something very familiar about the man in the middle.

At that moment she heard over the loud speaker, "Dr. Procter to the ER. Dr. Mark Procter to the ER."

The man in the middle looked up.

Candy felt like she'd been punched in the gut. "It is you! You lousy son-of-a-bitch! I always knew you were alive!"

Vic focused his eyes, "Candy? Is that you? When did you start cursing?"

Candy was livid, "How dare you criticize me! You don't even know me! You chose not to know me or your children, you arrogant asshole!"

Vic was struggling to breathe. "I'm … sorry, Candy. You… would not… have understood."

"Understood what? How do you know? You didn't give me a chance to understand. I had no choice. You took the choices away from me. I had to do the best I could alone with two babies."

Michele was looking back and forth from Vic to Candy. She didn't know what to say or do. She silently mouthed 'two babies'. One of the emergency staff brought a wheelchair and Jerrod tried to help Vic stand up but he was too weak. The orderly said he would get help and they would put him on a gurney.

Candy had never experienced such rage. She felt hot and flushed and knew that her face was red. She began to sweat. "You bastard. If I had a gun, I'd blow your fucking brains out!"

She pulled her lips back through her teeth and squeezed her eyes shut as she heard a familiar uneven gait behind her. She knew Mark was there. She took a deep breath and turned around.

"Mom, what are you doing here? What's wrong? Why are you cursing at this man? What's going on?"

Candy touched Mark's chest, "I'm so sorry, Mark. I didn't know you were there."

Mark took her hand, "Who is this person, and why are you cursing?"

Candy turned to Vic, "Well? Whatever you call yourself these days, do you want to tell him?"

Vic wheezed, "I'm... your... father."

Mark paled and began to tremble. He looked at Vic closely and turned to Candy, "Did you know he was alive?"

Candy said, "No. I didn't know. I suspected it all along. If I had known, I would have told you and Bea. I would have made the asshole accountable."

Wes and Judy watched what was going on in dismay. The twins ran to Candy and hugged her on either side saying, "Mommy, what's wrong?" They had never seen her so upset.

Two of the emergency staff came and lifted Vic onto the gurney and started to roll him away. Mark told them, "Wait just a minute before you take him away."

Wes said, "What's going on? Candy, I've never seen you like this."

She hugged the twins. "It's okay. I'm fine. It's okay."

They ran to Mark and hugged him. He knelt down and hugged them both. "What a surprise. I'm so glad to see you." He looked up at Candy with questioning eyes.

Judy tried to ease the tension by saying, "Surprise! We wanted to surprise you, and we did!"

Mark stood up and said, "It's a surprise in more ways than one." He clenched his teeth and with great effort took Judy's hand and held it to his chest, "This person is my father. We thought he was dead. Since I was three months old, he's been dead. He can stay dead for all I care."

Judy's eyes grew big as she took in the scene before her.

Vic said, "But she…"

Mark cut him off, "She's my wife. And this is my baby whom I would never desert," as he put his hand on Judy's stomach.

Vic struggled to say, "I… was… going to… say she… looks so… young."

Mark looked at him with disgust, turned and said, "Let's get out of here."

Candy said, "I'll be along in a minute. I have some things to say to him." She turned to Vic, "Did you know that your father died trying to save what he thought was you in that river? Turns out it was just your coat. He was a good man, and he deserved better than an ungrateful son like you. You didn't even bother to acknowledge his death, you selfish son-of-a-bitch."

Vic could hardly hold his head up, "I'm… so… sorry, Candy."

"Sorry for what? That you left your family? That you didn't respect your father or mother? Or that you got caught? I expect it's because your secret was exposed." She looked at Michele and Jerrod. "Some friend you've got here. You haven't even asked about your mother. I guess you don't care about her either."

Vic gasped, "Mother… what?"

Candy said, "She died last year. We got close towards the end. She was happy at last. She was a warm and loving grandmother to Bea and Mark and my twins, too. And here's something else for you to think about. Your grandmother, your mother's mother was a Negro. Yeah, Mark or whatever you call yourself, you're a Negro. Think about that as you die. You look like you're dying now. You look awful and I hope you suffer, you low-life."

Vic tried to raise his hand, "Don't... hate... me, Candy. Don't... be bitter."

Candy wiped tears from her cheeks and said, "Goodbye, Mark." She walked away and didn't look back.

Michele looked after Candy then back at Vic who had slumped back on the gurney. She went to him and said, "Oh, lord, Vic. What is it?" She saw that he had collapsed and she called out, "We need some help here! He's not breathing! Somebody come and help! Help!" As the attendants rushed over, Jerrod seemed paralyzed and stood shaking his head in disbelief.

Candy ignored the noise behind her and ran into Wes' waiting arms. She was trembling and Wes consoled her as best he could. Mark said, "I'll go sign out and we can go home."

When they got to the apartment, Mark called Bea and told her what had happened. "You heard right. Yeah, he's alive... It's hard to tell, he looked pretty bad... They have him in isolation... If you think you should... Fine with me... Okay, here she is. She wants to talk with you, Mom," and he gave the phone to Candy.

"Hello, sweetheart... I'm okay now. How about you? Yes, I'm sitting down. I know. That was a good surprise... Well Mark and Judy just told us... What do you mean? ...

You mean you and Ken are, too? Oh, baby, that makes me so happy. This makes up for what might have been a very bad day... Oh, good. Are you sure you'll be okay to fly? I'm so glad, honey... Okay, let us know... Love you, too." Candy turned to her family, "Bea is coming out to see the scum bag for herself and, guess what? She's pregnant, too! Our family just keeps growing and growing."

Judy said, "Mark, how do you know he's in isolation?"

Mark replied, "That's where they put all the AIDS patients. He's obviously in the last stages. If he lasts through the night, I'll check on him tomorrow. I'm curious about him and I have a lot of questions."

Candy started to protest, but Wes took her hand, "Let Mark do what he has to do, Candy. He has to work through this."

Candy replied, "You're right." She paused. "I said some horrible things to him. I should have thanked him. If he hadn't run away, who knows what our lives would have been like? I wouldn't have met you, Wes, or been blessed with the family that I have. I guess this shows there's a plan for us that we're not privy to. What looks like a tragedy, might be a blessing in disguise."

Bea arrived the next evening, and Mark went to pick her up. She wanted to go straight to the hospital. Vic was hooked-up to all kinds of equipment and looked like he was just barely holding on to life. Bea had to wear sterile garments and a mask. In the room she whispered, "Daddy? Wake up. It's me, Bea. Wake up and look at me, the daughter you left when she was just three years old."

Vic's eyes fluttered open and he had difficulty focusing, "Bea? Wha... Where? My daugh... Who?"

"It's me, Daddy. Open your eyes. It's me... all grown-up. The little girl who grew up without a father to look after her, or teach her about the world. The little girl who watched her mother have to do two jobs of raising us as well as make a living. The little girl who had no father to protect her. But you don't have to worry about us. Mother did a wonderful job with the help of Aunt Maggie. Looking at you now, I'm thinking you did us a big favor. At least we didn't have to live a lie. Can you say the same?"

Vic tried to talk, "Bea.... So....sorry... couldn't.... stay.... Too... hard... always... loved... you... and... son."

"Love is a verb, Daddy. You have to show it. You chose to run away. That's not love. That's cowardice." Bea took a breath. "I'm glad we had this little chat. Goodbye, Daddy." She left his room, tears streaming into the mask, which she ripped off as soon as she was out in the hall. Mark was there to hold her while she sobbed.

"It's okay, sis. It's okay. It's good to get it out of your system." When Bea seemed calmer, Mark said, "Let's go see our family. You and Judy can compare notes. Come on."

Bea looked up at Mark, "Thanks big bro. Is Mom okay?"

"You know Mom. She's strong. She's got Wes and Evan and Nicole, she'll be fine. She and Judy are cooking up a storm. We decided not to tell Auntie Mom over the phone.

Mom wants to talk to her face to face; she's worried the shock will be too much for her at her age."

As they were eating dinner, Candy said, "You know, in spite of the drama, this has been a good get-together. I've got all my family here with me except for Aunt Maggie and Kenneth. And I can't forget Fred, Amy and their little ones."

Bea said, "You're right, Mom. Judy, this is delicious. I've got to get the recipe from you. When are you due?"

Judy said, "In six months. How about you?"

Bea replied, "In five months." They compared bellies and laughed. "Auntie Mom will be so surprised."

Judy noticed that Mark was unusually quiet. She went over to him and said, "Go see him. You need to talk it out. I can see it's bothering you. Go see him."

Mark said, "Yeah, you're right. I've got to talk to him."

When Mark got to the hospital, the busy day shift was over and the isolation ward was eerily quiet. He looked into Vic's room. The low light cast a greenish glow on Vic's face. He looked like a skeleton. Mark talked with the night nurse and looked at his chart. The nurse helped him don the protective garb and a mask. In Vic's room he checked all the monitors, listened to his chest and felt his pulse. When he tried to take his hand away, Vic touched it and whispered, "Son... is... that... you?"

Mark took a deep breath, pulled his hand away and said, "Yes, it's me Mr. Newman. Can I get you anything?"

"No… thank… you. Just… talk… to… me. Tell… me… about… leg."

Mark thought, "The last thing I want to do is talk with you about my leg or anything else." Then he started telling Vic the story of the accident. As he spoke, he found himself sharing other times that had been important to him. Before he realized it, an hour had passed. Vic's eyes were riveted on Mark's face the entire time and he was smiling. Mark realized that he was tired. He said, "I've got to go now. Maybe I'll see you tomorrow, Mr. Newman."

"I'll… be… here, son," and he smiled.

As Mark walked out to his car, he realized he was not angry anymore. The man in that room was not his father. He was just another AIDS patient who needed medical care. He felt at ease and looked forward to getting home to Judy and his family. He chuckled to himself. That little apartment had never seen so much activity. Maybe I'll get a shot at the bathroom for ten minutes. He laughed out loud.

~~~~~~~~~~~~~~~~~~~~~~~~~~~~~~~~~~~~~~~

Bea didn't want to see Vic again. Two days later they all said goodbye to Judy at the apartment and Mark took everyone to the airport. He went back to the hospital where he checked on Vic then went on duty.

Bea arrived safely. In Middleton Aunt Maggie picked up Candy and her family at the airport. They went to her house for dinner. Evan and Nicole played with Buster in the back yard while Wes and Candy told Aunt Maggie about the trip. When Candy told her how she discovered Mark in the

357

emergency, Aunt Maggie looked like she would faint. She slumped down in a chair.

Candy said, "I was afraid it would be a shock, that's why we waited to tell you in person. Do you want some water?"

"No. This calls for some of my special tea."

Candy got a glass of tea for her. "We've got more news."

"I don't think I can take any more. What is it?"

Candy chuckled, "It's good this time. Mark and Judy are having a baby in six months, and Bea and Ken are having a baby in five months. How about that?"

"Well that's the best news ever. My word! Can you imagine what this old house will be like at Christmas time? We'll have wall-to-wall babies. I'll be a great-great aunt. That's just wonderful – just wonderful!"

After dinner Wes transferred the bags into their car and they went home. Candy said, "I've never been so glad to get home – just you and me and our babies."

From the back seat they heard, "We're not babies!"

Wes said, "You're right. So tomorrow you two will get a job," and they all laughed.

Aunt Maggie waved good-bye, fed Buster and Susie, cleared the dishes, locked-up the house, turned on the outside lights and said, "Come on Buster and Susie, let's go to bed."

She shuffled back to her room with Buster and Susie following close behind.

~~~~~~

Michelle and Jerrod were outside Vic's room when Mark went to check on him. They told Mark that they had been close friends to Vic for many years and asked if they could be with him now since he was obviously dying. Mark agreed and the three of them put on the protective gear. They went into his room together. The room smelled of hospital antiseptic and the low light made Vic look like a skeleton. Mark took Vic's hand to feel his pulse and Jerrod took his free hand. Vic's eyes fluttered open and he smiled. Michelle was sobbing with mascara running down her mask.

Vic looked from one face to the other and had a hard time focusing. He tried to say something, but it came out as a guttural croak. Jerrod said, "We know, Vic, don't try to talk."

When Vic took his last breath, Mark was still holding his hand. He never called him Dad or Father. He always referred to him as Mr. Newman.

About the Author

Jean Evans Robinson is a retired public school teacher who lives in Sacramento, California with her two cats, Thelma and Louise.

I would like to thank my family and friends for their support and encouragement.